DEATH MASQUE

P.N. ELROD

ACE BOOKS, NEW YORK

This book is an Ace original edition,
and has never been previously published.

DEATH MASQUE

An Ace Book / published by arrangement with
the author

PRINTING HISTORY
Ace edition / February 1995

ISBN: 0-441-00143-2

ACE®
Ace Books are published by The Berkley Publishing Group,
200 Madison Avenue, New York, New York 10016.
ACE and the "A" design are trademarks
belonging to Charter Communications, Inc.

PRINTED IN THE UNITED STATES OF AMERICA

10 9 8 7 6 5 4 3 2 1

For Mark,
Thanks for the best support, ever.

Thanks also to
Pegasus House,
may you always fly high!

As this story was written to give entertainment, not instruction, I have made no attempt to re-create the language spoken over two hundred years ago. There have been so many shifts in usage, meaning, and nuance that I expect a typical conversation of the time would be largely unintelligible to a present-day reader. As I have had to "shift" myself as well to avoid becoming too anachronistic in a swiftly changing world, modern usage, words, and terms have doubtless found their way into this story. Annoying, perhaps, to the historian, but my goal is to clarify, not confound, things for the twentieth-century reader.

Though some fragments of the following narrative have been elsewhere recorded, Mr. Fleming, an otherwise worthy raconteur, misquoted me on several points, which have now been corrected. I hereby state that the following events are entirely true. Only certain names and locations have been changed to protect the guilty and their hapless—and usually innocent—relations and descendants.

—JONATHAN BARRETT

CHAPTER

—1—

Long Island, September 1777

Molly Audy opened her eyes, smiled, and said, "I'm that sorry to lose you as a caller, Johnny boy, I really am."

"You're very kind, Miss Audy," I replied lightly, looking down at her with my own smile firmly in place. Her little bedroom was a place of smiles for both of us, but soon to end, alas.

"You're the kind one, I'm sure." She brushed a light hand over her bare breasts. "Some gentlemen I've known couldn't care less about how I feel, but you take the trouble to do things right by me—and every single time. It's just as well you call as late as you do. Come 'round any sooner and I'd not have the strength left to deal with the others."

"You mean none of them bother to—"

"I didn't say that. Some are just as nice, but if I let myself be as free with them as I am with you . . . well, I'd be an old woman in a month from all the good feeling."

I laughed softly. "Now you're just flattering me, Molly."

"Not a bit of it. On nights when I know you're coming over, I hold myself back with them and save it for you."

My jaw dropped quite a lot. "Good heavens, I had no idea. I *am* honored."

1

"And you really mean that, too. Some men don't give two figs for a whore's feelings, but not you." She tucked her lower lip in briefly, then lifted her head enough to kiss my cheek before dropping back onto her pillow. "You're a lovely, lovely man, Mr. Barrett, and I'm going to miss you terribly." Now her smooth face wrinkled up and her arms went hard around me and she abruptly hiccupped into a bout of sincere sobbing.

I held her close and made comforting noises and wasn't quite able to hold back a few tears of my own that unexpectedly spilled out. In a strangled voice I assured her that she was a lovely, lovely woman and I would also miss her, which was entirely true. In the year since we'd begun our pleasurable exchanges, she'd become a very dear friend, and it was a raw blow to realize anew that this was the last night we'd be together for some considerable time to come, if ever again.

"Just look at us," she said, finally straightening. She groped for a handkerchief from the small table next to the bed and used it thoroughly. "Goodness, you'd think someone had died. You'll be coming back, won't you?"

"I . . . don't know."

Her eyes, reflecting her spirits, fell, but she nodded. "We're all in God's hands, Johnny boy. Well, I can at least pray for a safe crossing for you, if there is such a thing these days."

"We've been told that there will be no trouble from the rebel ships."

"Rebels?" She snapped her fingers to dismiss their threat to my well-being. "It's the sea itself that's so dangerous. I lost my poor husband to it years back, so don't you be forgettin' your own prayers as you go."

"I won't," I promised.

"There now, you come here for cheering up and I've gone all serious."

"It's all right."

She made herself smile once more for me, then slipped from the mess we'd made of the bedclothes. She rose on her tiptoes, arms high overhead in a luxuriant stretch. I watched the easy movement of her rounded muscles, of how the candlelight caught and gilded the sheen of sweat clinging to her skin, and suddenly wanted her all over again. The need swept into me, playing over and through my body like a swift red tide.

"La, but I wish it were cooler," she murmured, lifting her thick hair from the back of her neck. "I've half a mind to sneak down to the stream for a quick wash before I sleep. Want to come along?"

The sight of Molly Audy splashing away like some woodland nymph was not something I was going to deny myself. On past occasions when we'd stolen off for such adventures, the outcome had ever proved to be a happy one for both of us. "I should be most delighted to provide you with safe escort, Miss Audy."

She turned and saw how I was looking at her. "Oh, you're a wicked 'un, all right, Johnny boy. Goin' to make an old woman of me before the night's done, is that it?"

She danced out of my reach and pulled on a light wrapper and some shoes; I left my coat, hat, and neck cloth, knowing I'd be back for them, and didn't bother fastening up my shirt. My breeches and boots I'd left on throughout our recent lovemaking. Perhaps it was not really gentlemanly, but Molly had often expressed to me that she sometimes found their retention on my person to be rather stimulating to her when she was in the mood for it. Being no fool, I was only too happy to comply with her preferences.

The street that her house faced was silent at this late hour, but we still left by her back door rather than the front. Besides being the quickest route to the little stream that flowed through this part of Glenbriar, it spared us from any unexpected observers who might also be wakeful from the warmth of the night. Witnesses for what we had in mind would have been an utterly unwelcome inconvenience.

There was enough of a moon showing to allow Molly to pick her way without much effort or noise. I could see perfectly well. As long as some bit of the sky was visible, the night was as day to me, and I kept an eye out for unwanted attention. The locals did not worry me so much as the Hessians. There had been many terrible incidents involving the army sent to protect us and put down the

Rebellion, but many of those troops had left our little portion of the island for other places by now, so perhaps I was being overly cautious. Then again, how could one be overly cautious during these turbulent times? Not only Hessians, but packs of booty-seeking rebels from across the Sound might be lurking about. My past experiences had taught me that avoidance was far preferable to encounter when it came to dealing with either of them.

We reached the stream without trouble, though, and walked upon its bank until coming to a spot lending itself to an easy descent. Giggling, Molly stripped off her thin garment and shoes and gingerly stepped into the shallows.

"It's just right!" she gasped. "Oh, do come in!"

I laughed, shaking my head. "You know it doesn't like me much." She was very well aware of my singular problem with free-flowing water, but chose to ignore it as part of her game with me.

"Coward," she called and bent to sweep her hand in the stream to splash me.

"Right you are," I called back. I made no move to dodge, but waved and teased her on, getting a good soaking before she tired from the play. My hair fell dripping and untidy about my face, and my shirt clung like a second skin. Though the heat of summer had even less effect upon me than the cold of winter, I must have had some sense of it for this state of damp dishevelment to feel so pleasant. Or perhaps it was Molly's undemanding company, her acceptance of me, of my shortcomings as well as my gifts.

I dropped upon our favorite grassy spot, where she'd left her clothes. Propped on my elbows, I had a fine view of her bathing. Moonlight filtered through the scattered branches overhead, making irregular patterns in black and silver over her body that shifted and shimmered as she moved. She didn't look quite real; she'd become a creature of mist and shadow. Even her laughter had been turned into something magical by the wide sky and the woods as it merged with the small sounds of hidden life all around us. I could scent it upon the warm wind, the green things, the musk of passing animals, the last of the summer flowers, the vitality of the earth itself where I lay. To my ears came the soft drift of leaves in the wind, the creeping progress of insects seeking to escape my presence, the annoyed call of a nearby bird and answering cries from those more distant.

This unnatural augmentation of my senses was all part of my changed condition, of course, and could not be ignored any more than I could ignore the blinding explosion of a sunrise. But I was well content, something that would have seemed quite impossible for me a year ago when a musket ball had smashed into my chest one sweltering morning, changing everything in a most extraordinary way.

Thinking me dead, my poor family had buried me, but it was not my lot to remain in the ground, for the legacy hidden in my blood soon expelled me from that early and unfair grave.

Sleeping during the day, abroad during the night, and able to command some very alarming talents, I had no name for this change or whether it was a curse or a miracle, though the latter seemed most likely, once the shock of my return had been overcome.

And now a very full and instructive year had passed; I'd learned of and explored my new gifts . . . and limitations, but was yet consumed with questions about my condition. Only one person in all the world could possibly answer them, but I'd exceeded the last of my patience in waiting for a reply to my many letters to her. The emptiness within could no longer be put off. The time had come for me to somehow find her again.

"What a dark look you have, Mr. Barrett," said Molly.

I gave a small start, then laughed at my own foolish lack of attention to her.

"Thinking about your lady, the one you left in England?" she asked, lying down next to me.

"How the devil did you know that?"

"Because you always wear that same long face when she's on your mind. I hope you don't hate her."

Molly was well known for her discretion. I'd long since confided to her about my other lover. About Nora Jones.

"Of course I don't hate her. I'm . . . disappointed. And hurt. I understand why she so ill-used me at our last parting, but that hardly makes it easier to live with."

"As long as you don't hate her."

"I could never do that."

"Then no more long faces, or you could frighten her away." One of her hands stole into the folds of my wet shirt. "You should take this off and let it dry out. Don't want to catch a fever, do you?"

"No, indeed. But are you quite comfortable yourself?"

She was still dripping from her bath, the ends of her loose hair sticking to her shoulders. "I feel just fine, though I should like to feel even better, if you please."

"And how might that be accomplished, Miss Audy?" I asked, falling in with her humor.

"Oh, in any way as seems best to you, Mr. Barrett." She helped me remove the shirt and tossed it out of the way on a convenient bush, then proceeded on to less prosaic pursuits. My arms were quite full of Molly Audy as we wrestled back and forth in the grass until she began panting less from the exertion and more from what I was doing to her.

"Off with them," she murmured, plucking at the buttons of my breeches.

"As you wish," I said, helping her. Soon my last garments were shoved down about my knees and Molly was straddling my most intimate parts, writhing about in a delightful expression of enthusiasm. I lay back and left her to it, reveling in the fever building within me as the central member of those parts began to swell under her ministrations.

We'd learned very early on that I had no need to make use of that portion of my manhood in order to bring us to a satisfying conclusion, but old habits die hard. So to speak. Though no longer able to expel seed, I was yet capable of using it to help pleasure a woman, though it was no more (or less, for that matter) important to my own climax than any other part of my body. My release came in a far different way from that which other men enjoy. It was far more intense, far longer in duration—far superior in every aspect; so much so that to return to the old way would have meant a considerable lessening of my carnal gratification.

And so, though it was active, if not functional, Molly made warm use of it as she pleased, bringing herself up to a fine pitch of desire, then, leaning far forward, gave me that which *I* most desired.

The marks I'd left upon her throat earlier in the evening were long closed, but that was easily remedied. Mouth wide, I brushed my lips over them, tongue churning against her taut skin. She gasped and drew back, then came close for more, playing upon this pattern until she could no longer bear to pull away. My corner teeth were out, digging into her flesh, starting the slow flow of blood from her into myself.

It had to be slow, for her own well-being as for mine. Thus was I able to extend our climax indefinitely without inflicting harm to her. She moaned and her body went still as I shifted to roll on top of her. Her legs twitched as though to wrap around me, to hold herself in place, but it was unnecessary for her to pursue that joining. The heat that lay between them would have spread throughout all her body by now, even as her gift of blood spread throughout mine.

A few drops. A scant mouthful. So *much* from so little.

Molly shuddered, her nails gouging into my back. In turn, I buried myself more deeply into her neck. The blood flow increased somewhat, allowing me a generous swallow of her life. Another, more forceful shudder beneath me, but I hardly noticed for my own sharing of the ecstasy. I was beyond thought, lost in a red dream of sensation that wrapped me from head to toe in fiery fulfillment.

Only Molly's cry brought me back. I became aware of her thrashing arms and extended my own to pin them down. She pushed up against me, urging me to take more, and I might well have done so, had we not already made love that night. Many long minutes later she gave a second, softer cry, this one of disappointment, not triumph, as she understood I was readying to end things, then came many a long sigh while I licked the small wounds clean, kissing away the last of her blood.

I took my weight from her, but we lay close together, limbs still entangled, bodies and minds slowly recovering themselves from that glorious glimpse of paradise. Molly's breathing evened out as she dozed in my arms. It would have been very good to join her in a nap, but my own sleep could only come with the sunrise.

Which wasn't all that long away, to judge by the position of the stars. Damnation, but the nights were *short*.

I let her rest another few minutes, then gave her a gentle shake. "I'm needing to leave soon, Molly."

She mumbled, more than half asleep, but made no other protest as she got up. I helped her with her wrapper and offered a steadying arm as she slipped on her shoes. She woke up enough to laugh a bit as I struggled to pull my breeches back into place. I made more of an effort than was needed for the task, in order to keep her laughing, and played the clown again when I donned my still damp shirt.

"You'll get a fever for sure," she cautioned.

"I'll risk it."

Taking her arm, I guided us back to her house. Quietly. Some of the very earliest risers of Glenbriar might be out and about by now; it wouldn't do to give them anything to gossip about. Or rather anything more to gossip about. Most of the village knew about Molly's nightly activities, but she made a good fiction of supporting herself with her sewing business during the day and otherwise held to the most modest behavior in public. Between that and a reputation for discretion, no one had cause to complain against her, and I wasn't of a mind to change things.

We eased through her back door and on to the bedroom, where I gathered up the rest of my clothes. I resolved to carry, instead of wear, them home and thus give my shirt a chance to dry.

"Don't forget what I said about sayin' your prayers, Johnny boy."

"I'll say one for you, too," I promised, giving her a final embrace.

"God, but I shall miss having you come by. Nights like tonight make me wish I didn't have to bother with the other chaps. None of them can do it as well as you. I'm that spoiled, I am."

"Then that makes two of us."

She began to sniffle. "Oh, now, there I go again."

"It's all right."

"Well, be off with you," she said, trying to sound brusque. "It won't do for you to be late."

"I know. God bless you, Molly." I kissed her hand and turned toward the doorway, then paused. "One more thing. I left a present for you under my pillow."

"La, Mr. Barrett, but you are—"

"And so are you, Molly dear." Then I had to dart outside and rush away because the sky was fractionally lighter than before. I trusted that she would find the ten guineas in coin—my parting gift to her on top of my normal payment for her services—to be most helpful in getting her quite comfortably through even the harshest of the coming winter.

I sped down the road leading home, feet hardly touching the earth.

The sun had become, if not an outright enemy, then an adversary whose movements must be respected. I had to keep close watch of the time or I'd find myself stranded all helpless in the dawn. That had nearly happened on my first night out of the grave. The old barn on our property had provided a safe enough shelter then, and it struck me that I might have to make use of it once more. The Hessians quartered in it over the last year were gone, thank God, so it would be secure, but my absence for the day would worry Father and my sister, Elizabeth.

I passed by that venerable landmark, ultimately deciding that there was just enough night left for me to make it to the house. Our open fields were tempting, clear of obstacles, unless one wished to count the ripening harvest. As it would be for the best to leave no traces of my passage, I willed myself into a state of partial transparency and, with my feet truly not touching the ground, was able to hurl forward, fast as a horse at full gallop.

It was one of my more exhilarating gifts and my favorite—next to the delight of drinking Molly's blood, of course.

Skimming along like a ghostly hawk, I sped across the gray landscape only a few feet above the ground. I might have laughed from the sheer joy of it, but no sound could issue from my mouth while I held to this tenuous form. Any verbal expression of my happiness would have to wait until I was solid again.

I covered the distance in good time, in better than good time, but saw that it would be a close race, after all. Too late to turn back. Our house was well in sight but still rather far away for the brief period I had left. The grays that formed the world as I saw it in this form were rapidly fading, going white with the advent of dawn.

Damnation, if I couldn't do better than this . . .

Faster and faster, until everything blurred except for the house upon which my eyes were focused. It grew larger, filling my vision with its promise of sanctuary, then I was abruptly in its shadow.

And just as abruptly found myself solid again. I couldn't help it. The sun's force was such as to wrench me right back into the world again. My legs weren't quite under me, and I threw my arms out to cushion the inevitable fall. My palms scraped against grass and weed, elbows cracked hard upon the ground, and any breath left in me was knocked out as my body struck and rolled and finally came to a stop.

If I could move as fast as a galloping horse, then by heavens, this was certainly like being thrown from one.

I lay stunned for a moment, trying to sort myself out, to see if I was hurt or not from the tumble. A few bruises at most, probably; I was not as easily given over to injury as before and knew well how to—

Light.

Burning, blinding.

Altogether hellish.

Even on this, the shadowed west side of the great structure, I could hardly bear up to its force. Fall forgotten, I dragged my coat over my head and all but crawled 'round to the back of the house and the cellar doors there. They were as I'd left them, thank God, unlocked. I wrenched one up and nearly fell down the stairs in my haste to get to shelter. The door made a great crash closing; if I hadn't already been keeping my head low, it would have given me a nasty knock.

The darkness helped a little, but provided no real comfort. That lay but a few paces ahead, deeper, in the most distant corner. My limbs were growing stiff, and it was with great difficulty that I staggered and stumped like a drunkard toward my waiting bed. I pitched into it, dropping clumsily on my face onto the canvas-covered earth and knew nothing more . . .

For what seemed only an instant.

Unlike other sleepers, I have no sense at all of time's passage when resting. One second I'm on the shrieking edge of bright disaster, and the next I'm awake and calm and all is safe. Adding to the illusion on this new evening was the welcome sight of my manservant, Jericho, standing over me holding a lighted candle. His black face bore an expression that was a familiar combination of both annoyance and relief.

"Hallo," I said. "Anything interesting happen today?"

The candle flame bobbed ever so slightly. "Half the house was roused at dawn by the slamming of a cellar door, sir. These are not easy times. A loud noise can be most alarming when one is unprepared to hear it."

Oh, dear. "Sorry. Couldn't be helped. I was in a dreadful hurry."

"So I had assumed when I came down to look in on you."

That was when I noticed that I was lying on my back, not my face, and bereft of soiled shirt, breeches, and boots. Some bed linen had been carefully draped over my body to spare the sensibilities of any kitchen servants who might have need to fetch something from the cellar stores. My hands had been washed clean of the grass stains they'd picked up, and my tangled hair was smoothly brushed out. Jericho had been busy looking after me, as usual. I'd slept through it, as oblivious as the dead that I so closely imitated during the day.

Further reproach for me to be more mindful of the time and to have more consideration for the others in the household was unnecessary. He'd made his point, and I was now thoroughly chastised and repentant. After putting his candle aside, he assisted as I humbly traded the bed linens for the fresh clothing he'd brought down. He combed my hair back, tying it with a newly ironed black ribbon, and decided that I could go one more night without shaving.

"You'll want a proper toilet before you have to leave, though," he warned.

"You speak as though you weren't coming along."

"I've been given to understand that the facilities aboard the ship may be severely limited, so I shall take what advantage I may in the time left to me."

No doubt, this advantage would be taken during the day. He got no arguments from me then. If ever a man was in thrall to a benevolent despot, that man was yours most truly, Jonathan Barrett.

Candle held high, Jericho led the way out of the cellar. We climbed the stairs, emerging into the stifling heat of the kitchen to be greeted as usual by Mrs. Nooth. She was busy with preparations for tomorrow's departure. Having decided that no ship's cook could possibly match her own skills, she was seeing to it my party would have sufficient provisions for the voyage. The fact I no longer ate food made no impression upon her; my gift for influencing other minds had seen to that. Except for Jericho, all the servants had been told to ignore such oddities in my behavior, like my sleeping the day through in the cellar. It was an intrusion upon them, yes, but quite for the best as far as I was concerned.

Jericho continued forward, taking me into the main part of the house. Now I could clearly hear my sister Elizabeth at her practice on the spinet. She'd borrowed something or other by Mozart from one of her friends and had labored to make a copy of the piece for herself, which I could only marvel over. From very early on it was discovered I had no musical inclinations to speak of; the terms and symbols were just so much gibberish to me, but I tried to make up for it with an appreciation of their translation from notes on paper into heavenly sounds. Elizabeth was a most accomplished translator, I thought.

I parted company from Jericho and quietly opened the door to the music room. Elizabeth was alone. A half dozen candles were lighted; wasteful, but well worth it as she made a very pretty picture in their golden glow. She glanced up but once to see who had come in, then returned her full concentration upon her music. I sprawled in my favorite chair by the open window, throwing one leg over an arm, and gave myself up to listening.

The last of the sun was finally gone, though its influence lingered in the warm air stirring the curtains. I breathed in the scents of the new night, enjoying them while I could. By this time tomorrow Elizabeth, Jericho, and I would be on a ship bound for England.

A little black spark of worry touched the back of my mind. Molly's concern for a safe voyage was not ill placed. The possibilities of autumn storms or a poorly maintained and thus dangerous ship or a discontented crew or—despite all assurances to the contrary—an attack by rebels or privateers in league with them loomed large before me. The night before I was too engrossed seeking the pleasures Molly offered to think much on them. Free of such distractions, I could no longer push them aside. I watched Elizabeth and worried on the future.

My initial invitation for her to come with me had been prompted by a strong wish to offer a diversion from the melancholy that had plagued her for the last few months. She'd been reluctant, but I'd talked her into it. With all the risks involved I was having second thoughts about having her along. And Jericho. But it was different with him. As his owner, I could command him to remain at home; with Elizabeth I could not. She'd been persuaded once and persuaded she would stay. The one time I'd raised the subject with her had convinced me of her commitment to come. We had not precisely argued, but she'd given me to understand in the clearest of terms that whatever perils that might lie ahead were of no concern to her and I would be advised to follow her example.

Too late to change things now. But as I'd told Molly, we were all in God's hands. I needed to listen better to myself. Sufficient unto the day is its own evil and all that. Or night, as the case was with me.

Elizabeth finished her piece. The last notes fled from her instrument and the contentment that always seemed to engulf her when she played faded away. Her face altered from a beatific smoothness to a troubled tightness, especially around her eyes and mouth.

"What did you think?" she asked.

"You did marvelous well, as always."

"Not my playing, but the piece itself."

"It's very pretty, very pleasant."

"And what else?"

No use trying to keep anything from her; we knew each other rather too well for that. "There did seem to be something of a darkness to it, especially that middle bit and toward the end."

That brought out a smile for me. "There's hope for you, then, if you noticed that."

"Really, now!" I protested, putting on a broad exaggeration of offense. Having played the clown for Molly last night, it was just as easy to do so once more for my sister. God knows, she was in sore need of having her spirits lightened. Elizabeth's smile did become more pronounced, but it failed to turn into laughter.

Then it vanished altogether as she looked back to her music. "That 'darkness' is my favorite, you know. It's the best part of the piece, the whole point of it."

"An interesting sentiment, no doubt."

Her eyes flicked over to mine as she caught my wary tone. "Oh, Jonathan, please stop worrying about me."

"It's gotten to be a habit, I fear."

"Yes, you and Father both. I'm all right. It's been awful and I'd never wish what happened to me upon my worst enemy, but I'm sure God had a good reason for it."

"I should hope it to be a very good reason, because for the life of me *I* can't fathom why. You certainly deserve better than what you've been served."

Her lips compressed into a hard line, and I knew I'd said too much.

"Sorry." I muttered. "But I just get so angry on your behalf sometimes."

"More like all the time. I've worked very hard to try and let it go. Can you not do the same?"

I shrugged, not an easy movement, given my position in the chair.

"You and Father have been of great help and comfort to me, but the need is past—I'm all better now."

Was she trying to convince me or herself? Or was I hearing things that weren't there? She certainly *seemed* better, especially with the trip to look forward to, but I wasn't quite over the shock yet, myself, so how could she be so fully recovered?

She wasn't, then. She was lying. But I'd heard that if one lies often and loud enough, the lie eventually becomes the truth. If that was Elizabeth's solution to living with the catastrophe that had engulfed her, then so be it, and she had my blessing.

"Did you enjoy yourself last night?" she asked, standing up and shuffling her sheets of music into order.

"Quite a lot," I said absently.

"I'm glad to hear it, I'm concerned for your . . . happiness." She paused to smile again and in such a way as to give me to understand that she knew exactly what I'd been doing. My vague stories to the rest of the household about going to The Oak to visit and talk were but smoke to her. And probably to Father. Most certainly to Jericho.

"Very kind, but this is hardly a topic I can discuss with you."

"Because I'm a woman?"

"Because I'm a gentleman," I said, with smug finality.

She chose to ignore it. "Meaning you don't discuss your conquests with other gentlemen?"

"Certainly not. Back at Cambridge you could find yourself bang in the middle of a duel for a careless boast."

"Ah, but I'm not a gentleman and have no wish to give challenge, so you're safe with me."

"But really—"

"I was just wondering who she was."

It wasn't much to ask, but damnation, I had my principles. If Molly could keep silent, then so could I. "Sorry, no."

Elizabeth finished putting her music away. By her manner I could tell she was not pleased, nor at all ready to give up.

"Why this curiosity over the company I keep?" I asked before she could frame another inquiry.

She paused and made a face. "Oh, I don't give a fig about who you're with."

"Then why—"

"Damnation, but I'm as bad as Mrs. Hardinbrook."

Now, *that* was an alarming declaration. "In what way?"

Elizabeth dropped onto a settee, her wide skirts billowing up from the force of the movement. She impatiently slapped them down. "The woman worms her way around, asking a dozen questions in order to work her way up to the one she really wants to ask. What a dreadful thing for me to be doing."

"Given the right situation it has its place, usually for questions that might not otherwise be answered, but I've discovered you out, rendering the ploy inappropriate."

She shot me a sour look. "Indeed, yes, little brother."

"Now, then, what is it you really want to ask me?"

The sourness turned into mischievous caution. "I was curious as to whether you dealt with your lady in the same manner that Miss Jones dealt with you."

Whatever I was using for a mind that night suddenly went thick on me for the next few moments. "I'm not sure I rightly understand your meaning," I finally said, straightening in my chair in order to face her.

"When you're with a lady and addressing certain intimate issues, do you conclude them by drinking her blood?"

"Good God, Elizabeth!"

"Oh, dear, now I've shocked you." And she did appear to be sincerely distressed by that prospect.

"That's hardly the . . . I mean . . . what the devil d'ye want to know that for?"

"I'm just curious. I was wondering about that, and that if you did, whether or not you *exchanged* blood with her, and what she thought about it."

My chin must have been sweeping the floor by then.

"Of course, if this is a breach of confidence, I'll withdraw the question," she continued.

"You can hardly do that! It's been said and . . . and . . . oh, good God."

"I'm sorry, Jonathan. I thought you might be a bit upset—"

A bit?

"But I thought that since you've already told me how things were between you and Miss Jones that you would not find it so difficult to . . ."

I waved a hand and she fell silent. "I think I have the general idea. I'm just surprised. This isn't the usual sort of thing one discusses with a woman. Especially when she's your sister," I added. "Why have you not raised the question before?"

"When this change first came to you, you were busy . . . and later on, I was busy."

"With your marriage?"

She snorted with disgust. "With my *liaison*, you mean."

"As far as anyone is concerned, it was a marriage."

"Words, words, words, and you're getting off the subject."

"I thought the two to be somehow related."

"In what way?"

Time for less bewilderment and more truth. "Well, you did sleep with the bastard—as his *wife*, so there's no shame in that—and for the short time you were together, we all got the impression that he pleased you."

It was Elizabeth's turn to go scarlet.

"My conclusion is that you're wondering if other women are also pleased with their men, so you ask me what I do and if the lady I'm with enjoys it."

Her gaze bounced all over the room since she could not quite meet my eyes. "You . . . you're . . ."

"Absolutely right?"

She ground her teeth. "Yes, damn it. Oh, for heaven's sake, don't laugh at me."

"But it *is* funny."

And contagious. She fought it, but ultimately succumbed, collapsing back on the settee, hand over her mouth to stifle the sound. God, but it was good to finally see her laughing again, even given these peculiar circumstances.

"All finished?" I asked.

"I think so."

"Curiosity still intact?"

"Yes. No more embarrassment?"

"No more. If you speak plainly with me, then I shall return the favor."

"Done," she said and leaned forward and we shook hands on it.

The issue settled, I twisted around to hook my leg over the chair arm again, affording myself a view out the window. Nothing was stirring past the curtains, which was a comfort. The events of the last year had taught me to place a high value on what others might consider to be dull: inactivity.

"Jonathan?" she prompted.

"Mm? Oh. As for your initial query, yes, I do consummate things in the same manner that Nora did with me. As for the other, no, I have never exchanged blood with the lady I have been seeing."

"Why not? You once said that Miss Jones found it to be exceedingly pleasurable."

"True, but we've also surmised that it led to this change manifesting itself in me."

"But it was a good thing—"

"I'll not deny it, but until I know all there is to know about my condition, I have not the right to inflict it upon another."

"But Miss Jones did so without consulting you."

"Yes, and that is one of the many questions that lie between us. Anyway, just because she did it, doesn't mean that I have to; it smacks of irresponsibility, don't you know."

"I hope you don't hate her." She said it in almost exactly the same tone that Molly Audy had used, giving me quite a sharp turn. "Something wrong?"

"Perhaps there is. That's the second time anyone's voiced that sentiment to me. Makes me wonder about myself."

"You do seem very grim when you speak of her."

"Well, we both know all about betrayal, don't we?"

Elizabeth's mouth thinned. "The nature of mine was rather different from yours."

"But the feelings engendered are the same. Nora hurt me very much by sending me away, by making me forget, by not telling me the consequence of our exchanges. *That's* what this whole miserable voyage is about, so I can find her and ask her *why*."

"I know. I can only pray that whatever answers you get can give you some peace in your heart. At least I know why I was betrayed."

We were silent for a time. The candles had burned down quite a bit. I rose and went 'round to them, blowing out all but two, which I brought over to place on a side table near us.

"Is that enough light for you?" I asked.

"It's fine." She gave herself a little shake. "I've not had my last question answered. What does your lady—the one you see now—think of what you do?"

"She thinks rather highly of it, if I do say so."

"It gives her pleasure?"

"So I understand from her."

"Does she not think it unusual?"

"I will say that though at first it was rather outside her experience, it was not beyond her amiable tolerance." I was pleased with myself for a few moments, but my smile faded.

"What is it?"

"I was just thinking of how much I'll miss her. Hated to leave her last night. That's why I was so late getting back. Won't happen again, though, Jericho took me to task on the subject of banging doors at dawn and waking the household."

"Father wasn't amused."

I wilted a bit. "I'll apologize to him. Where is he? Not called away?"

"On our last night home? Hardly. He's playing cards with the others."

Father was not an enthusiastic player and only did so to placate his wife. "Is Mother being troublesome again?"

"Enough so that everyone's walking on tiptoes. You know what she thinks of our journeying together—at least when she's having one of her spells. Vile woman. How could she ever come up with such a foul idea?"

I had a thought or two on that, but was not willing to share it with anyone. "She's sick. Sick in mind and in soul."

"I shall not be sorry to leave *her* behind."

"Elizabeth . . ."

"Not to worry; I'll behave myself," she promised.

Both of us had come to heartily dislike our mother, though Elizabeth was more vocal in her complaints than I. My chosen place was usually to listen and nod, but now and then I'd remind her to take more care. Mother would not be pleased if she chanced to overhear such bald honesty.

"I hope it helps you to know that I feel the same," I said, wanting to soften my reproach.

"Helps? If I thought myself alone in this, then I should be as mad as she."

"God forbid." I unhooked my leg from the chair arm and rose. "Will you stay or come?"

"Stay. It might set her off to see us walking in together."

True, sadly true.

I ambled along to the parlor, hearing the quiet talk between the card players long before reaching the room. From the advantage of the center hall, I could hear most of what was going on throughout the whole house. Mrs. Nooth and her people were still busy in the distant kitchen, and other servants, including Jericho and his father, Archimedes, were moving about upstairs readying the bedrooms for the night.

Long ignored as part of life's normal background, the sounds tugged at me like ropes. I'd felt it a dozen times over since the plans to leave for England had been finalized. Though not all that happened here was pleasant, it was home, *my* home, and who of us can depart easily from such familiarity?

And comfort. I hadn't much enjoyed my previous voyages to and fro. The conditions of shipboard life could be appalling—yet another reason for my second thoughts over having Elizabeth along. But I'd seen other women make the crossing with no outstanding hardship. Some of them even enjoyed it, while not a few of the hardiest men were stricken helpless as babes with seasickness.

Well, we'd muddle through somehow, God willing.

I shed those worries for others upon opening the parlor door. Within, a burst of candlelight gilded the furnishings and their occupants. Clustered at the card table were Father,

Mother, Dr. Beldon, and his sister, Mrs. Hardinbrook. Beldon and Father looked up and nodded to me, then resumed attention on their play. Mrs. Hardinbrook's back was to the door, so she noticed nothing. Mother sat opposite her and could see, but was either unaware I'd come in, or ignoring me.

The game continued without break, each mindful of his cards and nothing else as I hesitated in the doorway. For an uneasy moment I felt like an invisible wraith whose presence, if sensed, is attributed to the wind or the natural creaks of an aging house. Well, I could certainly make myself invisible if I chose. *That* would stir things a bit . . . but it wouldn't be a very nice thing to do, however tempting.

Mother shifted slightly, eyebrows high as she studied her hand. Her eyes flicked here and there upon the table, upon the others, upon everything except her only son.

Ignoring me. Most definitely ignoring me. One can always tell.

Home, I thought grimly and stepped into the parlor.

CHAPTER
—2—

Upon entering, I was able to see that my young cousin, Ann Fonteyn, was also present. She'd taken a chair close to a small table and was poring over a book with fond intensity. More Shakespeare, it appeared. She'd developed a great liking for his work since the time I'd tempted her into reading some soon after her arrival to our house. She was the daughter of Grandfather Fonteyn's youngest son and had sought shelter with us, safely away from the conflicts in Philadelphia. Though somewhat stunted in the way of education, she was very beautiful and possessed a sweet and innocent soul. I liked her quite a lot.

I drifted up to bid her a good evening, quietly, out of deference for the others. "What is it tonight? A play or the sonnets?"

"Another play." She lifted the book slightly. "*Pericles, Prince of Tyre,* but it's not what I expected."

"How so?" I took a seat at the table across from her.

"I thought he was supposed to kill a Gorgon named Medusa, but nothing of the sort has thus far occurred in this drama."

"That's the legend of Perseus, not Pericles," I gently explained.

"Oh."

"It's easy enough to mix them up."

"You must think me to be very stupid and tiresome."

"I think nothing of the sort."

"But I'm always getting things wrong," she stated mournfully.

That was my mother's work. Her sharp tongue had had its inevitable effect on my good-hearted cousin. Ann had become subject to much unfair and undeserved criticism over the months. Mother had the idiotic idea that by this means Ann could be made to "improve herself," though what those improvements might be were anybody's guess. Elizabeth and I had long ago learned to ignore the jibes aimed at us; Ann had no such defenses, and instead grew shy and hesitant about herself. In turn, this inspired even more criticism.

"Not at all. I think you're very charming and bright. In all my time in England I never once met a girl who was the least interested in reading, period, much less in reading Shakespeare."

"Really?"

"Really." This was true. Nora Jones had been a woman, not a girl, after all. And some of the other young females I'd encountered there had had interests in areas not readily considered by most to be very intellectual. Such pursuits were certainly enjoyable for their own sake; I should be the last person to object to them, having willingly partaken of their pleasures, but they were not the sort of activities my good cousin was quite prepared to indulge in yet.

"What are they like? The English girls?"

"Oh, a dull lot overall," I said, gallantly lying for her sake.

"Did you get to meet any actresses?" she whispered, throwing a wary glance in Mother's direction. Whereas a discussion of a play, or even its reading aloud in the parlor was considered edifying, any mention of stage acting and of actresses in particular was not.

"Hadn't much time for the theater." Another lie, or something close to it. Damnation, why was I . . . but I knew the answer to that; Mother would not have approved. Though I'd applied myself well enough to my studies, Cousin Oliver and I had taken care to keep ourselves entertained with numerous nonacademic diversions. Then there was all the time I'd spent with Nora. . . .

"I should like to go to a play sometime," said Ann. "I've heard that they have a company in New York now. Hard to believe, is it not? I mean, after the horrid fire destroying nearly everything last year."

"Very. Perhaps one day it will be possible for you to attend a performance, though it might not be by your favorite playwright, y'know."

"Then I must somehow find others to read so as to be well prepared, but I've been all through Uncle Samuel's library and have found only works by Shakespeare."

"I'll be sure to send you others as soon as I get to England," I promised.

Her face flowered into a smile. "Oh, but that is most kind of you, Cousin."

"It will be a pleasure. However, I know that there are other plays in Father's library."

"But they were in French and Greek and I don't know those languages."

"You shall have to learn them, then. Mr. Rapelji would be most happy to take you on as a student."

Instead of a protest as I'd half expected, Ann leaned forward, all shining eyes and bright intent. "I should like that very much, but how would I go about arranging things?"

"Just ask your Uncle Samuel," I said, canting my head once in Father's direction. "He'll sort it out for you."

She made a little squeak to indicate her barely suppressed enthusiasm, but unfortunately that drew Mother's irate attention toward us.

"Jonathan Fonteyn, what is all this row?" she demanded, simultaneously shifting the blame of her vexation to me while elevating it to the level of a small riot. That she'd used my middle name, which I loathed, was an additional annoyance, but I was yet in a good humor and able to overlook it.

"My apologies, Madam. I did not mean to disturb you." The words came out smoothly, as I'd had much practice in the art of placation.

"What are you two talking about?"

"The book I'm reading, Aunt Marie," said Ann, visibly anxious to keep the peace.

"Novels," Mother sneered. "I'm entirely opposed to such things. They're corruption incarnate. You ought not to waste your time on them."

"But this is a play by Shakespeare," Ann went on, perhaps hoping that an invocation of an immortal name would turn aside potential wrath.

"I thought you had some needlework to keep you busy."

"But the play is most excellent, all about Perseus—I mean Pericles, and how he solved a riddle, but had to run away because the king that posed the riddle was afraid that his secret might be revealed."

"And what secret would that be?"

Ann's mouth had opened, but no sound issued forth, and just as well.

"The language is rather convoluted," I said, stepping in before things got awkward. "We're still trying to work out the meaning."

"It's your time to waste, I suppose," Mother sniffed. To everyone's relief, she turned back to her cards.

Ann shut her mouth and gave me a grateful look. She'd belatedly realized that a revelation of the ancient king's incest with his daughter was not exactly a fit topic for parlor conversation. Shakespeare spoke much of noble virtues, but, being a wily fellow, knew that base vices were of far greater interest to his varied audience, sweet Cousin Ann being no exception to that rule.

I smiled back and only then realized that Mother's dismissive comment had inspired a white hot resentment in me. My face seemed to go brittle under the skin, and all I wanted was to get out of there before anything shattered. Excusing myself to Ann, I took my leave, hoping it did not appear too hasty.

Sanctuary awaited in the library. It was without light, but I had no need for a candle. The curtains were wide open, after all. I eased the door shut against the rest of the house and, free of observation, gave silent vent to my agitation. How *dare* she deride our little pleasures when her own were so empty? I suppose she'd prefer it if all the world spent its day in idle gossip and whiled away the night playing cards. It would bloody well serve her right if *that* happened. . . .

It was childish, perhaps, to mouth curses, grimace, make fists, and shake them at the indifferent walls, but I felt all the better for it. I could not, at that moment, tell myself that she was a sick and generally ignorant soul, for the anger in me was too strong to respond to reason. Perhaps it was my Fonteyn blood making itself felt, but happily the Barrett side had had enough control to remove me from the source of my pique. To directly express it to Mother would have been most unwise (and a waste of effort), but here I was free to safely indulge my temper.

God, but I would also be glad to leave *her* behind. Even Mrs. Hardinbrook, a dull, toad-eating gossip if ever one was born, was better company than Mother, if only for being infinitely more polite.

My fit had almost subsided when the door was opened and Father looked in.

"Jonathan?" He peered around doubtfully in what to him was a dark chamber.

"Here, sir," I responded, forcefully composing myself and stepping forward so he might see.

"Whatever are you doing here in the . . . oh. Never mind, then." He came in, memory and habit guiding him across the floor toward the long windows where some light seeped through. "There, that's better."

"I'll go fetch a candle."

"No, don't trouble yourself, this is fine. I can more or less see you now. There's enough moon for it."

"Is the card game ended?"

"It has for me. I wanted to speak to you."

"I am sorry about the banging door, sir," I said, anticipating him.

"What?"

"The cellar door this morning when I came home. Jericho gave me to understand how unsettling it was to the household. I do apologize."

"Accepted, laddie. It did rouse us all a bit, but once we'd worked out that it was you, things were all right. Come tomorrow it'll be quiet enough 'round here."

Not as quiet as one might wish, I thought, grinding my teeth.

Father unlocked and opened the window to bring in the night air. We'd all gotten into the habit of locking them before quitting a room. The greater conflict outside of our little part of the world had had its effect upon us. Times had changed . . . for the worse.

"I saw how upset you were when you left," he said, looking directly at me.

Putting my hands in my pockets, I leaned against the wall next to the window frame. "I should not have let myself be overcome by such a trifle."

"Fleabites, laddie. Get enough of them and the best of us can lose control, so you did well by yourself to leave when you did."

"Has something else happened?" I was worried for Ann.

"No. Your mother's quiet enough. She behaves herself more or less when Beldon or Mrs. Hardinbrook are with her."

And around Father. Sometimes. Months back I'd taken it upon myself to influence Mother into a kinder attitude toward him. My admonishment to her to refrain from hurting or harming him in any way had worked well at first, but her natural inclination for inflicting little (and great) cruelties upon others had gradually eroded the suggestion. Of late I'd been debating whether or not to risk a repetition of my action. I say risk, because Father had no knowledge of what I'd done. It was not something of which I was proud.

"I wish she would show as much restraint with Ann," I said. "It's sinful how she berates that girl for nothing. Our little cousin really should come with us to England."

"They had a difficult enough time getting her to take the ferry from New York to Brooklyn. She's no sailor and more's the pity."

Indeed. A trip to England would do her great good, but Ann was sincerely frightened and made ill by sea travel and had firmly declined the invitation to come with me and Elizabeth.

"What about yourself?" asked Father, referring to my own problem with water.

"I shall be all right."

At least I *hoped* so. The streams that flowed through our lands had come to be something of a barrier to me, a fact that I'd discovered the first time I'd tried crossing one on my own after my change. What had once been an easily forded rivulet had become a near impassable torrent as far as I was concerned. My feet dragged like iron weights over the streambed, and the water felt so chill as to burn me to the bone—or so it seemed to my exaggerated senses. Father and I had investigated the phenomenon at length, but could make no sense of this strange limitation I'd acquired. Like my ability to vanish, we connected it to my condition and had as yet found no cure for it.

Yet another question for Nora.

Thankfully, I was able to manage water crossings on horseback or in a wagon, though it was always hard going. I'd reasoned that taking a ship would entail about the same level of difficulty and was prepared to tolerate the inconvenience. It could be no worse than the bout of seasickness I'd suffered during my initial voyage to England four years ago. That had worn off as my body got used to the motion of the ship, and in this coming voyage I was counting on a similar recovery.

Not that I was giving myself much of a choice. If I had to put up with the discomfort for the next two months or more, then so be it. To England I would go.

"Your livestock was sent ahead this morning," said Father. "I hope to God it arrives safely."

"I'm certain it will."

His eyes gleamed with amusement. "You spoke to Lieutenant Nash?"

"At length. He'll provide as safe an escort as any might hope for in these times."

"My thought is that you've gotten a fox to guard your henhouse."

"This fox is very well trained, sir."

Nash, in charge of the profitable work of collecting supplies for the commissary, possessed the soul of a rapacious

vulture, but early in our acquaintance I'd been able to successfully curb his greedy nature to something more moderate. On more than one occasion, I'd been able to put the fear
of God into him by means of my unnatural influence, and
he took care to pay attention to any little requests we might
present to him as though they were written orders from the
King himself. In turn, we were most careful not to abuse
our advantage lest it draw unwelcome notice upon us.

In this instance, the request was to provide a safe escort
for the cattle I would be taking on the ship to England. He
was to make sure that all of them were put aboard without
incident. Such an undertaking was highly unusual, to say
the least, but my need was great enough that I had no heavy
weight on my conscience in suborning one of the King's
officers to play my private agent for such a task. Only he had
sufficient authority to protect them from others and see that
they and their fodder for the trip were safely delivered.

Also, with the British army and the Hessians on one
side and the rebels on the other and all of them hungry
as wolves for fresh beef, the idea of taking good cattle
out of the country bordered on madness. But I would need
to feed myself on the voyage, and for that I required a
ready supply of animal blood. I hoped a dozen would be
more than sufficient for my modest appetite, since I had no
plans for indulging in any unnatural exertions like flying or
vanishing while aboard. My only real worry was that the
animals might not survive an ocean voyage. Well, if they
all died, then so be it. I was not adverse to drinking human
blood for food if starving necessity forced me to such an
extreme.

Father and I had devoted much thought to the framing of
just how to ship the beasts and had planned things carefully.
Between us, fees (and bribes) were paid, documents were
issued, stamped, and made inarguably legal in ways that
only an experienced lawyer could devise. In the end we'd
obtained permission from His Majesty's servants in charge
of hindering honest travelers to ship one dozen heifers to
England ostensibly for the purpose of breeding them to
superior stock owned by the Fonteyn side of the family.
The logical thing to do, as was pointed out to us by the

first official we'd encountered, would be to purchase a bull in England and bring it here, thus reducing our expenses on the venture. I'd "persuaded" the fellow and all the others that came after not to argue, but to simply make the arrangements as we desired, without question.

None of it had been very easy, but there is a great satisfaction to be derived from the accomplishment of a difficult endeavor. Perhaps I would feel this particular satisfaction again once we made landfall in England, God willing.

"Trained or not, I shan't feel easy in my heart until I see the results of his work for myself," said Father.

His voice did not sound right to me, having in it an odd note of strain that I did not like one whit. "What is it, sir?"

He thought long before answering, or so it seemed to me as I waited. He gave a half shrug and nearly smiled, an expression remarkably similar to Elizabeth's own subdued efforts of late. "I shall have to tell you, I see that well enough, and hope that you can forgive me for adding another worry to the others you carry."

"Worry?"

His raised hand held back the formation of more specific questions from me. He pushed the window wide. "Come along with me, laddie," he said, and stepped over the low sill quick as a thief.

Too startled to comment at this unorthodox exit, I simply followed, though I did possess enough mind to finally remember to close my gaping mouth. He led the way toward the parlor window and stopped close enough that we might see those within, but yet be concealed from them by the darkness. Father signed for me to look inside, and I obeyed. It was a cozy enough scene to behold: Ann still read her book, and the others still played at their cards. All was peaceful. Familiar. Normal.

I turned back to Father and indicated that I did not understand his reason for showing this to me. He moved back a little distance now, so there would be no chance of anyone overhearing us.

"Is this what you thought might worry me?"

"I'm coming to the worry, laddie." He struck off slowly over the grounds, his eyes hardly leaving the house as we gradually began to pace around it. "It concerns the French," he stated.

Father had a manner about him when he was in a light mood and wanting to be humorous. That manner was lacking in him now, so I understood he was not trying to make some sort of an oblique jest. That was all I understood, though. "Sir?"

"The damned French. You mark me, they'll be coming into this war like wolves to a carcass. You've heard the news, but have you worked out what it means?"

"I've heard rumors that the French are sending ships loaded with holy water and rosaries and are determined to make us all Catholic."

Father paused and laughed at that one, just as I had done when I'd first caught wind of it at The Oak. Presumably, all good members of the English Church would be righteously horrified at the prospect of a forced conversion to an alien faith. Those who were less than firm in their loyalty to the King might then be persuaded to a more wholehearted support of his rule. It was an utterly ridiculous threat, of course, but some of our sovereign's more excitable subjects were taking it seriously.

"France will be sending shiploads of cargo," said Father, "but it will more likely be gunpowder, arms, and money. Some of their young rascals have already come over to lend their support to the rebel cause; it's only a matter of time before their government officially follows. We slapped them hard fourteen years ago, and they're still stinging from it. They want revenge against England."

"But they'll risk another war."

"Possibly. My thought is that they'll play the rebels against the Crown for as much as it's worth. Wars are expensive, but this one won't have a high price for them at all if they work it to their advantage. 'Tis a fine way to weaken both sides with little effort on their part."

"You'd think the Congress over here would see through the ploy."

"Some of the clever ones do, of that I have no doubt, but they're so desperate for help they dare not say a word to the people they claim to represent. I've no trust for them. My

God, barely a year before they came out with that damnable declaration against the King they were just as loudly voicing their undying loyalty to him. Bloody liars and rogues, the lot of them."

I made a noise to indicate my agreement with that sentiment. "And fools, if they will risk trusting the French."

"Indeed, yes."

"But this worry you spoke of . . ."

Father paused. We'd climbed a little rise and had the pleasure of viewing the house and much of its surrounding grounds. He glanced at me, then extended his arm to take in all that lay before us. "This," he said, "won't last." This was a flat and inarguable statement.

Inarguable, but needing an explanation. I asked for one.

"We've been safe enough here almost from the start. There have been raids and outrages and theft, but nothing like *real* war, Jonathan. The west end of the island saw that when General Howe's men landed. Stock was killed, crops burned to the roots, houses looted and burned, and the owners turned out to fend for themselves on what was left. 'Tis one thing to hear of it, but another to have the experience, and we were spared only by God's grace and Washington's prudence in running like a rabbit in another direction. I don't think we can count on many more such miracles."

"But the fighting is over. Gone from here, anyway."

"Who's to say it won't return, though? This has become a civil war with Englishman against Englishman, with each side regarding the other as the worst kind of traitor. Those are the most evil and the bitterest of conflicts, and when peace finally comes it won't matter which side you were on, for there will be reprisals for all."

"But the King must win. What else is possible? And I can't believe that he would be so ignorant as to punish those who have remained loyal to him."

"Stranger things have happened. Oh, don't be alarmed, I'm not speaking treason, I just want you to know that I've had some hard thought over how the world has changed for us and that it is likely to continue changing and not necessarily to our favor or liking."

"How can it not be in our favor once the rebels are subdued?"

"Reprisals, laddie. Not just in taxes to pay for the war, but court work and plenty of it. More than enough to keep me busy for the rest of my days . . . but I've no stomach for it."

I couldn't help but stare. Father loved his vocation, or so he'd always told me.

He was nodding at my reaction. "This won't be arguing the ownership of a stray sheep, or who's the rightful master of what parcel of land, or anything like that. This will be the trying of traitors, the confiscation of their property, jailings, floggings, hangings. Some have used the cloak of patriotism to cover their thefts and murders, and they will get all that they deserve, in this world or the next, but what of the others whose only crime may have been to read the wrong newspaper? I will not be a party to that, to punishing a man just because he *thinks* differently from me."

"You won't have to do any such thing, sir."

"Won't I? If I do not fulfill all the duties thrust upon me by the court, then might I not also be a traitor to the Crown?" He waved his hand against my protest and I fell silent, for I knew that he was right.

"What's to be done, then?"

He gave no answer, but sat down on the grass, still facing the house. I sat next to him, plucking up a stray bit of rock to play with. His somber mood had transferred onto me, and I wanted some distraction for my hands.

"What's to be done," he finally said in a heavy voice, "is to move back to England."

Had he picked up a stone himself and lobbed it square between my eyes, I could not have been more stunned.

He continued, "And before you say aught else, remember that I've first put all that hard thought into my decision."

In truth, I could not bring myself to say a damned thing for a considerable period. It seemed too much of an effort even to think, but think I must if I was to understand him.

But he seemed to anticipate the questions beginning to take form in my mind. "You know why we came here all those years ago? Your mother and I?"

"To put some distance between yourself and her father, you told us," I mumbled, too shaken yet to raise my voice. I made a fist around the little piece of rock so the edges dug hard into my palm.

"Exactly. Old Judge Fonteyn was a monster and no mistake. He did all he could to make our lives miserable, using his influence to intimidate your mother into obedience to his will long after she was a settled matron with a home of her own. How that old sinner could howl and rage, but I thought that that would end once I'd put an ocean between us. And it worked—for a time."

Until things had gone wrong between Father and Mother and she'd left him on Long Island to live a separate life for herself in Philadelphia.

He grimaced. "I won't repeat what you already know. What it has come to is this—the Judge is long dead, and his threat upon my marriage fulfilled itself long ago, so my reason for staying on here has quite vanished. Combine that with the fact that you and Elizabeth are grown adults and more than capable of being on your own, an endeavor you're about to undertake, anyway. Combine it again with the fact that the conflicts taking place all around us have made this into a most hazardous place in which to live. Ergo, I've no sane reason to remain here."

"But this is our *home*," I said, aware of the plaintive whine in my voice, but not caring.

"Only for as long as no one takes it from us. The rebels have confiscated property before, you've read the accounts and heard them. If there should be an unforeseen setback and our army is forced from this island, those bastards from Connecticut will be over here with the next turn of the tide ready to pick us clean in the name of their precious Continental Congress."

It was impossible to conceive of that ever happening, but the raids from across the Sound were real enough. We'd been watchful of our own and had been lucky, but many of our friends had not been so blessed. The story was still fresh in our minds of how two of the DeQuincey daughters had been burned out of their house and forced into the woods, barefoot, with only their nightdresses to protect them from

the March cold. They'd managed to reach the safety of
their uncle's home some miles away, but not without great
suffering and anguish. Their attackers had even chased them
for a goodly distance, hooting after them like schoolboys on
a lark. The great Sons of Liberty had given up the hunt, fortunately, wanting to return to their booty-laden whaleboat
before the coming of dawn.

That could happen to us, I thought. We were not immune.
No one could be so long as such men roamed free and
were base enough to think that two helpless girls were such
a grave threat to their miserable cause. I now understood
Father's worry, but that understanding did not make his
words any easier to accept.

He plucked a blade of grass and began to shred it, still
looking at the house. At *our* house.

"This is different for you, laddie, I know that, for you
were bred and born here. For myself, it has been a home,
but never really mine. The lands, the house, all that belongs
to your mother because of the agreement I'd signed before
our marriage. I've done well enough in my life. I've a few
pennies scraped together from my practice and that's all
I really need for my comfort, but not here, not anymore.
I've lived through one war and count myself blessed that
Providence saw fit to spare me, but there is no desire within
to go through another—nor do I want my children to have
any part of what's likely to come. You've had more than
your portion of grief already, as we all have." He let the
remains of the grass blade slip away unheeded. "Dear Lord,
but we don't need any more. Had it not been for your Miss
Jones, we'd have lost you last year. For a terrible time I
thought we had. . . ."

His voice caught and I put my hand on his shoulder.
My own throat had gone tight in reaction. "It's all right,
Father."

He sniffed and laughed a little. "Yes, by God it is, laddie.
I just want to keep it so."

"Are you saying that you're coming with us?"

He gave a thick cough and impatiently rubbed his nose.
"Not on this voyage, there's too much preparation to do first.
But soon. That's the worry I was meaning and I'm sorry to

thrust it upon you the night before you leave, but it wanted saying while there was still time to say it. Better now than later in a letter sent to England that will be months out of date by the time you get it."

"You've no need to apologize, sir."

"Well, I thought I should try to be polite about it, considering what a shock this must be."

I smiled and eased my grasp upon the rock. How appropriate. "When will you tell Elizabeth?"

"Tomorrow. When we take the carriage to the harbor."

"Why did you not tell us together?"

"I'd hardly planned on saying anything at all, but the time had come. Besides, one of you is formidable enough, but both at once . . ." He shook his head as though my sister and I could have overwhelmed him in some way, as we had done in play as children when trying to wheedle a special favor from him. But then as now, we knew when he could be persuaded and when he could not. Father had made up his mind, and it was not for me to question his judgment, though I yet had questions on other things.

"Sir, you had me look at the others through the parlor window, but I still do not quite have the purpose of it clear in my mind."

"So you could see how things are for us when compared to the rest of the world. There is a kind of peace here, but it's so damnably fragile. Any banditti claiming to be part of Washington's army can come day or night and shatter it forever. This is your home, but would you rather say good-bye to it now of your own volition and remember it as it is or wait, and live with the possibility that someone will come along to *take* it all away? If that were to happen, then nothing would ever be the same. This sanctuary and any others replacing it would ever and always be tainted by such an invasion."

And in that I could hear echoes of what his mistress, Mrs. Montagu, had frequently said to him on the subject. Last December her house had been broken into by rebels and thoroughly looted. Despite the repairs made and support he had given her over the months, she was still subject to vast distress in her own home and, though better prepared than before, was ever in fear of another attack. I asked after her.

"She's well enough."

"What I mean is, if you're planning a return to England, what will happen to her? Have you told her?"

"Laddie," he said, sounding amused, "it was *her* suggestion."

Well-a-day. Mrs. Montagu was a kind woman, for whom I had a great fondness. As I had lacked a mother for the greater part of my life, she had filled that need in me to some goodly degree. "Then she's preparing to leave as well? When?"

"Soon. That's all I can say. There's much that must be done first . . . like dealing with your mother."

Good God. My face fell at the very thought of her. She almost surely promised to be as fell an obstacle as any in Father's path. "What will you do?"

"I . . . haven't quite worked that out," he confessed. "I'm of a divided mind on whether to present it to her as a concluded arrangement, or to find a way for her to come up with the idea herself. The latter is more appealing to me as it is bound to be quieter."

"It would certainly appeal to Mother's nature, especially if she thought you might—" I cut off what was to come next, realizing how it would sound, but Father only smiled.

"Thought I might not like it? I know you meant no disrespect for me, only that you understand how her mind works. Then so be it. That shall be my strategy, though I doubt it will take much to put her onto the business. She has family in England she hasn't seen for decades, like that harpy of a sister who runs things."

And people. Aunt Fonteyn, as she chose to call herself. Horrible woman. At least I wouldn't have to be dependent upon her as were so many of her other relatives. I could thank my inheritance from Grandfather Fonteyn for that blessing.

"What about Dr. Beldon?" I asked. If Father intended to take Mother on a long voyage, Beldon and certainly Mrs. Hardinbrook would be necessary to help maintain his treasured peace.

"Gotten fond of him, have you?" His eyes twinkled.

"When he's not playing the toady, he's witty enough company," I conceded.

"First I'll see about persuading your mother, then I'll worry about the others."

I did not ask him if he had not thought of simply leaving on his own, for that would have been an unforgivable insult to his honor. He was a good and decent man, laboring to keep firm to the vow he'd made on his wedding day. No matter that their love had died, his promise to care for and protect his wife was still to be observed. To ignore that promise for his own convenience would violate all that he held sacred. He would sooner hang himself in church during Sunday services than forget it.

Many another man would not have put up with such a wife, but my Father was of a different heart than they. I was glad of him and proud of him and sorry for all the pain he'd endured and hopeful that the future might somehow be easier for him. For us all.

All. Thus was I reminded to speak on another's behalf.

"I must ask one thing of you, sir. Please don't wait until the morrow to tell Elizabeth. It wouldn't be fair to her. She needs . . . the time."

"Time?"

"So she can say good-bye."

He saw my point, nodding. We'd already made our partings with our friends, but not with the land itself. We might never see our beautiful house again, or the fields around it, or the thousand treasured places we'd explored while growing up. Certainly I'd said farewell before when I'd been packed off to Cambridge, but my home had ever been secure in mind and memory, waiting to welcome me back again upon my return.

No more. And that was a heavy sadness to carry along when, after quite a lot more talk and questions, I took my leave from Father and began walking. Aimless at first, I'd intended to wander the estate and simply stroll the night away. It seemed the best manner in which to bid farewell to my favorite haunts, but I found myself going instead to a place I'd been avoiding for far too long. Just over a year had passed since I'd last been there, and throughout that time the mere thought of it had never failed to make me physically ill.

Not without excellent reason.

As children, Elizabeth, Jericho, and I had played here. We were pirates hunting treasure or scouts and Indians; we gamed and quarreled and laughed and sang as our mood dictated; we called it the Captain's Kettle, this deep arena gouged out by an ancient and long-vanished glacier. A special place, a magical place, once protected by the innocence of young memory from all the harsh assaults of living.

At one time I'd regarded it as a refuge. Safe. But that illusion, like many others as my view of the world expanded, was gone.

Now I stood close by one edge, on the very spot where the musket ball had slammed into my chest, where interminable seconds later I'd gasped out the last of the life I'd known to fall helplessly into what would be the first of my daytime sleeps. If dreams had come to me during that period or if I'd been somehow aware of the goings-on about me, it was just as well no memories lingered to sear my mind. Those I did possess were sufficiently wretched, so much so that I had to cling hard to a tree to keep from collapsing beneath their sickening weight.

My knees had begun quaking long before reaching this ground, though I told myself that anticipation was making the endeavor more difficult than the actuality. Only by this inner chiding was I able to goad myself into coming, to attempt to look upon the last place on earth where I'd felt the then welcome blaze of sunlight and had breathed the free air without conscious effort.

Nothing had really changed here, nor had I expected it to, only my perception of it had suffered for the worse. A childhood playground had been corrupted into a vile pit of black dread, and since the possibility that I might never see it again had become a surety, I'd conceived the perverse necessity to come in the hope of ridding myself of the darkness by facing it. But as I held hard to the tree to keep steady, eyes squeezed tight against the view, the need was all but drowned by long-denied reaction. I hadn't anticipated it being this bad; I felt smothered, cold . . . my hands, my whole body, shaking, shivering.

This was a fool's errand. An idiotic mistake. A disaster. A . . .

No. God give me strength to fight this. And I started to mutter a prayer, but could not finish it. No matter. The mere intent to pray was a calming influence, reminding me that I was yet in God's hands.

The experience of my death had been hideous, but it was past and done. Fool or no, idiot or no, I would *not* let myself be defeated by a mere *memory*. Back hunched as though bracing for a blow, I forced my eyes open.

Grass, leaves, twigs, and rock sorted themselves into recognizable shapes, no different from those cloaking the rest of our estate, to be walked over or kicked aside as needed. Trees emerged next, then a bit of sky. High above, the branches had laced themselves together. I stared at their canopy and felt my belly twisting in on itself. Not good. To look made me dizzy, not to look made me a coward. But a little illness was preferable now than to suffer lonely recriminations later; so I stared until my guts ceased to churn and the world left off lurching every time I swallowed back bile.

Better. I straightened, discovering my legs were capable of supporting me unassisted. Releasing my grasp of the tree, I stepped unsteadily closer to the edge of the kettle and looked down. Looked across. Looked to the place where the Finch brothers had crouched, hiding from Hessian searchers. Looked to where I'd seen but not comprehended the meaning of a puff of smoke from a musket aimed at my heart.

I looked and waited for the next wave of illness to pass. It did not seem as severe as the others. The shakiness gradually subsided.

Much better. I sat on the once bloodied patch of earth where I'd fallen. Cautiously. It was impossible to rid myself of the notion that some trace of the agony I'd passed through might be lingering here to seize me once more.

An abrupt twinge through my chest did make me wince, but that, as I well knew, originated in my mind. A memory of pain, but not pain itself. No need to fear. No need. Really.

Father had taught us always to face our fears. Talk about them if need be, then look at them and decide if they're worth any further worry. That had ever and always worked in the past, and since my change I'd seen the need to face this one eventually. But I'd never once spoken of it; not even Jericho knew. Telling others meant I'd soon have to take action, and to come here was a labor I'd not yet been ready to assume, or so I told myself each time I put it off. But no longer. That luxury was no longer mine to have.

Drawing my knees up enough that I might rest my arms across them, I waited to see if more illness might overtake me.

Not exactly comfortable, I thought some little time later as a sharp stone ground against my backside. I shifted enough to allow a brief search for the offending rock, prying it free. I half expected it to be stained with old blood, but its rough surface proved to be as unblemished and innocuous as the rest of the area. Eventually I tossed it into the kettle, listening to it rattle through the trees and the faint thump when it struck the ground far below.

I looked and waited, taking in the night sounds as I'd done the previous evening on the banks of the stream, but it wasn't the same. The peace I'd known then had been sweet; was it so far from me now?

Yes, I grumbled, especially if I had to stay here much longer.

The tedium of waiting for another adverse reaction now became my chief adversary, not the illness. I began to drum my fingers, whistle without mind to the tune, and by degrees I came to think that I had more interesting things to do than this. But if I left now, would that be giving in?

Decidedly not.

Instead, I gave in to something resembling a laugh. It was breathy and had more than a small share of unease and subsided too quickly, yet was an indication of barely realized triumph.

It was absurd, of course. *I* was absurd.

My great and horrible fear had turned into boredom.

A second laugh, more certain than the first.

Absurd, and like many absurdities, it craved expression.

I found another stone and tossed it high. It arced through the trees and crashed into the tangle of growth far below. I grabbed another and another until none were left, then got up and searched for more, eager as a child. Circling the kettle, I let fly dozens of similar missiles. As though in a game of chase, I darted through the trees, shouting greetings at them just to hear the echoes.

Foolish, yes, but gloriously foolish. When one is suddenly liberated from a burden, one must celebrate. So I ran and jumped and called out bits of childish verse and song, careless and free.

The last thing I did was to throw myself over the edge of the kettle at a flat run. The world surged for a mad instant as I suddenly hurtled down, then vanished altogether. I'd swiftly willed myself out of all danger, spinning into that state of joyful weightlessness, like a leaf floating upon the wind. I drifted high, leisurely contesting the gentle pressure of the air, invisible as thought, yet in some way just as substantial.

I know not how long I played at this, but finally I tired and resumed solidity on the spot where I'd died. Whatever hurt I'd suffered, whatever anguish for that which I'd lost was no longer a part of this place. I laughed again, and this time the note of triumph was tempered only by a humble gratitude for that which remained: my life, changes and all, and my family.

My misgivings about a permanent parting from these lands was gone. Perhaps the reluctance most people feel when leaving a home has more to do with the inability to resolve any unhappiness that's occurred there, rather than the loss of the happiness they've had. The memories of dying were with me but could no longer instill their fear and pain. They had diminished; I had grown.

With a much lighter heart than before, I hiked back to the house.

CHAPTER
—3—

Much to Father's relief the cattle arrived at the ship and had been safely loaded along with the rest of the baggage we were taking to England. There was quite a lot of it, for at the last we'd applied ourselves to additional packing in light of Father's decision to soon follow. Not everything could come; Elizabeth was already mourning the loss of her spinet, but I'd promised to find her another, better one in London. My own major regret was having to leave behind my favorite hunter, Rolly. From the very start of the conflict I'd dreaded losing him to the commissary men, and I hated the idea of his falling into careless and cruel hands. It was one of the many questions I'd posed for Father during our lengthy talk, and one for which he had no ready answer.

I was held fast by my day sleep during the early morning rushing about as our things were piled into the carriage and wagon taking us to the ship. Though utterly oblivious to it all, I could count myself lucky to be well out of the maelstrom of activities attendant on our departure. That was the one positive aspect of my unconscious condition, and it stood alone against a legion of negatives, the chief of them being that I was forced to trust others to take proper care of me.

Not that I held anything in my heart but confidence for those in my family, but I didn't know the captain or crew of the ship, and it was easy enough to imagine the worst. Even the smallest lapse of attention during the process of putting me aboard could end with me plunging disastrously into the cold waters of the Sound. I'd received many assurances from Father that all would be well, but reluctantly surrendered to the effects of that morning's dawn with a feeling of dread and murmuring a hasty prayer asking for the care and preservation of my helpless body.

Elizabeth, with her talent for organization and the solving of problems, had early on determined the best means for me to travel while in this state. She had ordered the construction of a sturdy chest large enough for me to curl into like a badger in its dark winter burrow. As I was completely immobile while the sun was up, there was little need to consider the thing's lack of comfort. I'd tried out this peculiar bed and approved it, suffering no ill-effects from its confined space.

No pillows or mattress layered the bottom; instead, it was cushioned by several tightly woven canvas bags, each filled with a goodly quantity of earth from our lands. The grave had rejected me—or perhaps I had rejected it—but it was still necessary for me to carry a portion of it with me whenever traveling. Not to do so meant having to spend the entire day in thrall to an endless series of frightful dreams. Why this had to be I did not know. I hoped Nora would enlighten me.

I was later told that there were no mishaps of any kind in transporting my box to the ship. The only time a question was raised was when Elizabeth insisted that it be placed in the small cabin I'd be sharing with Jericho. For a servant to be in the same room as his master was irregular but not unheard of, but the quarters were very limited and it was logically thought that less baggage meant more space. But Elizabeth turned a deaf ear to any recommendations of stowing the box in the hold, and so I was finally, if obliviously, ensconced in my rightful place.

By nightfall the ship was well on its way, a favorable wind and the tide having aided our progress. Too late now to turn back, or so I soon had to remind myself.

Jericho had been hard at work, having thoughtfully freed me from the limits of the box with the intent of transferring me to the cabin's narrow bed. He'd placed my bags of earth over its straw mattress, concealed them with a coverlet, then eased me on top. The story we'd agreed upon to explain my daytime absences was to say that I was a poor sailor and having a bad attack of seasickness. It was a common enough occurrence and entirely reasonable; what we had not reckoned upon was it being so wretchedly true.

At the risk of making a supreme understatement, this was the second most disagreeable awakening of my life. The first, of course, was when I'd come to myself in that damned coffin over a year ago. That had been awful in terms of straightforward shock; this one was nearly as bad in terms of sheer physical torment.

Rather than my usual instantaneous alertness, I floated sluggishly back to consciousness, confused and strangely anxious. I was wholly aware of an unfamiliar discomfort afflicting every square inch of my body, inside and out. Had I felt an illness upon my return to the Captain's Kettle? Would that such a mild case of it would visit me now. Someone had taken my head and belly and tossed them around like dice in a cup, or so I might conclude in regard to their present lack of settlement. They *still* seemed to be rolling about on their own. Every hair on my head and all down my back stood on end, positively bristling with alarm at this unhappy sensation. My limbs seemed to weigh twice as much as normal, and my muscles seemed too spent to move them.

"Mr. Jonathan?" Jericho hovered over me, and if I read the concern in his face and voice rightly, then I was in a rather bad state.

"We're at sea," I whispered decisively. The very air seemed to press hard on me. My skin was crawling from it.

"I have been told that Sag Harbor is well behind us, sir."

"Oh, God."

"Sir?"

"*Mal de mer*," I gasped, closing my eyes. There was a lighted candle on the lid of the closed trunk and the motion of its flame was not in keeping with that of our surroundings.

"You look feverish." He put a hand to my forehead.

"Cold."

He found another blanket and tucked it around me. It did not help, but he was worried, and it gave him something to do. I was also worried, but unable to act, which made things worse.

"We can turn back, sir. You look ill enough to justify—"

"*No!*" No matter how awful I felt, I'd get through this somehow. But even if some freak of the wind should sweep us to Plymouth in the very next minute, the voyage would still be much too long for me.

"Perhaps you need something to—"

"If you have any care for me, for God's sake don't mention food."

There was solace in the fact that I had no need to breathe, else the odors permeating the very wood of the ship—tar and mildew and tallow and sweat and night soil and old paint and hundreds of others—would have sent me lunging for the chamber pot.

Someone knocked at the door. The room was so small Jericho had but to reach over to open it.

"Is he all right?" asked Elizabeth, peering in. "Good heavens!"

"He is not feeling well," he said, confirming her reaction to me. He moved past her to stand outside that she might come in. With her wide skirts it was not easily done, but she managed.

Unknowingly imitating Jericho, she put a hand to my forehead. "You're very hot."

"On the contrary—"

"I think I should fetch the ship's surgeon."

"No. I won't see him."

"But, Jonathan—"

"*No.* We don't dare. I'm too different now."

She didn't care for that; all her instincts were to do something for me.

"I forbid it," I said. "First he'd listen for my heart, and God knows what he'd do next when he couldn't hear it. Bleed me, probably, and I know that would be an extremely bad idea."

Elizabeth perceived the sense of my words. Even the most incompetent medical man could not be allowed to examine me. Besides being loath to part with a single drop of precious blood, I was incapable of drinking anything else that might be offered as a restorative. No glass of wine, no cup of brandy, no purge or sleeping draught could get past my lips; my changed condition would not allow it.

"But for you to lie there and just suffer . . ."

"It will pass away with time, I've seen as much happen to others. I don't plan to lie here, either." With an effort I made myself sit up, preparatory to standing.

My dear sister immediately objected.

"I will be the better for it, so indulge me," I said. "If I have something for occupation, the time will go more quickly, and I'll be less mindful of this irksome state."

She and Jericho exchanged places again, allowing him to help with my shoes and coat and offer a steadying arm when I was ready to stand.

"You're not at all ill, are you?" I said to him, making it half question, half accusation.

"No, sir, and that's just as well, don't you think?" He got me out the door into a dim and narrow passage.

By their very nature, all crafts that venture upon water are given a life as they move and react to that element. Our ship was very lively, indeed, as might be judged from the motion of the deck as I staggered along. It also had a voice, formed from wood creaking upon wood and the deep and hollow sound of the sea rocking us. These features I could note, but not in any way appreciate in a positive sense.

Elizabeth led us topside, and only then did I fill my lungs with fresh, cleansing air. The wind was cooler and helped somewhat to clear my head. Fixing my eye on the unbroken gray horizon beyond the rail was of no help to my unsettled stomach, but rather a powerful reminder that we had a lengthy and lonely journey ahead. Lonely, that is, if we were lucky enough to avoid contact with rebels or privateers. I remembered what Molly Audy had said about prayer and vowed to spend some time at that occupation later tonight.

I was introduced to the captain, certain of his officers, and a few of the other passengers who were also taking the air. No one had any comment for not having witnessed my ever coming aboard. For that I could thank the natural activity of preparing a ship for sailing, everyone being busy enough with their own concerns, having no time to spare for others.

Many of the people aboard were fleeing the unrest at home, preferring to take the longer sea voyage to England over risking the unknowns of a much closer Halifax. What news that had come to us on the latter locale had given everyone to understand that it was an altogether dismal place as well as dangerous. The winters there were said to be hellishly cold, plagued by too many other refugees, too few supplies, inadequate shelter, and outbreaks of the pox. *Much* better to go to England, where all one had to worry about was the pox and which coffeehouse to patronize.

As I'd expected, keeping myself busy with conversation helped to take my mind off my interior woes. Within an hour of introductions, several of us had found enough commonalties in our lives to form quick and comfortable friendships. An excellent situation, given the fact that we were going to have to share constant company with one another for the next two months or more.

The universal lament was the detestable unfairness that we, the loyal and law-keeping subjects of His Majesty, had to give way to the damned traitors who were running amok.

"It's too perilous to stay while the fighting's on," stated Mr. Thomas Quinton, an apothecary close to my age traveling with his wife and young daughter. The ladies in his life were in their cabin, feeling the adverse effects of sea travel themselves. We two stood by the rail, braced against the wind and rolling of the ship. Somehow Quinton had been able to light his pipe and was quite enjoying a final smoke before retiring.

"Many share that view, sir," I said. "It only makes sense to remove oneself from the conflict." I was far enough upwind of him so as to avoid his smoke, a little recovered, but still uncertain of my belly. It had a disconcerting habit of cramping at irregular intervals.

"Would that the conflict would remove itself from *me*. Surely the generals can find other places to fight their wars. Of course, the rogues that were raising the devil near my house weren't of any army."

"Who were they? More Sons of Liberty?"

"Damned Sons of Perdition is what I call 'em. For all the soldiers about, they still get up to enough mischief to curdle a butcher's blood. We had a fine house not far from Hempstead, and one night they came storming up demanding to see a neighbor of mine. They were so drunk that they'd come to the wrong door, and I was fearful they'd be dragging me out to be tarred and feathered."

"What incensed them? Besides the drink, that is."

"They'd taken it into their heads that my innocent neighbor was spying for General Howe . . . or Lord North. They weren't very clear about that point, but were damning both with equal fervor."

"What did you do?"

"Called at them from the upper window to disperse and go home. I had a pistol in hand, but one shot's not enough for a crowd, and there looked to be a dozen of them. They even had an effigy of my neighbor hanging from a pole, ready for burning. Took the longest time to convince them they were lost, then they wanted to know about me and whether I was a true follower of their cause. Told them that if their cause was to frighten good people out of their rest in the dead of night, then they should take it elsewhere and be damned."

"Given the circumstances, that doesn't strike me as having been a wise thing to say."

"It wasn't, but I was that angered by them. 'If you're not for us, you're against us!' they cried. They won't let an honest man mind his own business, not them. Some of the fools were for breaking in and taking me off for that sauce, but I decided to aim my pistol right at the leader and made sure he noticed. Asked him if he'd rather go back to his tavern and drink the health of General Washington or take a ball between his eyes right then and there. He chose the tavern and spared us all a great deal of trouble. My poor wife was left half-distracted by all that bother, and the next morning we were packing to leave. It's a hard thing to bear, but it won't be forever. Perhaps in a year or two we can return and resume where we left off."

"I hope all goes well for you, then. Have you any friends in London to help you when you arrive?"

"There are one or two people I know from New York who are now living in Chelsea. They left before Howe's landing and a good thing, too, for the fire last year consumed their houses."

No need to ask what fire. For those who lived within even distant sight of New York, there was only the one.

"Have you friends as well?" asked Mr. Quinton.

"Family. My sister and I will be staying with our cousin Oliver. I hope that he'll have received the letter we sent announcing our coming and will put us up until we find a place of our own."

"Has a large family, does he?"

"No, he just prefers his solitude." After a lifetime of having to account for himself every time his mother pinned him with her glare, my good cousin was positively reveling in his freedom. We'd shared rooms at Cambridge, but that's different from having one's own house and servants. Having also come into his inheritance from Grandfather Fonteyn's estate and with the beginnings of a fine medical practice bringing in a steady income, Oliver was more than content with his lot. "I'm very much looking forward to seeing him again; we had some fine times together."

Quinton's eyes lit up. "Ho, raised a bit of the devil yourselves, did you?"

"Our share, though we weren't as wild as some of our friends."

"But wild enough, hey?"

Compared to some of the others at the university, we were positively sedate, but then both of us would have to work for our suppers someday, so we did apply ourselves to study as it became necessary. Oliver wanted to be out and away from the restrictions of Fonteyn House—his mother's house—and I had pledged to Father that I would do my best. Not that our studies seriously interfered with the pursuit of pleasure, though.

"I suppose my wild days are over," said Quinton. His pipe had gone out and he knocked the bowl against the rail to empty it. "Not that I've any regrets. I've a real treasure in my Polly and little Meg. For all the unrest, I count myself a blessed man. We're all together and in good health, well . . . that is to say . . ."

"I'm sure they'll be fine, given time. This malady is a nuisance, but no one's died from it that I've ever heard."

"Thank you for that comfort, sir. Now that I've reminded myself of their troubles, I think I'll see as to how they're getting along." He excused himself and went below.

I leaned on the rail and fervently wished myself well again. Without his company for a diversion, the illness within rose up, once more demanding attention. As the ship heaved and plunged, so did my belly. My poor head was ready to burst from the constant ache between my ears. On each of my previous voyages I'd been sick, briefly, but it had not been anything as horrid as this. Was the difference in the ship, in the roughness of the sea, or in myself?

Myself, I decided unhappily. If I had difficulty crossing a stream, then a whole ocean would certainly prove to be infinitely more laborious. I gulped several times.

"Perhaps you should be in bed, sir." Jericho had appeared out of nowhere, or so it seemed to my befogged brain.

"Perhaps you're right. Where'd Elizabeth get to?" She'd made off with herself soon after I'd fallen into conversation with Quinton.

"In bed as well. It was a very tiring day for her."

Yes. Day. The one I'd missed, like all the others. And she'd been up for most of the night with packing. Having had more than my share of rest, it was damned inconsiderate of me to forget that she might need some, too.

"My insides are too disturbed for me to retire just yet. The air seems to help a bit."

Jericho nodded, put his hands behind his back, and assumed a stance that would allow him to remain sturdily afoot on the pitching deck. "Very good, sir."

And it was doubly damned inconsiderate of me to forget that of all people, Jericho might also be exhausted. Yes, he was; I could see that once I wrenched attention from myself to give him a close look. "None of that 'very good, sir' nonsense with me," I said peevishly. "Get below and go to sleep. I'll be all right sooner or later. If it turns out to be later, you'll need your strength to deal with me."

Along with the fatigue, amusement fluttered behind his dark eyes. "Very good, sir." He bade me a pleasant night and moved off, his walk timed to match the rhythm of the ship's motion. A natural sailor. Would that some of that inborn expertise could transfer to me.

Alone and with the whole night stretching ahead, I had ample time to feel sorry for myself. Hardly a new experience, but never before had it been so . . . concentrated. I couldn't just float off to visit Molly or gossip at The Oak. Any social activities I could enjoy were restricted to those swift hours between sunset and the time everyone had to sleep. No wonder Nora read so much. I'd brought a number of books, more than enough, but the idea of reading held no appeal as long as I was reacting so badly to the ship's rolling progress.

Despite my profession for not wanting to feed just now, it occurred to me that perhaps some fresh blood might be of help against this miserable condition. It was a wonderful remedy for anything that ailed me on land, after all. Jericho and Elizabeth had both made a point to mention that the cattle were secure in their stalls below and to provide directions on how to reach them, but I'd since forgotten what they'd said. Might as well use the time to see things for myself.

I spied one of the officers who had been introduced earlier and staggered over to make inquiries. He was on watch and could not leave his post, but detailed one of the seamen to take me below. The fellow led the way, surefooted as a goat and full of merriment for my own inept efforts at walking. Things improved somewhat below decks. The passages were so narrow that it was impossible not to remain vertical—as long as one fell sideways.

The darkness was so profound that not even my eyes would have been of use if our candle went out. We slipped through a number of confusing areas, occasionally spotting a feeble gleam from other candles as we passed other tiny cabins, and a somewhat larger chamber filled with hammocks, each one swinging heavily with the weight of a sleeping man. Snores filled the close air; the air itself made me more thankful than ever that I had no pressing need to use it.

Our journey ended in another chamber not far from the slumbering sailors, and the lowing sounds coming from it blended well with the deep noise of the ship. I thanked my guide and gave him a penny for his help, for which he volunteered to lend me any future assistance should it be required. He then sped away, leaving the candle behind, apparently having no need of it to make his way back topside.

The heifers appeared to be all right, given their situation, though none could be said to look very happy about it. Most were restless and complaining, which I took as a good sign; better that than with their heads hanging and voices silent with indifference. Father and I had picked the healthiest from our dwindling herd in the hope that they would last the journey, but sometimes one just could not tell. One moment you'd have a strapping, bright-eyed beast and the next it could be flat on its side, having dropped dead in its tracks. Those were the realities of life for a gentleman farmer. Or any farmer, for that matter.

Well, if it happened, so be it; I was nowhere near upon the verge of starvation, nor ever intended to get that far. I felt absolutely no hunger now, but the hope that blood might ease things impelled me to pick one of the animals to sup from.

I was very careful to make sure the thin partition between the cattle and the sleeping men was firmly in place. Only one other time had anyone witnessed my feeding. Two Hessians had chanced upon me just as I'd finished with blood smeared 'round my mouth and my eyes flushed red, presenting an alarming sight to them and a depressing aftermath for me. *Blutsäuger*, one of them had cried in his fear. I hadn't liked the sound of that appellation, but was more or less used to it by now. There were worse things to be than a bloodsucker in the literal sense . . . such as being one of those damned rebels.

Calming an animal was the work of a moment, then I dropped to one knee and felt for the vein in its leg. Conditions weren't exactly clean here, but that could be remedied with a little water. My God, we were surrounded by the stuff. All that was needed was to pay one of the sailors to try his hand at grooming.

Such were my thoughts as my corner teeth lengthened enough to cut through the flesh and reach the red fountain beneath. I hadn't fed from cattle for some time, preferring horses. Shorter hair, you know. The taste of the blood was nearly the same, though my senses were keen to the point that I could tell the difference between the two as easily as a normal man knows ale from beer.

I managed to choke down a few swallows and they stayed down, but only under protest. It was the same as it would be for any other person with the seasickness; food might be necessary, but not especially welcome.

I pinched the vein above the broken skin until the bleeding stopped, then rinsed my stained fingers in the dregs at the bottom of a slimy water bucket hanging in a corner. Well, something would have to be done about *that*. I'd paid plenty of good money for their care, which included keeping them adequately supplied with water. From the condition of the straw on the deck one could tell that they'd long since passed whatever had been in the bucket.

A quick search for more water was futile. Perhaps it was kept under lock and key like the crew's daily tot of rum. A note to Jericho or Elizabeth would sort things out.

I was about to quit the place and hazard the maze back to my cabin when I heard the achingly familiar snort of a horse. None of the other passengers had mentioned bringing stock aboard, though they'd all commented on my endeavor. Reactions varied from humor to curiosity at the eccentricity. Strange that no one had . . . whose horse was it?

Opening the partition between this stable and the next solved the little mystery. Inside, snug in his own stall, was Rolly. His ears were pricked toward me, his nostrils quivering to catch my scent.

Now was I flooded with understanding on why Father had said nothing about what was to be done about this, my special pet. He must have put himself to some trouble to arrange this last-minute surprise. God bless him and his accomplices. Elizabeth and Jericho had not given away the least clue.

I went in and lavished a warm greeting upon Rolly, rubbing between his ears and all down his neck; that was when I discovered a scroll of paper tied to his mane with a ribbon. A note?

A note. I cracked open the drop of sealing wax holding the ribbon to the paper and unrolled the brief missive.

My dear Jonathan,

I hope you will forgive me for this liberty with your property, but I deemed the risk to be worth the taking. I know how much Rolly means to you, and it would be a cruel thing to bear for you to have to give him up because of my plan to leave. Bereft as we are now of the influence you have over the commissary, it is not likely that so fine an animal could long escape their future notice.

He has sufficient food to keep him for the duration of even a lengthy voyage. Remember that throughout that time he will miss his usual exercise, so take care to bring him back to it gently once you're in England.

In prayer for a safe journey with God's blessings for all of you,
Your Loving Father.

The writing swam before my eyes. For the first time since awakening, a warmth stole over me. *God bless you, too, sir*, I thought, wiping my wet cheeks with my sleeve.

I spent an hour or more with Rolly, checking him over, petting and talking to him, letting him know why he was where he was. Whether he understood or not was of no importance, he was a good listener, and sharing his company was a much better distraction than conversation with Mr. Quinton. I discovered Rolly's tack and other things stowed in a box and filled the time by brushing him down and combing his mane and tail out until they were as smooth and shining as the rest of his coat. A groom's chore, yes, but for me it was pleasure, not work.

Having seen to his comfort and taken some for myself, I was ready to return topside and see how the night was faring. With occupation came forgetfulness and I had to keep track of the time, being determined to forevermore avoid further panicked diving into cellars to escape the dawn.

I had naught to fear; upon emerging, one glance at the sky told me that the greater part of the night still remained. It had to be but a glance; the sight of the masts swaying drunkenly against the background of the more stationary stars brought back the dizziness in full force. Shutting my eyes made things worse. Would to God this misery would pass away. I made a meandering path to the rail and held on for dear life, gulping air and cursing my weakness.

There was soon something else to curse when a wayward gust of wind splashed half a bucket of sea spray in my face. Ugh. I swatted at it, clearing my eyes and sputtering. It was colder than iron.

"Wind's freshening," said one of the ship's officers, by way of a comment on my condition as he strolled past. "Best to find some cover or you'll be drenched right through, sir."

Thanking him, I made a last look around, which convinced me that no further distractions were to be found this night—unless I wanted more chill water slapped in my face. Better to be seasick and dry than seasick and wet. I went below.

Jericho had left the cabin's small lamp burning for my return. He was deeply asleep in his cot jammed against the opposite wall. I was glad that he was getting some rest and took care to be quiet while slipping off my damp clothes. Not quite knowing what to do with them, I left them piled on the traveling box, then gratefully climbed into my own bed.

The presence of my home earth delivered an instant comfort so overwhelming that I wondered whatever had possessed me to leave it in the first place. Until this moment I hadn't realized how much I needed it, and lying back, I finally identified the feeling that had been creeping up on

me for the last few hours, one that I'd not had since before
my death: I was *sleepy*.

I'd known what it was to be tired, known all its forms,
from the fatigue of a dark and discouraged spirit, to the
weary satisfaction that stems from accomplishing a difficult
task. Much had happened in the last year, but not once had
my eyes dragged shut of their own accord as they were
doing now.

Damned strange, that.

But so wonderfully pleasant.

To escape into sleep . . . I'd thought that luxury forever
lost because of the changes I'd been through.

Out of old habit rather than necessity, I made a deep
inhalation and sighed it out again, pulling the blankets up
to my chin. Oh, but this felt good; my dizziness and bad
belly were finally loosening their grip on my beleaguered
frame. The earth-filled bags I rested on were lumpy and
hard, but at the same time still made the most comfortable
bed I'd ever known. I rolled on my side, punched the pillow
once to get it just right . . .

And then someone was tugging at my shoulder and calling my name most urgently.

Damnation, I thought, then said it aloud. "What is it?"

"Don't you want to get up, Mr. Jonathan?" Jericho asked.

"I just got to bed. Let me finish what I've started."

"But it's long past sunset," he insisted.

Ridiculous. But he was probably right or he wouldn't be
bothering me. I pried my eyes open. The cabin looked the
same as before, or nearly so. If his cot had not been made
up and my clothes neatly laid out on the box, I would have
had good cause for continued annoyance.

"Miss Elizabeth's been by to ask after you. She thought
you might still be ailing from the seasickness."

"It's not as bad as before."

"Do you wish me to convey that news to her?"

God, but I wanted to stay in bed. "No, I'll talk to her,
perhaps take the air."

He seemed about to ask another question, for he was
plainly worried, but I got up and requested my coat. That
was all that was required to change the subject. In the

next few minutes I was summarily stripped, dressed again, combed out, brushed off, and otherwise made ready for presentation to any polite company, though how he was able to accomplish so much in the tiny space we had was a mystery to me.

My hat in place, my stick in hand, I was bowed out into the passage.

"You're trying to get rid of me so you can tidy things, is that it?" I demanded.

His smile was one of perfect innocence. It was also his only reply as he shut the door.

There being little point in additional contest with him, I made my way topside. Long habit dictated I check the sky, which was clear, but I was surprised at the lateness of the hour. How could I have overslept for so long?

"I thought you'd never show yourself," Elizabeth called from a place she'd taken on the port rail. There was a good color in her cheeks and her mood seemed very light. Perhaps it had to do with the three young ship's officers who were standing about her. Apparently she was not in want of company or amusement.

"Must be the sea air," I said, coming over.

"You're feeling better?"

That subject again. "I wish you hadn't reminded me." I clutched the rail hastily, nearly losing my stick. Should have left it in the cabin as I'd done last night. Though an elegant affectation for walking in the city or country, it was quite the impediment on a shifting deck.

"Still seasick?"

"Oh, please don't say it. I'd forgotten until now."

"Sorry. You looked well enough a moment ago."

"It's rapidly reasserting itself, unfortunately."

One of the officers, anxious to make a good impression on Elizabeth, suggested that I consult Mr. Quinton. "He brought several cases of medicines with him. I'm sure he'd be only too happy to provide something to ease your difficulty," said the fellow with some eagerness.

"Thank you, Lieutenant George. I shall give that some consideration." About two second's worth, I thought.

"I can have him fetched for you," he offered helpfully.

"Not necessary, sir. I've no wish to disturb him just yet."

"But he's not at all occupied—"

"That's quite all right, sir," I said firmly, hoping he would accept the hint. Happily, Elizabeth smiled at him and told him not to worry so. He bowed and declared himself to be her most faithful servant, which inspired the other two to gainsay him by assuring her that they were better qualified to such a post by reason of their superior rank. One of them informed Elizabeth about the dates of their respective commissions in order to prove his case for being the senior officer. After that, I lost the thread of the discussion until she touched my arm, giving me a start.

"Are you bored?"

"Not at all. Where'd your suitors go?" I was mildly confused to note that they had quite vanished.

"Back to their duties. The captain caught their eye, raised his chin, and they suddenly remembered things they had to see to. It was very funny, didn't you notice?"

I shrugged, indifferent to her obvious concern.

She put a hand to my forehead. "A bit warm. Is the chill yet with you?"

"Not really, just the misery in my stomach and a spinning head. I was all right when I woke up, but it's returned. Maybe that's why I slept an hour later than usual."

"You look as though you could use even more rest."

"No need for concern, I shall seek it out," I promised, working to rouse myself, lest she continue on the matter. The topic of my well-being had worn rather thin with me. "I found Father's surprise," I said and explained how I'd come across Rolly.

She brightened. "Oh, I wished I'd been there to see. I'd promised to let him know everything."

"You can tell him that I was extremely happy. I plan to as well if I can bring myself to write in a steady hand on this vessel. I thought that a large ship like this would make for a smoother passage. The sea's not that rough."

"It's better than when we first set out. The other passengers are coming 'round from its effect. I hope you're next, little brother."

"As do I. Was I much missed from the table today?"

"Since you were never there to start with you could hardly be missed, though the captain and Mr. Quinton both asked after you. Even when you do recover, you won't want to look too healthy or people will wonder why you're not eating with them."

"Excellent point. I suppose I could be busy with some occupation or other. Tell them I'm involved with my law studies and will take meals in my cabin. Jericho can find some way of disposing of . . . the extra food."

"Jonathan?"

I shook my head. "Can't seem to wake up tonight. I don't remember the last time when I've felt so sleepy."

"Then pay mind to it and go to bed if it's rest you want."

"But so early? I mean, for me that's just not natural anymore."

"Perhaps the constant presence of being over water is especially tiring for you. You said as much last night before I left you in Mr. Quinton's company."

"I suppose I could lie down for a while. Jericho should be done by now."

"Done with what?"

"Oh—ah—doing whatever it is he does when I'm out of the room. The workings of one's valet are a mystery, and every good gentleman understands that they should remain so."

"It seems a one-sided thing."

"Such are the ways of the world when it comes to masters and servants. Believe me when I say that I'm very comfortable in my ignorance."

She fixed me with a most solemn look. "Get some sleep, Jonathan."

I gave a little bow, mocking the recent efforts of the absent officers. "Your servant, Miss Barrett."

"*Lots* of sleep," she added, brows high.

That was enough to carry me back to the cabin. It was empty of Jericho's presence, but not of his influence. My recently discarded clothes were gone and the bed was tidy again. What a shame to have to destroy such order.

Before collapsing, I rooted in the traveling box for something to read, but only for a moment. My eyes were already closing. Giving up the struggle, I dropped into bed.

At some point I became aware of another's presence, but it was a dim and easily ignored incident.

Jericho, probably. Shaking my shoulder again.

I muttered an inarguable order to let me sleep and burrowed more deeply into the pillow.

The next disturbance was more annoying. Elizabeth was calling to me. Being absolutely insistent.

Couldn't seem to respond. Not even to her. It hardly mattered.

Now she was all but bellowing right in my ear. My head jerked and I snarled something or other. It must have been forceful enough to put her off further attempts, for no more were made. I was finally left alone, left to enjoy my sweet, restorative oblivion.

The seasickness was quite gone when I next woke. The combination of my home earth, the extra rest, and last night's fresh blood must have done it. Of course, it might not be a permanent thing, for had it not returned when I'd abandoned my bed for a turn around the deck?

I made a kind of grumbling sigh and stretched. God, but I was stiff. And slow. I'd not been this sluggish since that time I'd been forced to hide from the day buried under a snowbank. At least I wasn't cold now, just moving as though half frozen. I was . . . numb.

My hands. Yes, they were flexing as I wished, but I had no sense of them belonging to me. I made fists and opened them, rubbed them against the blankets. There, that was better, I could almost feel that. Must have slept wrong, had them under me or . . .

Arms were numb, too.

Legs . . . face . . .

But wearing off. Just had to wake up a bit more. No need for alarm.

"Jonathan?" Elizabeth's voice. Thin. Odd mixing of distress and hope.

The room was dark—or my eyes weren't working properly. Rubbed them. Hard to work my fingers.

She said my name again. Closer this time. More pressing.

Had some trouble clearing my throat. Coughed a few times before I could mumble anything like an answer. Blinked my eyes a lot, trying to see better. The room was foggy as well as dark.

Her face hovered over mine. "Do you hear me?"

"Mm."

"Do you know me?"

What was she on about? "Mm-mu . . . niz . . . beh."

"*Oh, God!*" She dropped her head on my chest and began loudly sobbing.

What in heaven's name was going on? Was the ship sinking? Why was she acting like this? I touched her with one hand. She rose up and seized it, holding it against her wet cheek.

"Miss Elizabeth, please have a care for him." Jericho this time.

But she kept weeping.

"*Please*, miss, you're not helping him this way."

I had not been frightened before. His tone and manner were all wrong. Jericho was ever and always playing the role of imperturbable servant, but now he was clearly afraid, and that pierced right through my heart. And as for Elizabeth's reaction—I reached out to him.

"Wha . . . ss . . ."

"It's all right, Mr. Jonathan." His assurance was so hasty and sincere that I knew that something awful must be happening. I tried to sit up, but my apathetic limbs were as much of a hindrance as Elizabeth's close presence. "Lie still, sir. Please."

There was little else I could do as he got Elizabeth's attention at last and persuaded her to better compose herself. She soaked a handkerchief cleaning away her tears and blowing her nose. I looked to him for some clue to her behavior. He smiled at me, trying to make it an encouraging one, but creating a less positive response instead. His face was very drawn and hollow and . . . thinner? As though he'd not eaten well for some time. But he'd been perfectly fine last night. What in God's name . . . ?

With Elizabeth removed I was able to raise up on my elbows. We were not in the tiny cabin anymore. This room, while not palatial, was quite a bit larger. The walls were vertical, the ceiling higher. Why had I been moved?

"Forgive me, I just couldn't help myself," said Elizabeth. "It's been such an awful time."

"Whaz been?" I slurred. Coughed. Damned tongue was so thick. My voice was much deeper than normal, still clogged from sleep. "Whaz maa-er?"

"Nothing's the matter now, you idiot. You're all right. Everything's all right."

I made a sound to inform her that I knew damned well that everything was *not* all right.

"He doesn't understand, Miss Elizabeth. He's been asleep."

And it was past time to shake it off. With heroic effort, I pushed myself upright and tried to drag my legs from the bed.

It was a real bed, too, with fresh linen and thick dry blankets, not at all like the one in the old cabin. Had we taken over the captain's quarters?

I coughed and worked my jaw, rubbing my face. Yes. That was better. Feeling was returning once more, thank goodness. I could actually tell that my bare feet were touching the cold boards of the deck. Bare? Well, of course Jericho would have readied me for sleep. It was very remiss of me to have made extra work for him by falling into bed with all my clothes on.

Another stretch; this time things popped along my spine. God, but that felt good.

Jericho and Elizabeth watched me closely.

"Wha' iz the ma—matter?"

"You've been asleep, sir."

"S' you'f said. Wh'd 'f it?" Worked my jaw more. "What-of-it?" There, *now* I could understand myself.

"You remember nothing of the voyage?" asked Elizabeth.

"What do . . . you mean? What 'f the voyage? Something happened to Rolly?"

"No, he's fine. He's safely stabled. You—"

Stretched my neck, rubbing it. "Not making much sense, Sister." I saw that like Jericho, she was also very drawn and tired-looking. Circles under the eyes, skin all faded and tight over the bones. "Are you well? What the devil is wrong here?"

"For God's sake, Jonathan, you've been *asleep!*"

Was that supposed to mean something? Apparently so. Something most dreadfully important to them both.

"More than asleep, sir," Jericho put in. "You know how you are during the day. It was like that."

"Will you please be more clear? You're saying I slept, yes. Is it that I slept the whole night through as well as the day?"

"More than a night, Jonathan."

I abruptly fathomed that I was not going to like hearing what Elizabeth was about to say. "More?" I squeaked.

"You slept through the whole *crossing.*"

Oh, to laugh at that one. But I could not. Additional noises issued from me, unintelligible as speech, but nonetheless expressive.

"You went down to your cabin to get some rest on our second night out," she said, speaking carefully as though to prompt a poor memory.

"Yes, you told me to."

"You never woke up from it. You just wouldn't, and when you're that way, it's as if you're dead."

"Never woke up? Whatever do you mean?"

"You *slept* for the whole voyage! You were asleep for over two *months!*"

I was shaking my head. "Oh, no-oo . . . that's impossible."

Their expressions were sufficient to gainsay my weak denial.

"Impossible . . ." But I had only to look around to see that we were in a building, not on a ship. My own body had already confirmed as much. Gone were the raised hackles, the illness, the constant pressure inside and out. Nightshirt trailing, I boosted unsteadily from bed toward a small window.

The glass was cold and opaque with condensation. I fumbled with the catch and thrust the thing open. Cold wind slapped my face, bringing the scent of sleet, mud, coal smoke, the stable. I was on an upper story of a building taking in the view of its courtyard. An inn of some kind. Vaguely familiar.

The Three Brewers. The inn I'd stayed at while waiting to meet Cousin Oliver for the first time four years ago.

"This just cannot be." But the proof remained before my eyes, mocking my denial.

"Jonathan . . ." My sister's tone had taken on patient reproach. She could tolerate confusion, but not willful stupidity.

I stared dumbfounded at the prosaic scene below. Beyond the inn, past the lower roof of its opposite wing, were trees, other roofs, and church steeples stretching miles away into a cloudy winter night.

True, true, and true. We were most definitely, most undeniably, yet most impossibly in *London*.

CHAPTER
—4—

London, November 1777

"It was perfectly horrid, that's how it was," Elizabeth said, her voice a little high.

"I'm sorry, I truly am. If I'd any idea that—"

She waved her third sodden handkerchief at me and told me not to be foolish. "Of course you'd have said something. We both know that. But it's been such a wretched ordeal, and now that it's over I hardly know what to think or do."

"Tea," Jericho firmly stated.

"With lots of brandy," I added to his departing back. Would that I could have some for this shock. Two months? How could two *months* of my life have slipped away?

"You have no memory of *any* of it?" she asked.

"My last recollection was talking with you by the rail, going below, and dropping into bed. As far as I'm concerned, it happened last night."

She shook her head and kept shaking it.

"I don't disbelieve you, Elizabeth, it—it's just very hard to take in. Tell me all that happened, maybe that will help."

"Where to start . . . ?" She rolled her eyes to the ceiling, shut them a moment, then rested them on me. "First, I'll say that I am very glad that you are all right. You've no idea what we've been through."

"Then for God's sake enlighten me." I was sitting on the bed again, wrapped in my dressing gown now and wide awake, if still considerably shaken. By now it had thoroughly penetrated my skull that my mysterious lapse had been a singularly unpleasant experience for Jericho and Elizabeth. Better to concentrate on them than myself. It was more comfortable.

She gave a long sigh, then took a deep breath. "On the third night out Jericho tried to wake you, but you just refused to do so. I'd told him that you'd been very tired, and he let you rest a few more hours, then tried again. Nothing, except for a few grumbles, and you kept on lying there, not moving at all."

"I'm sorry."

She fixed me with a look that told me to cease apologizing. "We decided to let you sleep and try again the next night. Again, nothing. Finally Jericho went down to the hold and drew off some blood from one of the cattle and wet your lips with it. Then he tried putting a few drops in your mouth. Not even that worked."

I spread my hands. Apologetically. Couldn't help it.

"We didn't know whether to leave you alone or try something sterner, then Mr. Quinton, the apothocary, came 'round. Lieutenant George sent him to look in on you, the blasted toady." The tone she used with his name indicated that George was the toady, not Quinton. "Jericho tried to put him off, but he got curious and went in when we weren't around. He promptly ran straight to Mr. George to say you were dead."

"Oh, dear lord."

"That brought the captain down to see, and I was flooded with so much sympathy that I could hardly make myself heard. When I finally got them to listen, they thought I was a madwoman."

"What did you say?"

"That Quinton had got it wrong and you were only deeply asleep. No one believed me, and I was getting more and more angry. Oh, but they were very kind, telling me I was distracted by my grief and they were more than willing to spare me from the sad responsibility of seeing you decently taken care of. By that I understood you were to be in for a sea burial."

"How did you stop them?"

"By grabbing you and shaking you like a butter churn and screaming myself hoarse—"

"Wait, I remember that!"

She paused. "You do?"

"Just vaguely. I don't think I was very polite."

"You weren't. You damned my eyes, shrugged me off, and dropped asleep again."

"I'm terribly sorry."

"Don't be, it saved your life. They stopped trying to remove me from the cabin and had Quinton make another examination. He was very surprised and upset by then and anxious to redeem himself, and though I know he couldn't possibly have found a heartbeat any more than before, he said you were indeed alive, but unconscious. What a relief that was to hear. The captain and Mr. George wanted a closer look for themselves, but I'd caught my breath by then and an idea came to me of how to deal with them.

"Since they'd been so sympathetic, it seemed right to make use of it, so I got the lot of them out into the passage and lowered my voice the way Father does when he really wants people to listen. Then I told them in the strictest confidence that you were sadly addicted to laudanum and—"

"*You WHAT?*"

"I *had* to! It was the one thing I could think of that would explain your condition."

I groaned.

"I said you'd brought a supply with you and were taking it to help your seasickness and it was likely you would remain like this for most of the voyage. Afterward, they had quite a different kind of sympathy for me and were perfectly willing to leave you alone, and that was all I really wanted. Perhaps your reputation might suffer a little should there be any gossip—"

"A *little?*"

"But I doubt if anything will come of it; they gave me their word of honor to say nothing, and unlike some people I've known, I'm willing to believe them." She stalked across the room to rummage in a small trunk, drawing from it her fourth handkerchief. She blew her nose several times. "And so passed the first week."

"I'm afraid to ask about the rest."

"Well, happily they weren't as disruptive. Jericho took small meals to your cabin, supposedly for you, then either ate them himself or hid them in the chamber pot to be thrown overboard. He didn't have much of an appetite, nor did I, we were so damned worried. As the days passed and you kept sleeping, we almost got used to it. We reasoned that since you had survived the grave, you were likely to survive this, but it was such a thin hope to cling to with so much time on our hands and nothing to do but wait it out."

"It must have been awful."

"The word, little brother, is *horrid*."

"Ah . . . yes, of course."

She paced up and down and blew her nose again. Jericho was taking his time bringing the tea and brandy.

Two months. There was much about my changed condition that was unnatural, but this one was beyond comprehension. "It must in some way be connected to my difficulty in crossing water. . . ."

She gave me a sour look.

But I continued. "I was so seasick, perhaps it is meant to spare me the constant discomfort."

"Jericho and I had many, many discussions on the subject and came to the same conclusion."

"And you sound as though you're bloody tired of the subject."

"You are most perceptive."

I decided to be quiet.

She stopped pacing. "I do apologize, Jonathan. I shouldn't be so rude to you. You're safe and well and that's what we've been praying for all this time. I'm just so damnably weary."

"With much justification. Is it very late?"

"Not really. You woke up at sunset as usual—or what used to be usual. I'm glad to see your habit is reasserting itself."

"Is this my first night off the ship?"

"Yes."

Right. I was away from water and doubtless the solid ground below had aided my revival. "Uh . . . just how was I debarked?"

"Jericho put you back into your box and locked it up, same as when you were placed aboard. The sailors shifted it to the quay, I hired a cart—"

"Did no one notice I was missing from the other departing passengers?"

"It was too hectic. After those many weeks aboard, all everyone wanted to do was to get away from one another."

"Thank God for that."

I heard steps in the hall, recognized them, and hurried to open the door.

"Thank you, sir," said Jericho. His hands were fully occupied balancing a tray laden with enough tea and edibles for three. With the crisis past, he anticipated a return to a normal appetite. I got out of his way so he could put it down on the room's one table.

"That smells good." Elizabeth came closer. "Are those seedcakes? And eggs? I haven't had one in ages. . . ." She hovered over the table, looking unsure of where to begin.

The smells may have been toothsome to her, but were enough to drive me away. Cooked food of any kind had that effect on me. While she piled the beginnings of a feast on a plate, Jericho poured tea for her, adding a generous drop or two of brandy to the cup.

"All I really want is the tea," she protested, crumbs of seed cake flying from her mouth. "This only spoils the taste."

"You need it, Miss Elizabeth."

"Then so do you. Stop fussing and sit down. I shan't eat another bite until you have some as well."

This was a violation of custom, to be sure, but the three of us had been friends long before growing up had drawn us irretrievably into our respective stations in life. He hesitated a moment, glancing once at the door to be certain it was closed and once at me to be sure it was all right.

"Never argue with a lady," I told him.

He gingerly sat opposite her and suffered her to pour tea for a change.

"I've missed this," she said. "Remember how we used to take away a big parcel of things from the kitchen and eat in the woods, pretending we were pirates hiding from the king's navy?"

I gave a small chuckle. "I remember you insisting on playing Captain Kidd for all your skirts."

"Only because I'd made an eye patch, but I recall giving it to you when I became 'Scarlet Bess, Scourge of the Island' after Mrs. Montagu's gift of those red hair ribbons."

"Yes, and as Captain Kidd you were a much nicer pirate."

She threw a seedcake at me, and I caught it just to annoy her. She laughed instead. "I wish you could join us."

"But he can," said Jericho, garnering questioning looks from us. For an answer, he reached for a second teapot on the tray and held it ready to pour the contents into a waiting cup. He cocked an eye at me.

"What . . . ?" I drew closer.

He tipped the pot. From the spout came forth not tea, but blood.

Elizabeth gasped, eyes wide and frozen.

When the cup was full, he gently replaced the pot. Then he picked up the cup and a saucer and offered them to me.

Hardly aware that I spoke, I whispered a thanks to him. The scent of the blood filled my head. The sight of it . . . the whole room seemed to have vanished; all I saw was the cup and its contents. I reached out, seeing my fingers closing 'round it of their own accord. Then I was drinking.

My God, it was wonderful.

Still warm.

I drained it away in one glorious shuddering draught. Not until it was gone did I understand the breadth of my hunger. Muted by my long sleep, it snarled into life and was only slightly appeased by this minute offering.

"Another, sir?"

I could only nod. He poured. I drank.

So very, very wonderful. Eyes shut, I felt the glad heat spreading from my belly out to the tips of my limbs, felt the weight of need melting away, felt the *life* of it infusing every part of me. Each swallow restoring my depleted body with that much more strength.

Jericho cleared his throat. "I'm sorry, miss, I should have said something before . . ." He sounded mortally stricken.

I opened my eyes, abruptly reminded that I was not alone, and looked at Elizabeth. She was positively ashen. Her gaze fixed on the teapot, then Jericho, then me.

"I am most sincerely sorry." Jericho started to get up, but Elizabeth's hand shot out and fastened on his arm.

"No. Don't." For a long moment she did not move. Her breath was short and fast, then she forcibly slowed it.

"Elizabeth?" I hardly knew what to say.

Her head went down, then she gave herself a shake. "It's all right. I was just surprised. You did nothing wrong, Jericho, I'm just being foolish."

"But—"

"Nothing—wrong," she emphasized. She eased her grip on his arm and patted it. "You stay exactly where you are. Give Jonathan some more if he so desires."

"Elizabeth, I think I should—"

"Well, I don't," she snapped. "It's food to you, is it not? Then it's past time that I got used to the idea. For God's sake, some of our field-workers enjoy eating pigs' brains; I suppose I can stand to watch my brother drink some blood, so sit down with us."

Taking my own advice, I chose not to argue with her and obediently joined them.

In silence Jericho gestured inquiringly at the teapot. I cautiously nodded. Elizabeth looked on, saying nothing. She resumed her meal at the same time I did.

"How did you obtain it, Jericho?" she asked in a carefully chosen tone better suited for parlor talk about the weather.

He was understandably reluctant to speak. "Er . . . while the cook was making the tray ready, I excused myself and went down to the stables."

"There's such a quantity, though. I hope the poor beast is all right."

"I drew it off from several horses."

"And just how did you accomplish the task?"

"I—ah—I've had occasion to give aid to Dr. Beldon when he's found it necessary to bleed a patient. It was easy enough to imitate."

"The taste is agreeable to you, is it not?" Her bright attention was now focused on me.

Anything less than an honest answer would insult her intelligence. "Very agreeable," I said, trying not to squirm.

"How fortunate. What a trial your life would be were it not."

"Elizabeth . . ."

"I was only making an observation. You should have seen your face when Jericho gave you that first cup. Like my cat when there's fish in the kitchen."

Jericho choked on his egg. I thumped his back until he waved me away.

We three looked at one another in the ensuing silence. Very heavy it was, too. I wondered just how much of an effect that drop of brandy was having on her.

Then Elizabeth's face twitched, she made a choking sound of her own, and we suddenly burst out laughing.

"If anything, I feel cheated," I said sometime later.

Very much at ease once more, we lounged 'round the table, content to do nothing more than let peaceful digestion take its course.

"Of the time you lost?" asked Elizabeth.

"Yes, certainly. It's like that story Father told us about the calendar change that happened a couple years before we were born. They were trying to correct the reckoning of the days and made it so the second of September was followed by the fourteenth. He said people were in riot, protesting that they'd been robbed of two weeks of their lives."

Jericho, with both his natural and assumed reticence much weakened by the brandy, snickered.

"How absurd of them," she said. "However, that was a change made on paper, not in actual terms of living. Yours has definitely caused you to miss some time from your life."

"So instead of two weeks I may have been robbed of two months. Unfair, I say, most unfair."

"It's just as well that we will be staying in England, since you can expect a similar long sleep whenever you venture out to sea."

I shook my head and shuddered in a comical manner. "No, thank you. Though I might have to make a channel crossing if Nora is still on the Continent. It won't be pleasant, but it's short enough not to put me to sleep."

"Providing you can find a ship to take you across at night."

"I'm sure something can be arranged, but it's all speculation anyway until I can talk to Oliver. Have you sent word to him that we've arrived?"

"Not yet. I wanted to see if you were going to wake up first."

"I'll write him a letter if you'll have it sent tomorrow."

"Why not go over tonight and surprise him?"

"It's been three years and my memory of the city has faded. I may have his new address, but I don't think I could find it alone. You have the innkeeper find a trusty messenger in the morning."

"We could send one tonight—"

"Not without an army to protect him, dear Sister. London is extremely dangerous at night. I don't want either of you ever going out alone after dark. The streets are ruled by thieves, murderers, and worse; even the children here will cut your throat for nothing if it suits their fancy."

Both bore identical expressions of disgust and horror for the realities of life in the world's most civilized city.

"What about yourself, sir?" asked Jericho. "Will you not find your activities restricted as well since you're limited to the hours of night?"

"I suppose so, but I've got that Dublin pistol and the sword cane—and the duelers . . . but remember, I've also got certain physical advantages because of my change. I should be safe enough if I keep my wits on guard and stay away from the worst places. It's not as though we're imprisoned by the scoundrels, y'know. Once we get settled in and introduced we'll have lots of things to do in good company, parties and such. Oliver's a great one for parties."

"So you've often told us," Elizabeth murmured. Her eyes were half-closed.

I rose and pushed my chair under the table, making it clear that our own celebration was concluded. "Bedtime for you, Miss Barrett. You're exhausted."

"But it's much too early yet." She made an effort to straighten herself.

"For me perhaps, but you've had some hard going for a very long time. You deserve to recover from it. Besides, I've more than once boasted to Oliver about your beauty; you don't want to make a liar of me by greeting him with circles under your eyes, do you?"

She looked ready to throw another seedcake at me, but they'd all been eaten.

"Jericho, is there a maid here who can help her get ready for bed?"

"I can get ready myself, thank you very much," she said. "Though I might like to have some hot washing water. And soap. And a drying cloth."

Jericho stood. "I can see to that, miss. There's a likely wench downstairs who's supposed to help the ladies staying here. I'll send her up straightaway."

Faced with two men determined to see to her comfort, Elizabeth offered no more protest and took my arm as I escorted her across the hall to her room. She did not say good night, but did throw her arms around me in a brief, fierce embrace. I returned it, told her that all was well again, and to take as much rest as she needed. She was snuffling a little when she closed the door, but I knew the worst was over for her. Sometimes tears are the best way to ease a sorely tried soul; hers was on the mend. She'd be fine by the time the hot water arrived.

I felt in want of a good wash as well, and Jericho troubled himself to provide for me, unasked. He moved more slowly than usual because of the brandy, but his hand was as steady as ever while scraping my chin clean with the razor.

"Your beard did not grow much during the voyage," he said, wiping soap and bristles on the towel draped over his free arm. "I only had to shave you but once a week. Even then it hardly looked like half a day's growth."

"Good heavens, really?"

"It must have been a very deep sleep to do that."

"Deep, indeed. But never again. Too frightening."

He quietly agreed.

Hardly before I knew it, he'd finished my toilet and assisted my dressing for the evening. More than half the night remained to me, and I'd expressed a desperate need for fresh air despite the perils of the streets. Perhaps in my own mind I'd been at sea for only two nights, but that was still two too many. Though over solid ground at last, I badly wanted to *feel* it under my feet again.

"But this is my heavy cloak," I said as he dropped it over my shoulders.

"It's cold now, Mr. Jonathan, nearly December. The people here say they've had some snow and there's always a chance for more."

"Oh."

He put my hat in place and handed me my cane. It was so like the last time on the ship that I had a mad thought that their whole story was some sort of ugly trick. *Horrid* was indeed the word, this time to describe me for even thinking them capable of such a poor turn. I silently quelled my unworthy doubts and wished him a good evening.

"Please be mindful of the time," he said. "You've an hour more of darkness now, but there's no reason to take risks."

True. If I got caught out at sunrise, a near-stranger again in this huge and hasty city . . . I gave him my solemn promise to take all care, then exacted one from him to get some rest and not wait up.

Then I was downstairs and crossing the muddy courtyard of the inn, my stride long and free after the confines of the ship. The hour was early enough—at least for London—not more than eleven of the clock. Being used to the quiet of the country nearly half a world away, I found the continued noise and bustle of the streets hard to take in. My memories of previous visits had to do with the daytime, though; at night it was as if another, more wretched city emerged from some hidden concavity of the earth to do its business with a luckless world.

That business was of the darker sort, as might be expected. I kept a tight hand on my cane and my head up, alert to everything around me lest some pickpocket try making a profit at my expense. They were bad enough, but almost genteel compared to their wilder cousins, the footpads. Lacking the skill for subtle thievery, such rascals found it easier to simply murder their victims in order to prevent outcry and pursuit.

My pace brisk and eyes wide, I was well aware of the half-human debris skulking in the black shadows between the buildings. I avoided these by walking close to the street, though that put me to the risk of getting spattered by mud and worse from passing carriages and riders. Most of the thoroughfares were marked out by hundreds of white posts that separated the traffic from the pedestrians. No vehicle would dare cross that barrier, so at least I was safe from getting run over.

I could have made myself invisible, soared high, and easily floated over these perils, but that could have meant forsaking this glimpse of the city. Dangers aside, I'd missed London and wanted to get reacquainted with every square inch of it.

With some exceptions, of course. No man who was not drunk or insane would venture into certain streets, but there were myriad others to make up for that questionable lack. As I traveled from one to the next, I marveled anew at the lines of glass-fronted shops with their best wares displayed in an effort to tempt people inside. All were closed now, except for the taverns and coffee shops, but I had no interest in what they had to sell.

Nor was I particularly eager to sample the goods offered by the dozens of whores I encountered along the way. Most were my age or much younger, some of these desperately proclaiming their virginal state was mine to have if I but paid for it. A few were pretty or had put on enough paint and powder to make themselves so, but I had no desire to stop and bargain for their services or by doing so make myself vulnerable to robbery should they be working with a gang of footpads. I brushed past, ignoring them for the more pressing errand I had in mind.

I briskly crossed through one neighborhood after another, some fashionable, some so rank as to be a lost cause, and others so elegant that they seemed to have been birthed in another land altogether. It was to a particular one in this latter category that I eagerly headed.

Though she had moved to Cambridge to live near me while I pursued my studies, Nora Jones often returned to London to enjoy its pleasures. I just as often followed her whenever possible, for those pleasures were doubled, she said, by my company. We'd take her carriage across London Bridge to Vauxhall Gardens and stroll there, listening to the "fairy music" played by an orchestra located underground. Their sweet melodies magically emerged from the foliage by means of an ingenious system of pipes. Sometimes I would take supper in an alcove of the Chinese Pavilion, and later we would content ourselves with a tour of the Grand Walk. She never tired in her admiration of the innumerable glass lamps that made the whole place as bright as day. Other outings might mean taking a box at the theater or opera or going to Vauxhall's more formal rival, Ranelagh, but always would we return to her own beautiful house and in sweet privacy partake of more carnal forms of diversion.

To this house I now sped, holding a faint spark of hope in my heart that she might now be there.

Since my change I'd written Oliver many times asking him to find her, but his last missive to me on his lack of success was months old. There was every chance that she could have returned in the meantime.

Memory and anticipation are a tormenting combination. The familiarity of the streets brought her face and form back to me with the keenness of a new-sharpened knife. I found myself speaking her name under my breath as if it were a prayer, as though she could somehow hear and come to me. Gone was any shred of anger I'd harbored against her for the manner of our parting. It had been a cruel thing to try to make me forget her, crueler still to leave me with no warning or knowledge about the bequest of her blood, but I had no care for that anymore; all I cared about was seeing her again.

My heart sank as soon as I rounded the last corner and clapped eager eyes on the structure.

Nora was very careful to keep her homes in good order, and this one, though not at all fallen to ruin, yet exuded an unmistakable air of nonoccupation. Leaves and mud cluttered the dingy steps to the front door; its paint was in need of renewal. The brass knob and knocker were tarnished. All the windows were fast shuttered and undoubtedly locked from within.

I could hardly have felt worse if the entire building had been a gutted wreckage.

Slowly completing the last few paces to the door, I knocked, knowing it to be a futile gesture, but needing to do something. No one answered, nor did I hear the least sound from within. I looked 'round the street. It was empty for the moment.

Then it melted away to a gray mist and vanished.

I pressed hard against the door, aware of its solidity, but well able to seep past it like fog through a curtain. Grayness again, then shapes and shadows, then muted colors and patterns. I was standing in her foyer and it was very dark.

Only a few glimmers of illumination from the diffuse winter sky got past the shutters, not enough to really see anything. Opening a window would not be an especially good idea; I saw no advantage advertising my presence to her neighbors. They might come over to investigate the intrusion, and then I'd have to answer questions. . . . I could also ask some, perhaps obtaining a clue to her whereabouts, but Oliver had already done that, I remembered.

This much I could see: The furnishings were either gone or draped in dust sheets. No pictures adorned the walls, no books—no candles, either, I discovered. Not until I bumped my way to the kitchen in the very back of the house did I find one, a discarded stump no more than an inch long. Making use of my tinderbox, I got it lighted, but had no stick or dish to place it on. I made do by fixing it to the box with a drop of melted wax.

The kitchen was not as deserted as the rest of the house. Though clean enough, there were probably still crumbs to be had for the rats and mice. I could hear them scuttling unseen inside and along the walls. Leaving them to their foraging, I went back to the central hall and hurried through the door to her bedroom.

Emptiness, both in the room and in my heart. The walls were stripped, the curtains gone, even the bed where I'd so wonderingly lost my virginity was taken. The dust coating the floor was such as to indicate things had been in this deserted state for a very long time.

All the other chambers were echoes of this one. Everything that was important to her—everything that *was* her—was missing, removed to God knows where. Oliver had said she'd left for the Continent, but he'd not mentioned just how thoroughly she had removed herself.

Feeling ten times worse than dejected, I came down again, this time to investigate one last room. Its door was just off the foyer and locked. Untroubled by this barrier, I passed through it; the candle in my hand flickered once, then resumed a steady flame. The tiny light revealed long-unused steps leading down into overwhelming darkness.

Dank air, more scuttlings; filled with the kind of oppression that's born from morbid imaginings, I'd no desire to be here, but also no choice. I had to see one last thing for myself and not give in to childish trepidations about lurking ghosts. It was a dark cellar and nothing more. The place would be no different if I had a company of soldiers along all armed to the teeth. On the other hand, perhaps it would be. Not so quiet. More light.

No key or bolt on this side of the door, so I couldn't open it and provide myself with an easy escape. Considering my ability to disappear at the least provocation, I was only being foolish. I forced myself down to the landing.

Nothing more threatening awaited here than some old boxes and broken furniture. I threaded a path through them, holding the candle high, squinting ineffectually against the gloom, until I found what seemed to be the opposite wall. Seemed. I knew it to be false.

It had been built out from the actual wall as a carefully constructed duplicate, even down to the coloring of the stones and mortar. There was no opening of any kind; she'd not found one to be necessary. To enter, she had but to vanish and pass through as I was now doing.

Within was a silence so complete that I had to fight to retain solidity. My mind had instantly cast itself back to the hideous moments when I'd first awakened to this life and realized I was in a coffin and *buried*. There was even a strong smell of damp earth here the same as there had been then. They'd put me in my best Sunday clothes, drawn the shroud up past my head and tied it off, then nailed me into a box, and lowered it into the weeping ground.

A sudden hard sob rose up, choking me.

I'd missed the service that they'd said, missed the hymns, missed the prayers, the tears, the hollow impact as the first clods were shoveled into the grave. Asleep. I'd been oblivious in the sleep of the dead until the sun was gone and consciousness returned.

There had been nothing to *hear*, nothing but my own screams.

My hand began to shake in remembrance of that damnable terror.

I wanted out, I had to get *out*.

Nothing to *see*. I'd have sold my soul for even this tiny flame.

And then it began to fade, to diminish.

No . . .

Getting smaller . . . dying.

No . . . If it went out now I might never return later, not with this fresh fear close atop the old ones.

I made myself watch the little drop of fire in my hand as though I could will it back to strength again.

And most remarkably, it did grow brighter.

Only then did I understand it was not the candle but myself that had faded. Trying to escape from a memory. From a shadow alive only in my mind. A fool's occupation, I impatiently thought.

Not a fool. Only a frightened man, with a perfectly reasonable fear.

So face it, laddie. I could almost hear Father's comforting voice in my head, gentle and at the same time so practical and firm.

Would that the laugh I conjured up from within had some of his tone, but I settled for the thin noise that did come out. It struck flat against the close walls of this chamber, but the fear holding me frozen retreated somewhat. Not far, but far enough.

Able to look around now, I was well aware that no one else other than Nora had been here since the workmen had sealed up the cracks. My shoes scraped over dust that had last been disturbed by her passage. There lay the marks of her own slippers and long swirls where her skirts had brushed the floor.

They led to a sizable rectangular shape rising from the floor; like the remaining furnishings above, it was also protected by a dust sheet. I flipped back a portion of it, revealing a plain oaken construction some two feet high and wide and long enough to serve as a bed.

Lifting the lid, I found that the interior of the box was filled right to the top with what appeared to be small pillows made of thick canvas. They were actually bags hauntingly like those I'd had made, and like mine, were heavy with a quantity of earth. *Her* home earth. This was where she rested during the day. Not inside, of course, as there was no room, but above on the closed lid, thus sparing her clothing from the siftings from the bags.

Now I released a sigh, thanking heaven for this happy discovery. As precious and necessary as it was to my day-time rest, I could expect her need for this portion of the grave to be identical to mine. Certainly she would have taken some with her to wherever she now lived, but if she never intended to return to this house, she'd have removed this cache along with the rest of her things.

Unless something had happened to her.

Her goods could have been carried off and sold and this box left behind because no one knew about it. Or if anyone did, they'd placed no value on it, not bothering to knock down the wall to . . .

Stop it. Nora was all right. Until and unless I heard anything different, she was all right.

God, but she was the most cautious soul I'd ever met. Had she not been able to safely juggle the attentions of a dozen or more of her courtiers, taking care that none of them should harm her or each other? There had been the one exception with Tony Warburton, but she'd survived his madness well enough. With my own rough experiences as a guide, I knew it would be difficult, if not impossible, for her to come to permanent physical harm. Sunlight was our only real enemy and, of course, fire, but this chamber was ample proof of the measures she'd taken to ensure her safety should such a calamity occur. With its stone walls and a strong roof made of slate, this sanctuary was as fireproof as a . . . a tomb.

Better not to dwell on that point, Johnny Boy, I thought with a shiver.

I replaced the lid and pulled the dust sheet back. A note, then, was necessary. I'd prepared one against this possibility and could leave it here where she was sure to find it . . . no . . . perhaps not. Better she directly learn from me the results of our liaison than to infer it by my invasion of this most private place. I'd leave it upstairs, then.

The outside air, for all its stench of coal smoke and night soil, seemed sweet and fresh after my exploration of Nora's empty house. The wind was not too bad, though it whipped my cloak around a bit on some of the street corners. It had a wet bite, promising rain, but not cold enough for sleet. The sky was still clouded over, but very bright to my eyes, for the most part casting a diffuse and shadowless illumination over the city. Those areas still held fast by the darkness I avoided, having already had a glut of it.

Though I'd gotten past my adverse reaction to the sealed room, I was yet a little shaken. The strength of it surprised me, but what else might I have expected? Perhaps this was a fear I needed to face down the same as I'd done at the Captain's Kettle; however, there was absolutely no desire lurking in me to attend to it in the near future, if ever. For the present, I had other things to think about, with finding Nora being the most pressing.

Since most of her near neighbors appeared to have retired for the night, I could not impose myself upon them to ask questions. That would have to wait until early evening tomorrow. Oliver might have the names of some of them or even know them; he had a very wide circle of friends. My chief hope was that none of this would be necessary. If Oliver had located Nora since his last letter, then all would be well. And if not, then I had at least one other person I could consult, though that would be attempted only with the greatest reluctance.

Again, nothing could be done until the morrow. Well, so be it, but what to do until then?

As ever in these early morning hours, I had much time for thought and little choice for anything else. I wanted conversation, but could hardly be so rude as to inflict my restlessness upon Elizabeth or Jericho. The best entertainment I could expect back at the inn was either to pass the time with some sleepy porter or delve into the stack of books I'd brought along for the voyage.

All two months' worth.

I'd have to widen my own circle of acquaintance in this city unless I wanted to spend the greater part of my life reading. Not that the prospect of a good book was so awful— I was quite looking forward to lengthy expeditions at the many booksellers on Paternoster Row and adding to my collection—but the printed word isn't always the best substitute for cheerful companionship.

My current choices for distraction were small. Winter weather would have closed Vauxhall for the season; I wasn't sure about Ranelagh. It did have that magnificent rotunda with the huge fireplace in the center for the comfort of its patrons. But it could only be reached by a ferry ride across the Thames, and I'd had a surfeit of water travel. Other, lesser gardens remained on this side, but they wouldn't be the same without Nora, and it was so very late now.

Perhaps I could go to Covent Garden. No one slept there at night; they had better things to do in their beds. I felt no carnal stirrings right now, but that might change fast enough if the lady was sufficiently alluring. She'd also be much more expensive than sweet Molly Audy. It was only to be expected in so great a city, though I had coin enough and time. To Covent Garden, then, for should pleasing company not be available, then I could at least find amusement observing the antics of others.

Quickening my steps, I headed with certainty in the right direction. Four years may have passed since my last visit, but there are some things one's memory never gives up to time. On many, many occasions Oliver and I had gone there for all manner of entertainments, sometimes trying the theater or more often offering our admiration to any ladies willing to accept it. My particular favorite had been arranging watery trysts at the Turkish baths, though Oliver always maintained that I was running a great risk to my health with such overly frequent bathing. He blamed my recklessness on the rustic influence of the wild lands where I'd been raised. I blamed my own inner preferences.

Before I'd quite gone half a mile toward my goal, I was stopped short by a commotion that literally landed at my feet. About to pass by the windows of a busy tavern, I was forced to jump back on my heels to avoid a large heavy object as it came hurling through one of those windows.

The object proved to be a half-conscious waiter, and the unfortunate man was bleeding from several cuts. The bloodsmell mixed with wine rolled up at me along with his pitiful groans. From inside the tavern came cries of dismay and outrage and drunken laughter, very loud.

A slurred voice bawled out, "Ha, landlord, put him on the reckoning, there's a good chap."

CHAPTER
—5—

The jest was followed by more laughter. The man at my feet, his forehead and hands gashed, moaned and cursed. Heads appeared in the remains of the window and jeered at him for being a bloody fool. This witticism inspired more drunken hilarity, and one of them threw out the remains in his tankard, splashing both the injured man and myself.

"Damned louts!" I yelled.

"And you're a thrice damned foreigner," came the return, its originator having taken exception to my simpler clothes and lack of a wig.

Two people cautiously emerged from the door of the tavern, hurried toward the fallen waiter, and lifted him up and away. For their trouble, they were pelted with more drink and several tankards, the uproar within growing each time someone struck true. Their targets hastily removed themselves, leaving me in command of the field. Not unexpectedly, I became the next target of abuse. A tankard was launched at me, but I foiled the attack by catching it as easily as I'd caught Elizabeth's seedcake hours before. Unable to resist the temptation, I returned the missile with as much force as was in my power, which was considerable, if I could judge from the resulting crash and yelp.

This only incensed the aggressors, and before I could also

remove myself from the area, several men came boiling
through the window. Too many, I thought, with vast alarm.
I backed away from them, but several more rushed from the
tavern door and cut off my escape. But a second passed and
they had me encircled, their swords out and leveled.

"Here's a pretty lad who doesn't know his manners. What
say you that we give him the favor of a sweat?" Thus spoke
their leader, or so I assumed him to be by his size and
manner with the others.

His suggestion was met with sniggering approval.

Though I'd never met them before, I knew who they were,
having wisely avoided contact with their ilk on my previous
visits to the capital. They were called "Mohocks," perhaps
after the Indian tribe, and I'd have preferred the company
of the latter over these particular savages. They were well
dressed as any of the gentry and quite probably were of that
class. Their chief form of pleasure came from terrorizing
the helpless citizenry with cruel bullying that ranged from
passing water in public to throwing acid.

To think I'd been worried about mere footpads. At least
they murdered and maimed for a reason; these beauties did
it for the sake of the dirty mischief itself.

The assault planned for me identified them as devotees of
"the sweat," the purpose being to raise a warm one on their
victim. If I was so rude as to present my back to any of
them, I would find my rump pierced by that person's sword.
Naturally, I'd be forced to jump around, allowing whoever
was behind me at any given moment an opportunity to stab
in turn, continuing the grim frolic.

I couldn't expect help from the watch; they were often the
frightened victims of the Mohocks themselves, nor would
the other patrons of the tavern dare interfere. Being skilled
in its use, I could draw my own sword for defense, but they
were eight to my one. Even the great Cyrano might hesitate
at such odds. I'd left my Dublin revolver at the inn, else I
might have been able to account for six of the worst.

All this flashed through my brain so quickly I hardly
noticed its passage. As the hooting fools closed in to begin
their sport, I took the one excellent advantage left to me
and vanished.

My sight was nonexistent and my hearing was grossly impaired, but not so much as to deny me the pleasure of eavesdropping on their cries of shock and fear at this startling turn. I sensed their bodies falling back in confusion as they tried to sort out what had happened. They were very drunk, though, which added to my entertainment. One of them suggested in awestruck tones the possibility of a ghost and got only derision for his thought. I attached myself to the one who laughed the loudest.

Elizabeth had long ago informed me that when assuming this state, I produced an area of intense cold in the place where my body had been. By draping an arm—or what should have been an arm—around this fellow in a mock-friendly fashion, I was soon rewarded by his unhappy response, which was a fit of violent shivering. He complained to indifferent ears about the cold, then hurried off. I clung fast until I realized he was returning to the warmth of the tavern, then abandoned him to seek out another to bedevil.

The remaining men were now searching the area, having muzzily concluded that I'd slipped away by means of some conjuring trick. I picked another man at random and followed until he was well separated from the group. Resuming solidity, I tapped him hard upon the shoulder to gain his attention. He spun, roaring out a cry to his friends as soon as he saw me. His sword was up, but I was faster and put the broad handle of my cane to good use by shoving it into his belly. His foul breath washed into my face. He doubled over, then dropped into whatever filth happened to be lying in the street. I hoped it to be of an exceptionally noxious variety.

I also was not there when his friends came stumbling over.

They had much speculation as to how he'd come to be in such a condition, and found it amusing. None seemed to have any sympathy for their comrade's plight, only disgust that he'd let himself be so used. The big leader was for further search, his frustration growing in proportion to the time consumed trying to find me. He became the next one upon whom I lavished my attention.

As with the first, I gave him good cause to start shaking and moaning as though with an ague. Instead of seeking shelter in the tavern, he stubbornly continued to look, filling the street with a string of curses that would give offense to a sailor. I'm no stranger to profane speech, but I had my limits. When I judged him to be well enough separated from the rest, I took solid form again. Though his clothes proclaimed him a gentleman, I had cause to disagree with the possibility and acted accordingly. Without a thought for being fair or unfair, I struck across the backs of his knees with my cane and, while he was down, followed with another sturdy blow to his sword arm.

His bellow of rage was enough to rattle windows in the next street. He dropped his sword, of course. I'd gotten him hard in the thick meat halfway between the shoulder and elbow. He lunged at me with his other arm, but I swatted that away and danced out of his reach, causing him to fall flat on his face. Perhaps I should not have been laughing, as it only increased his fury, but I couldn't help myself. Mud and worse now stained his finery, an excellent return for that splash of beer I'd gotten.

Someone suddenly laid hands upon me from behind, dragging me backward and off balance. I flailed about with my stick, connected sharply once, then had to fight to keep hold of it. The half dozen remaining men were getting in one another's way but still managing to provide me with a difficult time. I vaguely felt some blows landing on my body, and though there was no real pain, it took damned few to send me back to the safety of an incorporeal state.

If my initial disappearance surprised them, this latest act left them first dumbfounded, then panicked. Those who had been holding me now yelled and reeled into others. The effect was like that of the rings spreading out from a stone dropped in a pond; all they wanted was to remove themselves from where I'd been in the center.

Their leader cursed them for cowardly blockheads, but they were having none of it, calling for a return to the tavern with thin, high voices.

That seemed a good scheme to me as well. One more nudge would do it, I thought.

Rising over and behind the leader some three or four yards above the street, I willed myself to become more and more solid. I could just see them as gray figures against a gray world. As they assumed greater clarity, so did I, until I had to halt my progress or drop from my own weight. As it was, I was substantial enough to be firmly affected by the wind and had to fight to hold my place, instinctively waving my arms like a swimmer.

By their aghast expressions, I must have been a truly alarming vision. Two of them shrieked, threw up their hands, and dropped right in their tracks; the rest fell away and fled. As for the leader, just as he began to turn and look up toward the source of the disturbance, I vanished once more to leave behind a mystery that would doubtless confound them for some time to come.

I remained in the area to descend upon the big fellow because I thought he deserved it. Quaking with cold and surly from his thrashing, he demanded an accounting from the two that remained, but did not get much sense from them. They talked of a flying ghost and how I'd swooped upon them breathing fire and screeching like a demon. He called them—correctly—drunken fools and stalked away. Like dogs at heel, they clattered after him, whimpering.

Time to abandon the game. Doubtless they would comfort themselves with more drink and vent their displeasure upon some other person, but I'd had enough of their demeaning company. I surrendered my amorphous form to the wind and drifted away from the asses. When I judged myself well clear, I cautiously came back into the world, the caution derived from a wish to avoid frightening some undeserving soul into hysterics by my sudden appearance from nowhere.

The street was empty of observers, unless I desired to count a pack of mongrel dogs. They were startled, but after a few warning barks, slipped off on their own business. A pity the Mohocks hadn't done the same, though I was feeling strangely cheered about the whole business. I'd bested eight of them, by God; what man wouldn't enjoy the triumph? My sudden boom of laughter echoed off the buildings and set the dogs to barking again. A not too distant voice called for me to keep the peace or face the wrath of the local watchman. An empty enough threat, but I was in a sufficiently genial mood to be forgiving and subside.

I wondered at my good spirits, for except for finding Nora's cache of earth, this had been a singularly fruitless outing. Also, the loss of those two months still disturbed me mightily, though I'd been shy with myself in thinking about it. It seemed to mean a loss of control as well as a loss in time. Of the two, the lack of control over myself was the greater burden, but unpleasant as it had been, my success against these English vandals had altogether lightened it.

Putting my clothes back into order, I made sure my money was intact and the tinderbox and snuff box were still in place. At least my attackers had not been pickpockets, but perhaps that fine talent was well beyond their limited skills. And just as well, for had it been necessary to reclaim my property, I'd no doubt that my return would have been greeted with much adverse excitement.

London life certainly presented its dangers, but this time I was well pleased with the outcome, though my clothes had suffered. I reeked of beer. Jericho would have a few words to say to me, and Elizabeth would probably admonish me against further nocturnal rambles. Excellent thought, that.

The extranormal activity was having its toll, leaving me feeling both shaken and wan. I wondered at this until recalling that I'd been as one dead for the last two months. Father's note concerning Rolly had warned me to gently ease him back into exercise. The practice held true for a horse, then why not for a man? If so, then my venture to Convent Garden might be too much for my health. Tomorrow night, then, if I was up to it.

Feet dragging, I pressed forward, seeking out what streets I'd used earlier, and took myself back to The Three Brewers Inn.

I returned around four of the clock and made a short visit to the stables to look in on Rolly. He was a little worse from his journey, thinner than he should be, but he'd been cared for if I could judge anything from his well-groomed coat. His teeth were fine and there was no sign of thrush on his hooves. He eagerly accepted an extra measure of oats I found for him, finishing it quickly and shoving his nose at me to ask for more. That was a good sign. Tomorrow night I'd see about giving him a stretch for his legs, but only a moderate one. He'd been without saddle or bridle for far too long.

Before leaving I provided myself with a second supper from one of the other animals. Refreshed somewhat, I solved the problem of making a quiet entry to my room by once more employing my talent for walking through doors. Jericho was asleep, but he'd left a candle burning in a bowl of water against my return. On the verge of sputtering itself out, but I rescued it, putting it in a holder on the table.

From my traveling box, I softly removed my cherrywood writing case, opened it, and sorted things. The ink had since dried, but there was plenty of powder to mix more using water from the bowl. For the next hour or more I was busy composing a short letter to Oliver and a much longer one for Father. In it, I detailed my various experiences concerning the crossing—or rather lack thereof—and my joyful gratitude to him for arranging to send Rolly along. As for the cattle, Elizabeth said that five had died and their fresh meat had been gratefully consumed by the passengers and crew. The remaining seven were penned in a field near the inn, awaiting disposition.

I'd been too much occupied with the voyage itself to think on what to do with the beasts upon arrival. Now I speculated it to be an excellent idea to continue the story we'd given the shippers and have the creatures bred to some of the Fonteyn stock. By the time Father arrived in England, I could have a fine herd well started for whatever future he chose to follow. There were plenty of opportunities for his practice of law here in the city, but others might also be made in the country should he want to resume farming again.

My pen flew over quite a number of pages before I'd finished. It would cost more than a few pence to send this letter a-sailing, but no matter. Writing him was almost like talking to him, so I willingly drew out the conversation, closing it with a promise to write again as soon as we were settled with Oliver. I sanded, folded, and sealed it. On a bit of scrap paper I asked Elizabeth if she wanted to include some of her own thoughts before posting swept the packet away to America.

By this time it was very close to dawn and people were well astir below as the inn began to wake. Jericho would probably soon be roused by the disturbance, and I had no desire for a whispered and possibly reproachful inquiry about the state of my clothes. I stripped out of them and into my nightshirt, raised the lid of the traveling box, and whisked inside, quick as a cat. Just as I lowered it, I heard his first waking yawn. Then I was incapable of hearing anything at all.

Not until the day had passed, anyway.

Jericho stood ready as I emerged, armed with my brushed-off coat, clean linen, and polished shoes.

"Good evening," I said, full of cheer for my rest. "Any news from Cousin Oliver?"

"Mr. Marling arrived some time ago. Miss Elizabeth did ask him to come by in an hour more suitable to your habits, but he stated that he couldn't keep himself in check a moment longer. Miss Elizabeth is presently with him in the common room below." There was a note of disapproval in his tone, probably to do with Elizabeth mixing with the rest of the herd. I knew my sister, though; she'd likely insisted on it herself.

"Best not keep them waiting, then. I'm anxious to see him, too. It's been ages."

"There was a strong smell of beer on your coat, Mr. Jonathan," he began.

"Just a stupid accident. I was in the wrong place at the wrong time. Not ruined, I hope?" I looked vaguely at the coat in question, which was draped over a chair.

"I sponged it with vinegar and tried to air it, but the coal dust is so thick in this city, I feared—"

"And quite right. London is a horribly dirty place, but it can't be helped. Have to hurry now, I don't want to keep

Oliver waiting more than necessary." On went my stockings, up went my breeches, on went my shoes. Throughout this and without a word, Jericho managed to convey to me his knowledge that I wasn't being entirely forthright and that a reckoning was in store for me at his next opportunity.

Coat in place and ready for the public, I fled downstairs.

Oliver was as I remembered him, but for being a couple years older and even more fashionably dressed than during our Cambridge days. Same wide mouth, same bright blue eyes in a foolish face, and happily retaining a certain genteel boisterousness in his manner. He knew well how to enjoy himself, but not to the point of causing offense to others, allowing the contradiction to exist.

The second he spotted me coming in, he shouted a good, loud view-halloo in greeting and rushed over. There followed a hearty exchange of embraces and considerable slappings on the back with both of us talking at the same time about how pleased we were to see each other again. It took some few minutes before we were able to troop arm in arm back to the table he'd been sharing with Elizabeth, both of us grinning like apes, with the other occupants of the room looking on in amusement.

"Thought you'd never show yourself," he said, resuming his seat across from her. "Which isn't to say that I'm not enjoying Cousin Elizabeth's company, far from it. Every man in the room has been throwing jealous looks my way since we've been here. I can't wait to take her around the town and make all the rest of the lads in our circle envious for my good luck."

Elizabeth, though she lived up to his praise, had the decency to color a bit. "But I've no wish to impose—"

"Oh, rot—that is, never you mind. I'd count it a distinct honor to introduce you. You can't get out of it, anyway. Since that letter your good brother sent arrived I've been able to speak of nothing else but your visit, and now everyone's mad to meet you. Both of you, of course. Jonathan's met most of 'em, but there's a few new faces in the crowd these days—some of 'em are even worth talking to."

"God, but I've missed this," I said with warm sincerity.

"And so have I, Cousin. Remember all those riots at Covent Garden and—er—tha—that is to say we had excellent good fun at the theater there."

Elizabeth understood that he was making an attempt to protect her sensibilities, but took no exception to it. This time. After she got to know him better, he was likely to be in for something of a shock at just how much I'd confided to her about my previous time in England.

"We'll have even more fun now," I promised.

"I should hope so, enjoy everything you can while you're able. How long are you planning to stay, anyway?"

"Elizabeth didn't tell you?"

As an answer, she shook her head and shrugged. "We never got 'round to it."

"Got 'round to what?" he demanded.

"We're coming to live in England," I said. "For good."

His wide mouth dropped fully open. "Well-a-day! But that's splendid news!"

"I'm glad you think so, Cousin. We'll need your help finding a house—"

"Well, you won't get it, my lad. The both of you are most welcome to live with me for as long as you like."

"But you're being much too kind," said Elizabeth.

"But nothing. It will be my pleasure to have the company of my two favorite relatives. It'll be like Cambridge again with us, Jonathan, except for the added delight of your sister's presence to grace the household."

"And Jericho's," I added.

"Yes, I'd heard that you'd brought this paragon of a man with you. Can't wait to meet him. Have you freed him yet?"

"Freed him?"

"We've slaves here, but the business isn't as popular as it is in America. The fashionable thing these days is freeing 'em. Of course, you'll have to pay him a wage, then."

"I think I can afford it." The only reason I'd not done so before was that Mother would have insisted on then and there dismissing Jericho to replace him with an English-bred valet of her choosing. Though she no longer controlled my purse strings, she would have vigorously exercised her right as mistress of her own house, as well as made life a living hell until she'd gotten her way. Far better for everyone if Jericho remained my legal property until circumstances were more in his favor. Then he could himself choose to leave or not. Not that I harbored the least thought that he would ever forsake my service. We got on very well and I knew he enjoyed playing the despot within his sphere of influence, which was not inconsiderable.

My cousin was chattering on about the splendid times we'd soon be having. "It may not make up for being parted from the rest of your family, but we'll do what we can to keep you in good cheer."

"But, Oliver, it won't be just me and Elizabeth; our father is planning to move to England as well."

"The devil you say! Oh, I do beg pardon, Elizabeth. The whole Barrett clan coming back to the homeland? That *is* good news."

"It also means we still need to find a house."

"But I've *lots* of room," he protested.

"Not enough to accommodate your aunt Marie."

At this mention of Mother—for I had written much to him about her over the years—Oliver's unabashed enthusiasm suddenly shriveled. "Oh, dear God."

"More like the wrath of, Coz. You can see why we're eager to find a separate place for us to be than in your home."

"Maybe she could stay at Fonteyn House," he suggested. "My mother will be glad to see her."

Alone against the whole island of England, I thought, but then Aunt Fonteyn and Mother were cut straight from the same cloth. Human nature being what it is, they'd either despise each other or get along like the kindred spirits they were.

"That's fine for Mother," said Elizabeth, "but what about Father? I can't see him living at Fonteyn House. Please forgive me, Oliver, but from some of the things I've heard said about Aunt Fonteyn . . ."

Oliver waved both hands. "No forgiveness is needed, I *do* understand and have no blame for you. God knows I left the place as soon as I was able. She's a terrible woman and no mistake."

"Elizabeth . . ." An idea popped into my head. "We're forgetting what it was like before."

"Before what?"

"Before Mother left Philadelphia to come live with us. She only came because of the danger in the city. There are no damned rebels at Fonteyn House—"

"Only the damned," Oliver muttered darkly.

"—they might go back to that again, with Mother in her own place and Father in his. Certainly they must. I'll lay you fifteen to five she proposes the idea herself once they've landed."

"Good heavens, yes. After two months or more aboard ship, she'd leap at the chance to get away from him."

"I say," said Oliver. "It doesn't exactly sound right, y'know, two children so enthusiastically talking about their parents parting from each other like that. Not that it bothers me, but I just thought I'd raise the point, don't you know."

"But we aren't just anybody's children," she said, with meaning.

"Yes, I see, now. This has to do with the *Fonteyn* blood, which taints us equally. Good thing I've my Marling half and you've the Barrett side to draw sense from, or we'd all be in Bedlam."

That inspired some laughter, but in our hearts we knew he was speaking the grim truth.

"Now what about a bit of food and a lot of drink?" he suggested. "They didn't christen this place in vain, y'know. Let's have a celebration."

Elizabeth confessed that she was in need of supper, then shot a concerned look at me. I winked back, hoping to reassure her. Eyes sharp and lips compressed into a line, she understood my intent all too well. She then removed her gaze entirely. Ah, well, with or without her approval, it couldn't be helped.

"You two may celebrate with my blessing," I said, "but I'm still unsettled from the traveling. Couldn't eat or drink a thing tonight."

"Really?" said Oliver, brows rising high and making lots of furrows. "Perhaps I can prescribe something for you. There's got to be an apothecary nearby and—"

"No, I'm fine in all other respects. I've had this before. It will pass off soon enough."

"But really, you shouldn't let anything go untreated—"

"Oliver . . ." I fixed my eyes on him.

He blinked and went very still.

"You need not concern yourself with my lack of appetite. It doesn't bother you now, and you need not ever notice it in the future. All right?"

"Yes, of course," he answered, but without his usual animation.

I broke my hold. Elizabeth was very still as well, but nodded slightly. She wasn't happy that I could influence people in this manner, but time and again—at least on the topic of my not eating—it prevented a multitude of unanswerable questions.

"What will you have?" I asked Oliver. As I expected, he was absolutely unaware of what had happened.

"Some ham, I think, if that's what smells so good here. Hope they cut it thicker than at Vauxhall. You'll love Vauxhall, Elizabeth, but it won't be open for months and months, but it's worth the wait even if their ham's so thin you can read a paper through it."

He babbled on and she began to smile again. I called a serving lad over and ordered their supper. That task finished, I assumed another, more important one, the whole point of our long journey.

"Oliver, have you any news of Nora Jones?"

By his initial expression I saw that he had none. He glanced once at Elizabeth and shifted as if uncomfortable.

She correctly understood what troubled him. "It's all right, Jonathan's told me everything about his relationship with Miss Jones."

"Oh—uh—has he, now?"

"So you may speak freely before us both."

With that obstacle removed, Oliver squared his shoulders and plunged forward, addressing me with a solemn face. "Sorry, but I've not heard a word on the lady. I've asked all around for you, called on everyone who'd ever known her or had her to a party, but nothing. The Warburtons saw her last and that was just before they left Italy to come home for the summer. She was a frequent visitor with them while they were there; they had quite a high regard for her. Seems she was always very kind to poor Tony, spent time with him and read to him a lot, which went very well with his mother. She said he was often a bit improved afterward."

"But they'd no idea of her whereabouts?"

"Mrs. Warburton had reckoned that Miss Jones would be returning to England as well and was surprised as any when she did not, what with her attachment to Tony and all."

Not the news I'd been hoping for, but not unexpected after my exploration of her empty house. "Have you talked to her neighbors lately?"

"I took supper with the Everitts only last week—they live next door on the left—and they've not had the least sight of her. Even spoke to one of their footmen when I'd learned she'd given him a special vale to keep the lamp in front of her house charged with oil and lighted after dark. He had nothing to say, either."

"Probably because he's been lax in his duty."

"Eh?"

"I went by there last night and found it singularly deserted. I'd have noticed a lighted lamp."

"So that's where you'd got to," said Elizabeth. "Jericho told me that you'd made some sort of expedition, but he couldn't guess as to how your clothes had gotten into such a state."

"Oh, ho," said Oliver. "Having adventures, were you?"

"Misadventures, more like," I answered. "I happened to have gotten splashed with beer by a careless drunkard, that's all. Next time I'll hire a sedan chair if I want to go anywhere. You said Tony was improved?"

Another glance at Elizabeth.

"I'm also acquainted with Mr. Warburton's plight," she assured him.

He gave a self-deprecating shrug and continued. "Yes, much better than before. The Italian holiday must have helped. He still drifts off while you're talking to him, but not as much as before. Sometimes he can even hold a conversation, as long as it's brief and fairly simple. He enjoys a carriage ride when the weather's nice, and going to St. James's Park. His body's healthy enough, but his mind . . . a most curious case. I'm his physician now, you know; I've got a keen interest in nervous disorders, and Tony is my favorite patient."

"I'm happy to know he's in your capable hands," I said. "The poor fellow didn't ask for what happened to him, whatever that was." Though he'd certainly brought it upon himself with his murderous attack on Nora and me. He'd failed only because of Nora's extranatural abilities, but she'd lost control of her temper and that had resulted in his present condition. Nora had regretted her action against him and had no doubt sought to make amends, but where was she now? Why had she ceased to see Tony when he was apparently recovering a little? Was she afraid of that recovery? I couldn't imagine her to be afraid of anything.

"I'm thinking of trying a course of electrics on Tony," Oliver was saying.

"But I thought such things were for parlor games," said Elizabeth.

"There's use and misuse of anything in the scientific arts. Heaven knows the town is full of quacks, but I've seen favorable results on many hopeless cases by the use of electricity. I've almost got his mother talked into it. A few years ago she was eager enough to try earth baths for Tony, but now when I come along with something that may really help, she becomes the soul of caution. I suppose it's because she remembers me during all those times Tony and I dragged ourselves home at dawn drunk as two lords."

Elizabeth wrinkled her nose. "Earth baths?"

"Oh, yes, it's still very popular, supposed to draw out bodily impurities or something like that. I went to one establishment to see for myself, but the moment they found out I was a doctor, they refused me admittance. Claimed that I'd be stealing their secrets. I might well have done so, if they'd been worth the taking. What I did was simply to go to another place offering the service, claim an imposition, and go inside for a treatment."

"Which involves . . . ?"

"They have you in a state of nature and then bury you up to your neck in earth for as long as is necessary for your complaint. It's quite an elaborate operation, I must say. You don't expect to go into an otherwise respectable-looking house to discover several of the rooms looking like a street after the ditch diggers have had their way with it. Imagine whole chambers piled high with ordinary dirt. Thought I'd walked into some kind of a gardener's haven. Wonder what their landlord makes of it, though they probably pay him well. The only evidence I saw of any kind of 'drawing off' was how they drew off money from their patients."

"And you expect your electrics to be superior?"

"Most anything would be, but yes, I have great confidence that a judicious application of electricity in this case would effect a change for the better."

"One can hope and pray so," Elizabeth said. She looked at me.

"Oh, yes, absolutely," I added. I hardly sounded believable in my own ears or to hers since she knew the truth of what had happened to Tony, but Oliver accepted it well enough.

Their food began to arrive and our talk moved on to other subjects.

The evening was highly successful. Elizabeth took to Oliver as if he were a long misplaced brother and not a first cousin she'd never seen before. He had her laughing over his jokes and dozens of amusing stories and gossip of the town, for which I was exceedingly grateful. I hadn't seen her sparkle with such an inner light for so long I'd forgotten what she'd been like before tragedy had crashed into her life.

We kept our revels going as long as we were able, but the wine and excitement had its way with them. The signs of fatigue had set in, and not long after midnight Oliver said he needed a bed more than another bottle of port. Elizabeth also announced her desire to sleep, and we gave her escort upstairs, bidding her good night at her door, then going across to my own room.

Jericho had taken pains to do some cleaning, or to have it done, so despite the intrusion of our baggage into every corner, the chamber was more livable than before. I made introductions and he gravely bowed, assuming the near-royal dignity he wore as easily as his coat. Oliver was highly impressed, which was a relief to me. As we were intending soon to encroach ourselves upon him, it was important that everyone, including the servants, got along with one another. I told Jericho what had been planned, then asked my cousin if there would be a possible problem between his valet and mine.

"Don't see how there can be since I threw the chap out last week," he responded.

"Heavens, what did he do?"

"What didn't he do, you mean. Said he knew how to barber, but he was the ruin of two of my best wigs. Told him to give my favorite yellow velvet coat a brushing, and the fool washed it in vinegar. 'Enough of you,' I said, and out he went. He had a confident manner about him, that's why I took him into service, acted like he knew everything, but he had less brains than a hedgehog."

Jericho nodded sympathetically, his eyes sliding toward mine with one brow rising slightly for but a second.

"Perhaps Jericho can fill his place until you can secure another," I said, obedient to this silent prompting.

"That would be damned kind of you. You don't mind?"

I professed that I did not.

"As matters stand, I could use a bit of help. I've only got the one scullery and a lad who comes in with the coal," he confessed.

"What?"

"Well, it's bloody hard to get good help, though the city's full of servants if you can believe the notices they post. But I'm busy with my calls all day and haven't the time. I was rather hoping your sister would take things in hand and get me set up, if she had no objection."

"I'm sure she won't, but how long have you been without a household?"

"Couldn't really say," he airily evaded. "You know how it is."

No, but I could deduce what had happened. On his own for the first time he'd found it difficult to get fully established and dared not ask for help from his family or any friends. Word would filter back to to his mother, and she'd upbraid him for incompetence in addition to all the thousand other things she upbraided him for on a regular basis. In our four years of correspondence, he had also filled quite a lot of paper up on the topic of maternal woes.

"Yes, I know," I said. "But we'll have things sorted out soon enough."

"Excellent!" He dropped into a chair and propped his feet on the table. I followed his example and we grinned at one another for a moment. "God, but I've missed your company, can't wait to go drinking and whoring with you again—that is, if it won't interfere with your search for Miss Jones."

"We'll sort that out, too. Perhaps if you found her bankers . . ."

"Already tried that. She hasn't any."

"No bankers?"

"Went to everyone in this city and Cambridge. No one had ever heard of her. I also tried the agent who had sold her the London house. She'd paid him directly in cash, no bank draft. Then I asked around for her solicitor and finally found him last spring, but he had no knowledge of her whereabouts or how to contact her."

"Good God, but her solicitor must know of all people," I said.

"Apparently not. I did leave a letter with him to forward to her. I also wrote care of the Warburtons, but they said they never got it. The Italian post, if there is such a thing, would likely explain that. I am sorry, I know this must be frightfully important to you."

"You did your best."

"There's good reason to hope that she'll turn up soon enough."

"Indeed?"

"The coming holidays. There's going to be all sorts of fetes going on next month and for the new year, and you know how she enjoyed going to a good party."

I had to laugh. His unabashed optimism was enough to

infuse me with a bit of fresh hope as well. "You may be right."

"Now I've a few questions to pose," he said, raising his chin to an imperious height so he might look down his nose.

"Question away, Cousin."

"About Elizabeth, don't you know, and this Norwood business. My mother had gotten a letter from yours saying that Elizabeth had married the fellow and was now Lady Norwood, but she can't be because there is no Lord Norwood, and all I know about it is the chap was killed and in your last letter you told me for God's sake not to ask her about it or refer to it in any way, that it was very complicated and you'd tell me everything once you were here. I am awaiting enlightenment."

"But it's a long tale and you're sleepy."

"I'm only a little drunk; there's a difference."

True. He looked quite awake and expectant. "I hardly know where to begin. . . ." But I eventually determined a place and filled his ears with the whole miserable story. Jericho brought in tea halfway through, but Oliver was so engrossed he never touched it.

"My God," he said when I'd finished. "No wonder you wanted it kept quiet. The scandal would be horrible."

"The facts are horrible enough without worrying about any trivial gossip, but for Elizabeth's sake we decided to be less than truthful about them. What did my mother write to yours?"

"Only that Norwood had died an honorable death fighting the rebels. From her manner I got the impression she wholly believed it."

"Because that's what my mother was told; thank heavens she believed it, too. Only Father, Elizabeth, and of course Jericho know the truth of the matter. And now you."

Sadly, we had found it necessary to maintain the lie before our neighbors at home. Better that Elizabeth be thought of as the widow of a man who had died defending his family and king, than for her to endure the torment of pointing fingers and whispers if the truth came out. As things were, she'd put up with a certain amount of whispered speculation on why she'd discarded her married for her maiden name, but with our relocation to a new home, perhaps the whole thing could be buried and forgotten along with Norwood.

"I shall keep it in the strictest confidence," Oliver vowed.

"She'll appreciate that."

"She won't mind that you've told me?"

"I was instructed to do so by her. She said that since you were the one who discovered the truth of the matter, you were certainly entitled to hear the outcome of the revelation. If not for you, my dear sister would have been hideously murdered by those bastards. We're all very grateful to you."

Oliver flapped his mouth a bit, overwhelmed. "Well," he said. "Well, well. Glad to have been of service." He cleared his throat. "But tell me one more thing . . . about this 'Lady Caroline' . . . you said the shock that she'd been discovered had brought on a fit of apoplexy that left her simpleminded. What has since happened to her?"

What indeed? Just as Nora had shattered Tony Warburton's mind, so had I broken Caroline's. Like Nora, I'd lost control of my anger while influencing another, but unlike her I had no regrets for the frightening results. Father had been hard shaken by this evidence of the darker side of my new abilities, but placed no blame upon me.

"It was more than justified, laddie," he'd said. "Perhaps it's for the best. At least this way we're spared the riot of a hanging." Not too surprisingly, he'd asked me to avoid a repetition of the experience. I'd willingly given him my word on that endeavor.

"She's being cared for by our minister's family," I answered. "His sister runs a house for orphans and foundlings and was persuaded to take Caroline in as well."

Father had been worried that a creature like Caroline might prove a danger to the children, but that had lasted only until he'd seen she was unaware of them. She was unaware of the world, I thought, though she could respond slowly to any direct request. "Stand up, Caroline. . . . Caroline, please sit down. . . . There's your supper, Caroline. Now pick up your fork. . . ."

She passed her days sitting with her hands loose in her

lap, her eyes quite empty whether staring out a window, into a fire, or at the ceiling, but I had not a single regret and never would.

"God 'a' mercy," said Oliver, shaking his head. "I suppose it's all just as well. There'd have been the devil to pay otherwise. Is Elizabeth quite recovered? She seemed fine with me, but you never know how deep a wound might run in these matters."

"She's a woman of great strength, though I can tell you that the voyage was hard on her."

"Not a good sailor, is she?"

"Actually, I was the poor sailor. She and Jericho had their hands full with worry about me."

He cocked a suddenly piercing blue eye in my direction. "Usually a person subject to the seasickness comes away looking like a scarecrow. You look fine now, though, better than fine."

"They made me eat for my own good."

He grunted approval. "It'd be a trial to have to get you fattened up first before indulging in the revels to come. What do you say that we ready ourselves for an outing?"

"At this hour?"

"It's not that late. This is London, not the rustic wilds of Long Island."

"I fear I'm still in need of recovery, but you go on if you wish."

He thought about it and shrugged, shaking his head. "Not as much fun when one is by oneself. Also not as safe—but another night?"

"My word on it, Cousin."

With that assurance, he heaved from his chair, suffered to let Jericho relieve him of his coat and shoes, then dropped into bed. His eyelids had been heavy with long-postponed sleep for the last few minutes, and now he finally surrendered to their weight. Soon he was snoring.

"What shall I do about tomorrow?" Jericho asked. "He will be curious that you are not available."

"Tell him I had some business to see to and did not confide the details to you. I'm sure Elizabeth can put him off until sunset."

"Since we are to all live in his house, would it not be fair to let him know about your condition?"

"Entirely fair," I agreed. "I'll sort it out, but not just yet."

Oliver had not been especially fond of or comfortable with Nora. At one time he'd been one of the courtiers who supplied her with the blood she needed to live, but she'd sensed his lack of enthusiasm and had let him go his own way—after first persuading him to forget certain things . . . like the blood drinking. Though she could have influenced him into behavior more to her liking, it would not have been good for him. She preferred her gentlemen to be willing participants, not slaves under duress.

"I'll be taking a walk," I told Jericho.

Without a word, he shook out my heavy cape. It still had a faint smell of the vinegar he'd used to combat the beer stink. "You will be careful tonight, sir." It was more of an order than an inquiry.

"More than careful, as always. Take good care of Oliver, will you? He shouldn't be much trouble, but if he asks for tea, don't waste any time getting it. I think he consumed the landlord's entire supply of port tonight and will be feeling it in the morning."

With any luck, he'd be in such misery as to not notice my absence for many hours. Hard for my poor cousin, but very much easier for me, I thought as Jericho held the door open, allowing me to slip away into another night.

CHAPTER
—6—

Church steeples rose from the city fogs like ship masts stripped of their crosspieces. Some were tall and thin, others short and thin, and overtopping them all in terms of magnificence was the great dome of St. Paul's. It was this monument in particular that I used as a landmark to guide me toward the one house I sought in the smoky murks below.

Upon leaving the inn, I lost no time in quitting a solid form in order to float high and let the wind carry me over street and rooftop alike. And mansion and hovel did look alike at first, because of the thick air pouring from the city's countless chimneys. The limitation this form put on my vision added to the illusion, and I'd despaired of reaching my goal until spying the dome. With this friendly milepost fixed in my mind, I varied my direction, wafting along at a considerable pace, far faster than I could have accomplished even on horseback. I was free of the confusing turns otherwise necessary to the navigation of London, able to hold a straight line right across the clustered buildings and trees.

Free was I also of the squalor and danger of the streets, though I was not immune to risk. Anyone chancing to look up or peer from his window at the wrong time might see my ghostly form soaring past, but I trusted that the miserable weather would avert such a possibility. What windows I saw were firmly shuttered, and any denizens out at this hour were likely to be in a state of inebriation. Then might the sight of a ghost be explained away as being a bottle-inspired phantasm and easily discounted.

The time and distance passed without incident until I reached a recognizable neighborhood, though I could not be sure from this lofty angle. To be certain, I materialized on the roof of one of the buildings for a good scout around.

The house I wanted was but a hundred yards distant. I felt quite absurdly pleased at this accurate bit of navigation, but did not long indulge myself in congratulation. The coal dust was thick on my perch, and needle sharp sleet had begun to fall in earnest. Fixing my eye on one window from the many overlooking the street, I made myself light and pushed toward it. Upon arrival, the glass panes proved to be only a minor check. Once fully incorporeal I had but to press forward a little more until their cold brittle barrier was behind me, and I floated free in the still air of the room beyond.

By slow degrees I resumed form, alert to the least movement so as to vanish again if necessary. But nothing moved, not even when I was fully solid and listening with all my attention.

Quite a lot came to me—the small shiftings of the structure itself, the hiss and pop of fires in other rooms, tardy servants finishing their final labors for the night—but I discounted all for the sound of soft breathing very close by. Quietly pulling back the window curtains to avail myself of the outside light that allowed me to see so well in an otherwise pitchy night, I discerned a shape huddled beneath the blankets of a large bed. From the size, it was a man, and he was alone. As I softly came closer, I recognized the wan and wasted features of Tony Warburton.

He was older, of course, but I hadn't expected him to have aged quite so much in the last four years. I hoped that it was but a trick of the pale light that grayed his hair and put so many lines on his slack face.

But no matter. I could not allow myself to feel sorry for him, any more than I could have compassion for Caroline. But for the chances of fate both of them would have murdered me and others in their madness. Another kind of madness had visited them, overwhelmed them, left them in the care of others with more kindness of heart than I could summon. Though I sponsored Caroline's care with quarterly bequests of money, I did so only because it was expected of me. I'd have sooner provided for a starving dog in the gutter than succor one of the monsters who had tried to murder Elizabeth.

Enough of that, old lad, I thought. Put away your anger or you'll get nothing done here.

I gently shook Warburton's shoulder, calling his name.

His sleep must have been very light. His eyes opened right away and looked without curiosity at this post-midnight intruder. He gave not the least start or any hint that he might shout for help. That was no small relief. I'd been prepared for a violent reaction and was most grateful that he'd chosen to be quiescent.

"Do you remember me, Tony?" I kept my voice low, putting on the manner I used when calming a restive horse.

He nodded after a moment.

"I have to talk to you."

Without a word he slowly sat up, slipped from his bed, and reached toward the bell cord hanging next to it.

I threw my hand out to catch his. "No, no. Don't do that."

"No tea?" he asked. The expression he wore had a kind of infantile innocence, and on a face as aged as his, it was a terrible thing to see.

"No, thank you," I managed to get out. "Let's just sit down a moment."

He removed himself to a chair before the fireplace and settled in as though nothing at all were amiss. The room must have been cold after the warmth of the bed; I noticed gooseflesh on the bare legs emerging from his nightshirt, but he gave no complaint or sign of discomfort. The fire had been banked for the night; I stirred it up again and added more coal.

"Is that better?" I asked as the heat began to build.

No answer. He wasn't even looking at me. His eyes had wandered elsewhere, as though he were alone.

"Tony?"

"What?" Same flat voice. I recalled how animated he'd once been.

"Do you remember Nora Jones?"

He blinked once. Twice. Nodded.

"Where is she?"

He drew his right hand up to his chest, cradling and rubbing the crooked wrist with his left. It had never healed properly since that awful night of his attack on myself and Nora.

"Nora has come to visit you, has she not?"

His eyes wandered first to the door, then to the window. He had to turn slightly in his chair to see.

"She's visited you in the late hours? Coming through the window?"

A slow nod. He continued to stare at the window and something like hope flickered over his face. "Nora?"

"When was she last here?" I had to repeat this question several times, after first getting his attention.

"Don't know," he said. "A long time."

A subjective judgment, that. God knows what he meant by it. "Was it this week? This month?"

"A long time," he said mournfully. Then his face sharpened and he sat up a little straighter. A spark of his old manner and mind flared in his eyes. "She doesn't love you. She loves me. I'm the one she cares for. No one else."

"Where is she?"

"Only me."

"Where, Tony? Where is she?"

"Me."

I gave up for the moment and paced the room. Should I attempt to influence him? Might it not upset whatever progress Nora had made for his recovery? Would it even work?

One way to find out.

I knelt before him, got his attention, and tried to force my will upon him. We were silent for a time, then he turned away to look at the fire. I might as well have tried to grasp its smoke as influence Tony.

"Is she even in England?" I demanded, not bothering to keep my voice low.

He shrugged.

"But she's been here. Has she been here since your return from Italy?"

Nothing.

"Tony, have you seen her since Italy?"

He blinked several times. "She . . . was ill."

"What do you mean? How was she ill?"

A shrug.

"Tell me!" I held his shoulders and shook him. "*What* illness?"

His head wobbled, but he would or could not answer.

I broke away, flooded with rage and the futile, icy emptiness of worry. Warburton was focused full upon me, his mouth set and hard as though with anger, but none of it reached his eyes. He reached forth with his left hand, and his fingers dragged at my neckcloth. I started to push him away, but he was swift and had the knot open in an instant. Then he pulled the cloth down to reveal my neck. Unresisting now, I let him have a close look. It was the first sign of interest he'd shown in me.

He smiled, twice tapping a spot under my right ear. "There. Told you. She doesn't love you. Only me. Now look you upon the marks of her love." He craned his head from one side to another to show his own bared throat. "See? There and there. You see how she loves. I'm the only one."

His skin was wholly innocent of any mark or scar.

He continued smiling. "The only one. Me."

The smile of a contented and happy man.

A man in love.

Elizabeth looked up from the household records book she'd been grimacing over to regard me with an equal sobriety. "Is it our new surroundings or is something else plaguing your spirits?"

"You know it's the same trouble as before."

"I was hoping for a change, little brother."

"Sorry I can't accommodate you," I snapped, launching from my chair to stalk from Oliver's parlor.

"Jonathan!"

I stopped just at the door, back to her. *What?*

"You are—"

Anticipating her, I snarled, "What? A rude and testy ass?"

"If that's what you think of yourself, then yes. You're going through this torture for nothing, and by that you're putting the rest of us through it as well, which is hardly considerate."

She was entirely right; since my frustrating interview with Warburton last night, I'd been in the foulest of moods. Not even the move from the inn to the comforts of Oliver's big house had lifted my black spirits to any degree. Oliver had noticed my distraction, but had received only a cool rebuff from me when he made inquiry about it. I had spoken to Elizabeth about what I'd done—briefly—so she knew something of the reason for my boorishness. She also wasn't about to excuse it. Unfortunately, I was still held fast in its grip and was perversely loath to escape.

"Then what am I supposed to do? Act as though nothing was wrong?"

"Use the mind God gave you to understand that you can't do anything about it right now. Oliver and all his friends are doing their best. If Miss Jones is in England, they'll find her for you."

And if she was not in England or lying ill and dying or even dead? I turned to thrust these bitter questions at her, but never got that far. One look at Elizabeth's face and the words withered on my tongue. She sat braced in her chair as though for a storm, her expression as grim and guarded as it had ever been in the days following Norwood's death. By that I saw the extent of my selfishness. The hot anger I'd harbored in my heart now seemed to cool and drain away. My fists relaxed into mere hands and I tentatively raised, then dropped them.

"Forgive me. I've been a perfect fool. A block. A clot. A toad."

Her mouth twitched. With amusement perhaps? "I'll not disagree with you. Are you finished?"

"With my penance?"

"With the behavior that led you to it."

"I hope so. But what am I to do?" I repeated, wincing at the childish tone invading my voice. "To wait and wait and wait like this will soon make me as mad as Warburton."

She patiently listened as I poured out my distress for the situation, only occasionally putting forth a question to clarify a point. Most of my mind had focused upon the one truly worrisome aspect of the whole business: that Nora had fallen ill.

"What could it be?" I asked, full knowing that Elizabeth had no more answer than I'd been able to provide for myself.

"Anything," she said unhelpfully. "But when was the last time you were sick?"

"On the crossing, of course."

"And since your change, nothing. Not even a chill after that time you were buried all day in the snow. And remember how everyone in the house was abed with that catarrh last spring? You were the only one who did not suffer from it. Not natural was what poor Dr. Beldon said, so I am inclined to connect your healthful escape to your condition. Perhaps it's because you don't breathe all the time that you are less likely to succumb to the noxious vapors of illness."

"Meaning that Nora could be just as hardy?"

"Yes, and you might also consider that Mr. Warburton may have last seen Nora when they were crossing the Channel. To him she might appear to be very poorly, if her reaction to sea travel is anything like yours. She could have even told him she was ill so as to gracefully quit his company for some reason."

"It's possible. But Tony's mother said she hadn't seen Nora since Italy."

"There is that, but Nora could have wished to cross incognito to avoid questions on her whereabouts during the day. However, we are straying much too far into speculation. All I intended was to provide you with some comforting alternatives to the dark thoughts that have kept you company all this time."

"I do appreciate it, Sister. Truly I do." God, why hadn't

I talked to her before like this? Like the anger, my worries and fears were draining away, but not all, alas. A goodly sized block still remained impervious to Elizabeth's logic, though it was of a size I could manage. "I've been such an oaf. I'm very sorry for—"

She waved a hand. "Oh, never mind. Just assure me that you're back to being your own self again. And Oliver, too. The dear fellow thinks you're angry at him for some reason."

"I'd better go make amends. Is he home yet? Where is he?"

"Gone to his consulting room with the day's post."

"Right, I'll just—"

Before I could do more than even take a step in the door's direction, it burst open. Oliver strode in, face flushed and jaw set. He had a somewhat crumpled piece of paper in one nervous hand.

"Oliver, I've been uncommonly rude to you lately and I—"

"Oh, bother that," he said dismissively. "You're allowed to be peevish around here, it's certainly my natural state."

"You are not."

"Well, I am now and with good reason. We're in for it, Cousins," he announced. "Prepare yourselves for the worst."

"What is it? The Bolyns haven't canceled their party, have they?"

We had hardly been in town long enough to know what to do with ourselves, when the festive Bolyn tribe had yesterday sent along our invitation to their annual masqued ball. It had been the one bright point for me in my self-imposed darkness, for it was at one of their past events where I'd first met Nora. I had a pale hope that she might be in attendance at this coming revel.

"No, nothing like that," he answered.

"More war news?" I'd thought we'd left behind the conflicts of that wretched disturbance forever.

"Oh, no, it's much worse." He shook the paper in his hand, which I perceived to be a letter. "*Mother* has sent us a formal summons for an audience at Fonteyn House. We dare not ignore it."

Elizabeth's face fell, and I mirrored her reaction.

"It was an inevitability," he pronounced with a morbid air. "She'll want to look the both of you over and pass judgment down like Grandfather Fonteyn used to do."

"I'm sure we can survive it," said Elizabeth.

"God, but I wish I had your optimism, Coz."

"Is she really that bad?"

Oliver's mobile features gave ample evidence of his struggle to provide an accurate answer. "Yes," he finally concluded, nearly choking.

She looked at me. I nodded a quick and unhappy agreement. "When are we expected?" I asked.

"At two o'clock tomorrow. God, she'll want us to stay for dinner." He was groaning, actually groaning, at the prospect. Not without good cause, though.

I frowned, but for a somewhat different cause. "Ridiculous! I've other business to occupy me then and so do you. We'll have to change the time."

Oliver's mouth flapped. "But we couldn't possibly—"

"Of course we can. You are a most busy physician with many important calls to make that day. I have my own errands, and Elizabeth is only just getting the house organized and requires that time as much as we do to accomplish what's needed. Why should we interrupt ourselves and all our important work to accommodate the whims of one disagreeable person? Good heavens, she didn't even have the courtesy to ask first if we were even free to attend the engagement."

Elizabeth's eyes were a little wide, but she continued to listen, obviously interested to see what other nonsense I could spout. Full in the path of this wave, Oliver closed his mouth. His expression might well have belonged to a damned soul who had unexpectedly been offered an open door out of hell and a fast horse. All he needed was an additional push to get him moving in the right direction.

So I pushed. Lightly, though. "Just send 'round a note to tell her it will have to be six o'clock instead. That way we can avoid the torture of eating with her and make our escape well before supper." Desperation to avoid anything to do with daylight had inspired me mightily.

"But . . ." He crushed the paper a little more. "She'll be very angry. Horribly angry."

"She always is," I said with an airy wave. "What of it?"

"I—I—well, that is—"

"Exactly. It's not as though she can send you to Tyburn for it."

"Well, that is . . . when you put it that way . . ." Oliver arched one brow and squared his shoulders. "I mean, well, damnation, I'm my own man now, aren't I? There's no reason to dance a jig every time she snaps her fingers, is there?"

"Not at all."

He nodded vigorously. "Right, then. I'll just dash off a letter and inform her about when to expect us."

"Excellent idea!"

Behind him, Elizabeth tapped her fingertips together in silent applause for me, breaking off when Oliver wheeled around to get her approval. She folded her hands and offered one of her more radiant smiles, which was enough to send him forth to the task like a knight into battle for his lady.

"Be sure to send it," I added to his departing back.

He stopped short and glanced over his shoulder. "Oh. Well, yes, of course."

"Are you ever going to talk to him about your condition?" Elizabeth asked *sotto voce* after he'd gone.

"When the time and circumstances are right. There's not been much chance for it, y'know."

She snorted, but abandoned the subject, trusting me to address it when I was ready.

We did not ignore Oliver's advice to prepare for the worst, but beyond fetching out and putting on our best clothes the following evening, there wasn't that much to do. At least Oliver and Elizabeth could bolster themselves with brandy; I was denied that luxury. Oliver found it puzzling, but again, I urged him to pay no attention. Elizabeth, having just heard several ghastly tales about our aunt, had too much to think about to provide her usual frown for this liberty I'd taken upon his will.

We piled into the carriage that had been sent over and rode in heavy silence. I was thinking that standing with bound hands in an open cart surrounded by jeering crowds might have been more appropriate to our dour mood. We arrived at our destination, however, without such fanfare and much too quickly.

Fonteyn House had been designed to impress those who viewed it from without rather than to provide much comfort to those living within, certainly an architectural reflection of the family itself. The rooms were very large, but cold rather than airy, for the windows were few and obscured with curtains to cut the drafts. When I'd first come here four years past, I'd commented to Oliver on the general gloominess of the place, thus learning that nothing much had been changed since Grandfather Fonteyn's death years before, and it was likely to remain so for the life of its present guardian, Elizabeth Therese Fonteyn Marling.

Once inside again after so long an absence, I saw this to be true, for nothing at all had been altered. I rather expected the same might be said for Aunt Fonteyn when the time came for our audience.

An ancient footman with a face more suited to grave digging than domestic service ushered us into the main hall and said that Mrs. Marling would send for us shortly.

"What's this foolishness?" Elizabeth whispered when he'd gone.

"It's meant to be a punishment," said Oliver, "because I was so impertinent as to insist on changing the time of this gathering."

"Then let us confound her and entertain ourselves. Jonathan has told me that you have an excellent knowledge of the paintings here. Would you be so kind as to share it with me?"

Oliver gave her to understand he would heartily enjoy that distraction and, pointing out one dark portrait after another, introduced her to some of our long dead ancestors. I followed along more slowly, hands clasped behind, not much interested in the lecture since I'd heard it before. Oliver paused in his recital when the doors leading to the main parlor were opened, but instead of the footman come to fetch us, some other guests emerged. I thought I recognized a few faces, but no one paid us any mind, intent as they were themselves to leave.

"Hm. More cousins," said Oliver, scowling. "There's Edmond and the fetching Clarinda. Remember her, Jonathan? Very lively company, and just as well, since her husband's such a rotten old stick."

Edmond Fonteyn wasn't that old, but his sour and surly disposition always made him seem so.

"Yes, I do remember. Lively company, indeed," I murmured.

"Really?" asked Elizabeth. "Lively in what way?"

"Oh, er, just lively," he said, shrugging. "Knows all the best fashions, all the dances and games, that sort of thing. How she and Edmond get along is a major mystery, for the man never has time for any frivolity. Mother doesn't like her at all, but Clarinda was married to Mother's favorite brother's son and provided him with an heir. The poor boy got sent away to school several years back; I doubt if he's ever seen his little half brother."

"I'm sorry, Oliver, but you've quite lost me. Who is Edmond?"

"Clarinda's *second* husband. He's a distant Fonteyn cousin. When Clarinda became widowed, he put forth whatever charm he possessed and managed to marry her. It pleased Mother, not so much that Clarinda had a protector, but that her grandnephew had no need to change his name. As for her other grandnephew, Mother largely ignores him, and he's probably well off for it."

The people in the hall were donning cloaks against the cold outside. They should have retained them for protection from the chill of Aunt Fonteyn. One of the more graceful figures looked in our direction. Cousin Clarinda, without a doubt. She nodded to Oliver and Elizabeth, who offered a slight bow in return. Then she cocked her head at me. I somberly bowed in my turn. She smiled ever so slightly, and I hoped that the dimness of our surroundings would prevent anyone noticing the color creeping into my cheeks. Her eyes were on me a moment longer than they should have been, then she abruptly turned back to her husband.

Edmond paid her no mind, concentrating instead upon me. There was a strange heat in his dark-eyed glare, and I wondered if he knew. I bowed to him, but got none back. A bad sign, that.

He broke off to hustle Clarinda out the door. A very bad sign. It was likely that he did know, or at least strongly suspected. Perhaps his reaction was the same for all the men who could count themselves to be admirers of his beautiful wife. If so, then I need not feel so alone in the face of his ill regard.

Besides, the cause had been well worth it, I thought, turning my own attention inward to the past, allowing sweet memory to carry me back to a most unforgettable celebration of the winter holidays, specifically, my first Christmas in England.

I was to spend it at Fonteyn House, and despite Oliver's mitigating presence, had come to regard the idea with the same enthusiasm one might reserve for acquiring a blister. I hoped this experience would heal into a simple callous on the memory, but leave no lingering scars. And so I joined with a hundred or more Fonteyns, Marlings, and God knows what other relations as they merged to cluck over the deaths, coo at the births, shake their heads at the marriages, and gape at me, their colonial cousin. It was Aunt Fonteyn's idea to call this annual gathering, it being her opportunity to inflict the torture of her presence equally throughout all the families.

I was promptly cornered by the men and subjected to an interrogation not unlike my last round of university exams. They were most interested in politics and wanted my opinion of the turmoil going on between the Colonies and the Crown. I told them that it was all a damned nuisance and the pack of troublemakers calling themselves the Continental Congress should be arrested for sedition and treason and hanged. Since my heart was in my words, this resulted in much backslapping and a call for drink to toast my very good health.

They also wanted to know all about my home, asking, like my new friends at Cambridge, the same dozen or so questions over and over. A pattern emerged that had first been set by Oliver as they expressed exaggerated concern over Indian attacks and displayed a serious underestimation of the level of civilized comfort we enjoyed. (They were quite astonished to learn of the existence of a theater house in New York and other cities.) Some colonists lived in isolated forts in constant fear of the local natives, or hand-to-mouth in crude huts, but I was not one of them. The only hardship I'd ever suffered up to that point in my life had been Mother's return from Philadelphia.

Unlike Oliver, they weren't very interested in the truth of things when I tried to correct them on a few of their strange misconceptions. Dispelling the romantic illusions of a reluctant audience turned out to be a frustrating and exhausting exercise. It also made me feel miserably home-sick for Father, Elizabeth, Jericho, Rapelji, and oh, God, so many others. This stab of loneliness led to another as I wistfully thought of Nora. She was very much elsewhere, having remained behind in Cambridge. Her aunt, Mrs. Poole, had developed a cough and needed close care lest it become worse.

It just wasn't *fair*, I grumbled to myself, then halfheartedly looked for some distraction from my mood.

I made friends with the cousins of my own age easily enough, though several of the girls had been eagerly pushed in my direction by their ambitious mothers. Apparently they'd developed some hopeful ideas of getting closer to my pending share of Grandfather Fonteyn's money by way of an advantageous marriage. I suppose I could have gathered them all together and told them to cease wasting their time, but something as logical and straightforward as that would have offended them, and I knew better than to give offense to such a crowd. Some acting was required, so I was ingratiating, painfully polite, conservative in talk, and careful to comport myself in a dignified manner, for every eye was upon me. Anything out of the ordinary would certainly be passed on to Oliver's mother, and I was very keen to avoid her displeasure at all times.

Actually, I was just keen to avoid her, period.

In pursuit of this aim I finally quit the crowded rooms to seek out some peaceful sanctuary, trying to remember how to get around in her huge house again. My recollection of the initial tour Oliver had given me earlier that year was pretty fogged, no doubt due to the brandy I'd consumed then.

Brandy. What an excellent idea. Just the thing to get me through the rest of the evening. Surely I could bribe one of the servants to produce a full bottle and guide me to some spot well away from the rest of the family and the threat of Aunt Fonteyn in particular. The problem was choosing the right fellow. An error in character judgment on my part and all would be lost before it could ever begin.

There was one man that Oliver trusted; now if I could just come up with his name . . . so many names had been thrust at me today. Given time, and I'd get it. I had a picture in my mind of a rat on a shelf or something like that. Long ago Rapelji had taught me to associate one thing with another as a spur to memory. Rat on a shelf . . . no, rat on a cliff. Radcliff—that was the fellow. Excellent. Relief was at hand.

While busy thinking this through, I found I'd wandered from the busiest rooms into one of the remoter halls and by accident had gained at least half of what I desired. I wasn't exactly alone, though, not if one wished to count the dozen or so family portraits hanging from the walls. I snarled back at some of the poxy faces glowering down at me and gave thanks to God that I took after Father for my looks rather than the Fonteyn men.

At the far end of this hall a door opened. The light here was very poor; the windows were narrow and the day outside dark and dull. I made out the form of a woman as she entered. She paused, spied me, then pulled the door closed behind her. Heavens. Yet another female relative with a daughter, I thought. She floated toward me, her wide skirts rustling and shoes tapping loud upon the length of floor between us.

"Dear Cousin Jonathan," she said with a joy-filled and decidedly predatory smile.

How many daughters did this one have? I struggled to come up with her name. That I was her cousin was no clue—the whole house was positively crawling with cousins of all sorts. It had something to do with wine . . . claret . . . ah . . .

"Cousin Clarinda," I said smoothly and bowed over her hand. Deep in my mind I once again blessed old Rapelji for that very useful little trick. But I was out of practice, since her last name eluded me. She could be a Fonteyn or a Marling. Probably a Fonteyn from that eager hunter's look she wore. She was in her thirties, but graceful as a girl, with a slim figure and a striking face.

She slipped her arm through mine. "The other rooms are so crowded and noisy, don't you think? I had to get away for a breath of air. How nice we should end up in the same place," she concluded brightly, inviting me to agree with her.

"Indeed, ma'am, but I have no desire to intrude upon your meditations. . . ." Before I could begin a gentle disengagement from her, her other hand came around to reinforce her grip. We—or rather she—started to slowly stroll down the hall. I had to walk with her to be polite.

"Nonsense. It is a positive treat that I should have you all to myself for a few minutes. I wanted to tell you how much I enjoyed hearing you speak about your home so far away."

"Oh. Well. Thank you." I'd been unaware that she'd even been present.

"I'm unclear on one thing: Do you call it Long Island or Nassau Island?"

"Both. Many people use both names."

"Is it not confusing?"

"No, we all know what island it is." ·

"I meant to strangers."

"Hadn't really thought of it, ma'am."

"Please, you must call me Clarinda. As cousins, we need not be so formal, you know." She squeezed my arm. If affection might be measured by such pressure, then she seemed to be *very* fond of me.

"Certainly, Clarinda."

"Oh, I do like the way you say my name. It must be the oratory training you get at the university."

Even when the flattery was all too obvious, I was not

immune to it, and her smile was both charming and encouraging. I stood up a little straighter and volunteered an amusing story about an incident at Cambridge having to do with a debate I'd successfully argued. I hadn't quite gotten to the end of it when we ran out of hall. It terminated with a sitting room that had been stripped of seats; the chairs had been moved elsewhere in the house where they were more needed. All that remained was a broad settee too heavy to lift and a few small tables.

"What a pleasant place this is!" Clarinda exclaimed, breaking away from me to look around.

I didn't share her opinion, but nodded to be amiable. The draperies were partly drawn, and the gray light seeping past them was hardly worth mentioning. The fireplace was bare, leaving the chamber chill and damp. A bust of Aristotle—or maybe it was one of the Caesars—smiled warily from the mantel. So far his was the most friendly expression I'd yet seen represented in the art treasures of the house.

"It is just the kind of restful room one needs now and then when things become too pressing," she continued.

"Indeed." Since she was evidently so distracted by the—ah—allure of the place, I concluded she had no interest in hearing the rest of my story. This would be the best time to make my bows and go hunt up Radcliff, but before I could get away she seized my arm again.

"You know, you are not at all what Therese led us to expect."

Good God, what had Aunt Fonteyn been telling them? Despite my good record at Cambridge, she'd not relinquished the preconceptions set up by my mother's letters, so what . . . ?

"I thought you'd be some horrid, hulking rustic, and instead I meet a very handsome and polished young gentleman with the most perfect manners and a dignified bearing."

"Er . . . ah, thank you. You're very kind." She'd maneuvered herself directly in front of me, and I could not help but glance right into her brilliant eyes. It is amazing how much may be read from a single, piercing look. She held me fixed in place until, like the sun breaking through an especially thick cloud, I suddenly divined her intent.

I was at first unbelieving, then doubtful, then shocked, then strangely interested. The interest was abruptly dampened by a worried thought for Nora. What would she think? I wavered and wondered, then considered that she had time and again expressed her repugnance for any kind of jealousy. She seemed to harbor no ill feelings toward those of her courtiers who saw other women. Taking that as an example that the principles she asked of us also applied to herself, then I was certainly free to do as I liked. On the other hand, I—we—were special to each other. In our time together she'd not slept with another man, nor I with another woman, though I had, admittedly, a singular lack of opportunity for encountering women within the sheltering walls of the university.

And here was a definite opportunity. And I was interested. Perhaps I should at least hear the lady out before refusing.

Then it struck me that such a liaison, if discovered by Aunt Fonteyn—especially if discovered while being consummated in her own house—might have the most disastrous of consequences. The details of such a scene eluded me, but they would be awful, of that I was sure. My blood went cold remembering the disgusting accusation Mother had made against myself and Elizabeth, of which we were entirely innocent. How much worse would it be with Aunt Fonteyn—particularly with a decided lack of innocence in this case? No. No amount of transitory pleasure could possibly offset *that* storm.

All this and more passed through my mind in less time than it took me to blink. I steeled myself to graciously turn down the lady's generous offer.

Truly, I *did*.

Clarinda, however, was not ready to hear my decision, much less accept it. As I stumbled to find the right words to say, she placed herself closer to me. I had an unimpeded and unsettling view of just how low the bodice of her gown went and just how much filled it.

"Oh, dear," I gulped. My blood ceased to be so cold. Just the opposite, in fact.

"Oh, yes, my dear," she murmured. Without looking down to guide it, her other hand unerringly pounced upon a very vulnerable and now most sensitive portion of my person. I jumped and stifled an involuntary yelp at this action. As if to gainsay me, the hand's quarry began to traitorously rise and swell to full life in my breeches.

"I . . . ah . . . think, that is . . ." *Oh, dear. Again.*

"What *do* you think, dear Cousin Jonathan?" She was all but purring.

"I think . . . it would be best to shut the door. Don't you?"

As a romantic dalliance it was brief in duration, but compensatingly intense in terms of mutual satisfaction. The fact that Clarinda was already more than halfway to her climax before I'd even lifted her skirts had much to do with it. When a woman is that eager it doesn't take long for a lively man to catch up; something I was only too happy to do for this enchanting lady once the door was securely shut. Though the danger of being caught was a contributing factor to our speed, it added a strange enhancement to the intensity of our pleasure.

I was puffing like a runner when we'd finished and, after planting a last grateful kiss on her mouth, gently let myself drop away to the floor to catch my breath. Clarinda was content to recline back on the settee with her legs still invitingly extended over its edge. From my present angle it was all I could see of her, as the upper portion of her body was hidden by what seemed to be an infinite number of petticoats and the fortunately flexible pannier that supported them. It was an absorbing view: white flesh, flushed pink by activity and friction and embellished with silk ruffles all around like a frivolous frame on a painting. I found the study of her upper thighs as they emerged from her stockings to be very fascinating, the fascination growing the farther north I went.

Now that I had the leisure for study, I could not help but make comparisons between Clarinda and Nora. Of their most intimate place, I noticed that Clarinda had more hair and that it was of a lighter color, nearly blond, causing me to speculate on the real color that lay under her wig. Her skin was equally soft, but with a slightly different texture under my hand.

The view—and my exploring hand—was suddenly engulfed by a tumble of underclothes as she straightened up.

"Goodness, but you are a restive young man," she said with a glowing smile.

My hand was still up her dress and I gave her leg a tender squeeze by way of reply.

"I'm not your first, am I?" She had a trace of disappointment in her expression.

It seemed wise to be honest with this woman. "No, dear lady. But if you had been, no man could have asked for or received a better initiation."

"Oh, I *do* like your manners." She leaned forward to brush her lips lightly on my temple. "Whoever your teacher was, she has my admiration. She must be a remarkable woman. You are doubtless one of the most considerate lads to have ridden me in many a year."

I writhed happily under her praise. A pity I would not be passing her compliments on to Nora, but I instinctively knew she might not appreciate them. "Would I be too impertinent if I asked you if . . ."

"If I always go around seducing young men? Yes, that is impertinent, but no more so than I have been with you just now. I hope you will give me pardon."

"With all my heart, dear lady. But as for my question—"

"Not always. Only when I see a handsome fellow who stirs up my . . . my curiosity, then I can't resist the temptation of finding out what he's like. In all things," she added, to clarify her meaning.

"I trust the answer you found was fulfilling?"

She made a catlike growl in her throat that I interpreted as contentment. "May I know the name of this lady to whom I also owe my thanks?"

"I gave her my word I would always be discreet. I am honor-bound to that pledge."

"You gentlemen and your honor." She sighed, mocking me a little. "But I do see that it is a wise practice. May I ask your pledge to apply to ourselves as well?"

Whatever other differences lay between Nora and Clarinda, their desire for discretion was identical. I wondered if the trait was true for all women. It seemed likely. I readily gave my promise, easing the lady's mind and at the same time providing me with a very legitimate reason to refrain from confiding this episode to Nora.

Clarinda produced a handkerchief and dabbed at my face where some of her powder and paint had rubbed off, then offered it to me for any other cleaning I required. In a flash of interested insight, I noticed that it was a plain bit of linen with no initials. I felt a surge of amused admiration for her forethought as I pocketed her favor.

"May I see you again, soon, dear Cousin?" I asked hopefully. I'd regained my feet and was buttoning my breeches.

She smoothed out the fall of her skirts. "Not soon, perhaps. We live here in London, you see, such a long way from Cambridge."

"How disappointing, but should I get a holiday . . ."

"Then we must certainly arrange for a visit. Of course we can't meet at my home. My husband's there and the servants will gossip."

"Husband?" I squeaked.

"I would rather he not know. I'm sure we can work something out when the time comes."

"Yes, I'm sure we can," I said vaguely, swatting away any dust lingering on my knees and seat.

Husband, I thought with a flash of panic. *I've just committed adultery.*

It had happened so easily, so quickly. Surely the breaking of one of the Ten Commandments should have been accompanied by some kind of thunderclap in one's soul. There had been no hint. Nothing. I felt betrayed. Would God hold it against me that I'd done it in ignorance? Possibly not. My knowledge of biblical laws on that point was hazy, but He certainly would if, with this in mind, I repeated the sin.

Clarinda remained serenely unaware of my wave of guilt. I was one of many to her, a happy memory. We parted company on friendly terms, albeit separately. I remained in that cold sitting room for a long time, walking in slow circles, the pacing an outer reflection of inner musings.

Why was I so bothered? Father had his mistress. I'd heard the other lads talking freely about their women, and some of them had mistresses who were married. It was such a common practice as to seem normal and right. But what was right for them was wrong for me in a way I could not yet define. Being with Nora was one thing; neither of us was married. But being with Clarinda—or with any other woman who belonged to another man—was quite something else. It troubled me. Deeply.

As well as betrayed, I also felt rather stupid that I could initially assume her to have children, but fail to consider they might also have a father.

There and then I made a private vow that no matter how pleasurably provoked by a woman, I would first determine whether she was free or not before engaging in any activity that might cause . . . problems later. For either of us. For any of us, I thought, including the husbands. I had no wish to encounter this odd, creeping emptiness again. Clarinda and others might be able to live with it; I could not.

My God, but life was full of surprises.

I'd been very young then and, in matters of the heart and body as well as the mysterious ways of women, still somewhat inexperienced. But after the passage of four very full years, the negative memories of that day had long faded, though I had kept my promise about not bedding married women. Even dear Clarinda. At subsequent gatherings, I avoided being alone with her, but made an effort to be exceedingly polite about it so as not to hurt her feelings. I now could look back upon the interlude and smile with a surge of genuine affection for my sweet, passionate cousin.

Cousin by marriage only, I reminded myself. All the better that she was free of the taint of Fonteyn blood, if not the companionship. I wondered what had ever possessed her to marry again into the same family. Money, perhaps. There was a vague recollection in me that Cousin Edmond had a good income from somewhere. Clarinda might want a share of it to add to her deceased husband's bequest, thus maintaining her preference for the finer comforts of living and assuring a good future for her small brood.

"What amuses you, little brother?" Elizabeth seemed to

have suddenly appeared before me, unknowingly interposing herself between me and the past. I did my best not to jump.

"The long face on that one there," I said smoothly, pointing to a handy portrait behind her. "It may surprise you to hear that once when a hunt was called, his grooms put a bit in his mouth and saddled him for the chase."

"Few things would surprise me about this family," she said, narrowing her eyes against my jest. "I suppose once the bit was in, he could not protest further indignities, the poor fellow."

"Far from it," put in Oliver, joining the game. "He was always the first one away over the fences. Might have even done a bit of racing in his time except he'd had the bad luck to break a leg and was shot. Cousin Bucephalaus they all called him."

This was delivered with a perfectly sober demeanor, and for an instant Elizabeth gaped at him in near-belief before her own good sense prevailed, and she began to laugh. Oliver pretended to ignore her reaction and was drawing her attention to another painting, doubtless with a similar eccentric history attached, when the gravedigger footman approached and bowed.

"Mrs. Marling is ready to receive you, sir," he announced. I couldn't help but think of a judge intoning a death sentence upon the guilty.

"Well," Oliver growled, his cheerful manner quite vanished. "Let's get it over with."

CHAPTER

—7—

We entered and marched slowly down the length of a room that was really much too large for the purpose of an intimate reception. Aunt Fonteyn must have found the great distance between herself and the door to be a useful means of studying her prey as it approached.

The room itself had but one window away to the left. Candles were needed in the daytime to illuminate the more isolated corners. Many candles had been lighted, but these were concentrated at the far end. The only other light came from a massive fireplace large enough to burn a tree trunk. Indeed, a great pile of wood was flaming away there, filling the room with suffocating heat.

Above the mantel, bracketed by candelabra, was the full-length life-size portrait of Grandfather Fonteyn, the wicked old devil who started it all as far as my view of the world went. If not for his influence on Mother, then Mother's influence on me, I mightn't be standing here now, braced against whatever onslaught his eldest daughter had readied. On the other hand, without it I might never have met Nora Jones or survived past perils had I been spared so strange a progenitor. Still, it was no small amount of hardy resolution on my part that kept me from thumbing my nose at his fearsome, frowning image on the wall.

The stories that had come to me about him varied. According to Mother and Aunt Fonteyn, he was a stern but fair saint possessing a bottomless wisdom, who was never wrong in his judgments. According to Father, he was an autocrat of the worst sort, subject to impassioned fits bordering on madness whenever anyone crossed him. Having much respect for my father's opinion, I was wholly inclined to believe his version. Certainly the evidence was there to see, since Grandfather's bad temperament had been passed down to his daughters as surely as one passed on hair and eye color.

Enthroned in a big chair below and to one side of the portrait was Aunt Fonteyn, and seeing her again after such a lengthy absence was anything but a pleasure. For a wild second I thought that it was Mother, for the woman scowling at us as we came in had the same posture and even wore a dress in a material identical to one of Mother's favorite gowns. The fashioning was different, though, leading me to recall that about a year ago Aunt Fonteyn had sent her younger sister a bolt of such fabric as a gift.

Her hair was also different, being in a much higher and more elaborate style, but like Mother, she grasped a carved ivory scratching stick in one hand to use as needed, whether to poke at irritations on her long-buried scalp or to emphasize a point when speaking.

She had not aged noticeably, though it was hard to tell under the many layers of bone-white powder caking her face. The frown lines around her mouth were a bit deeper; the laugh lines around her eyes were nonexistent. We each received a cold blast from those frosty orbs before they settled expectantly on Oliver and he formally greeted her with a deep bow. I copied him, and Elizabeth curtsied. Such gestures were better suited for a royal audience, but Aunt Fonteyn was, for all purposes, our royalty. By means of her father's will she controlled the family money, the great house, and in turn the rest of the clan. She never let anyone forget it.

"And it's about time you got here," she berated him, her voice matching her cold eyes. "When I invite you to this house, boy, you are to come at the time specified and without excuses. Do you understand me?"

"Yes, Mother," he said meekly. His own gaze was fixed in its usual spot, a place just beyond her left ear.

"You may think you're well occupied wasting time getting drunk and worse with your so-called friends, but I'll not be mocked in this way ever again."

And what way would you care to be mocked, madam? I thought irreverently. Awful as she was, I'd met worse people than Aunt Fonteyn. The realization both surprised and gratified me.

"What are you finding so amusing, Jonathan Fonteyn?" she demanded.

"Nothing, ma'am. My nose tickles." To demonstrate the truth of this, I rubbed it with the knuckle of one finger. Not the best substitute for thumbing, but better than nothing. I stole a glance at Elizabeth, who raised one warning eyebrow. She'd somehow divined the irreverence lurking in me and, being prudent, wanted it curbed.

Aunt Fonteyn noticed the interplay. "You. Elizabeth Antoinette."

Elizabeth, though she despised her middle name as much as I did my own, remained calm and offered another cautious curtsy. "Madam. It is a pleasure and honor to meet you at long last."

Had we been alone, how I might have teased my sister for lying through her teeth with such ease.

Aunt Fonteyn looked Elizabeth up and down for a long moment, obviously disapproving of what she saw. "Why aren't you in mourning, girl?"

The question struck Elizabeth hard enough to rock her. She blinked and her color deepened. "Because I choose not to wear it."

"You *choose?* I've never heard such nonsense. Who put that idea into your head?"

"I did myself. My husband is dead, his name and his body are buried, and with them my marriage. It is a painful memory and I am doing my best to forget it." True enough.

"Ridiculous. Custom demands that you be in mourning for at least a year. You are in a civilized country now, and you will maintain civilized manners. I'll not have it said that my niece denied respect to the memory of her husband. It is especially important that you set an example to others because of your raised status."

"Status?" This one thoroughly puzzled Elizabeth.

"Your being Lady Norwood of course."

"I have forsaken that name for the one I was born with."

"Which is of no value whatever in genteel society. You are Lady Norwood until such time as you might be allowed to remarry."

I felt the mute rage rolling off Elizabeth like a wave of heat from an oven. "I am Miss Barrett again until such time as *I* say otherwise," she stated, carefully grinding out the words.

Aunt Fonteyn was obviously not used to such face to face rebellion. Her jaw tightened to the point of setting her whole body aquiver. Her grip on the scratching stick was so tight it looked ready to break in her hand.

Elizabeth read the signs correctly and added, "My mother was in complete agreement with me on this, Aunt Fonteyn. She knows the depth of pain I have suffered and deemed it best for me to put it all behind me. So it is with her full approval and blessing that I have returned to the use of my maiden name."

And very true that was, too. It was one of the few times Elizabeth had applauded my talent for influencing others.

Now it was Aunt Fonteyn's turn to look as if she'd been slapped. A mighty struggle must have been going on behind all that face paint, to judge by the twitchings beneath its surface. We did our best to remain unmoved ourselves, waiting with keen interest for her reply.

"Very well," she finally puffed out. "If Marie thinks it is for the best, then I shall respect her wishes."

"Thank you, Aunt."

"But it's not a good thing for a female to display any stubbornness in her nature. I expect you to cease such blunt behavior, for you are only hurting yourself. You are forgiven on this occasion. I'm keeping in mind that you are probably still unsettled from your sea voyage."

Oliver and I held our breath, but Elizabeth simply murmured a quiet thank you. She had, after all, won the round and could afford to be generous.

"It took you long enough to get here," Aunt Fonteyn added, addressing me again. I hardly need mention that she made it into an accusation.

"We came as soon as we could, ma'am," I said. "The captain of the ship assured us that we had a very swift crossing." Actually, Elizabeth and Jericho had gotten the assurance, but it was easy enough to repeat what they'd told me.

"I was referring to the fact that you wasted time stopping over at that disreputable inn when you should have sent for my coach to bring you straight from the docks to Fonteyn House."

As there seemed no advantage for any of us to offer comment to her on the subject, we remained silent.

"It was a sinful waste of money and time, and there will be no more of it, y'hear?"

"Yes, ma'am."

"And as for your present arrangements—I suppose Oliver talked you into staying at his house?"

"We accepted his invitation, yes, ma'am. And very comfortable it is, too. Your son is a most generous and gracious host."

"Well, that's fine for you two, but Elizabeth Antoinette will be moving into Fonteyn House. She will remain here tonight. When the coach takes you both back, you will see to it that her things are loaded in and—"

"I will not!" Elizabeth cried.

Aunt Fonteyn turned a calculating eye upon her niece. "Did you say something, girl?"

"I prefer to remain where I am," she stated, lifting her chin.

"Do you, now? Well, I do not, and you can't tell me that you have your mother's support on this one, because I know you don't."

"Nevertheless—"

"You will not argue with me on this, Elizabeth Antoinette. It isn't seemly for an unmarried girl to be living with two unmarried men, any idiot knows that."

"There is nothing unseemly about it," Elizabeth protested.

"You have no chaperon, girl, that's what's—"

"Oliver is my first cousin and Jonathan my own brother—what better chaperons and protectors could I want?"

Aunt Fonteyn abruptly fell into a silence so cold and so hard that Elizabeth instantly halted any further comment she might have put in. Aunt Fonteyn was exuding a near-palpable air of triumph.

Oh, dear God, not *that* again, I thought, groaning inside.

"And so it comes out at last, does it?" she said, and there was a truly evil glint in her small, hate-filled eyes.

Elizabeth must have also seen what was coming. Her whole body stiffened, and she glanced once at me.

Our aunt leaped on it. "I see that it does. See how she blushes for her shame!"

Blushing with anger would have been the correct interpretation of Elizabeth's high color.

Aunt Fonteyn went on, clearly enjoying herself. "You dirty, shameless slut! Did you think I would tolerate such blatant sin under my own nose?"

Shaken beyond words, Elizabeth could do nothing more than tremble. I feared her temper might overtake her as it had once done with Mother and that a physical attack was in the offing. An interruption was desperately needed.

"Tolerate what, Aunt Fonteyn?" I asked in a lazy voice, all bland innocence.

Her stare whipped over to me, but I stared back, quite impervious to any threat this one dungheaded woman might hold. I could feel Oliver's eyes hard on me as well. No doubt he was trying to fathom what had happened to set her off.

"How *dare* you raise such an impertinent face to me, you filthy fornicator!" she screeched. "You know very well what I'm talking about. Your mother has long written to me about your unnatural liaison, and since she cannot get your blind father to end what's been going on, she's begged me to put a stop to it."

Oliver choked with shock as the dawn started to break. "What—what are you saying?"

I readily answered. "It seems that my mother, who suffers from a singularly unstable mind, has the disgusting delusion that Elizabeth and I are engaged in incestuous relation with one another, and that your mother is imbecile enough to believe her lunatic ravings."

"Oh, my God!" That was as much as he could get out before Aunt Fonteyn's shriek of outrage burst forth.

It was more than sufficient to rattle the windows in the next room; it certainly brought the footman running. The parlor door was thrown open, and he and some other servants crowded through. Their swift appearance gave me to understand that they'd been listening all along. Excellent. I'd hand them something worth the hearing.

If I got the chance. Aunt Fonteyn was doing some considerable raving herself, calling me a number of names that a lady in her position should not have even known, much less spoken. She'd risen from her chair and was pointing at me with her ivory stick in such a way as to make me thankful it was only a stick and not a dagger. I held up against this tide of ill-feeling well enough, but Oliver had gone quite pasty. It was difficult to tell whether he was more upset by my revelation or by seeing his mother in such an extreme choleric state. Elizabeth had backed far out of the way and watched me with openmouthed astonishment, but by God I'd had enough of this sly and festering falsehood. It was past time to put an end to it.

When Aunt Fonteyn ran out of breath, I seized the opening and continued, doing a fair imitation of a man bored with the topic. "Of course you're aware that my poor mother has been under a doctor's direct care for several years now. She's often deluded by the heavy influence of the laudanum she takes, and so is hardly responsible for herself or anything she says."

"*Be quiet!*" roared my aunt.

"I only speak the truth," I said, full of offended dignity.

"You! All of you out of here!" she bellowed at the servants. It was quite amusing to watch their scrambling escape into the hall. The door slammed shut, but I had every confidence that their ears were glued fast to the cracks and keyhole.

"You know, Oliver," I went on in a carrying tone, "this display convinces me that your poor mother may also suffer from the same complaint as mine. She seems quite out of control."

Oliver could not yet speak, but Aunt Fonteyn did. Her voice was low and murderous.

"You vicious young *bastard!* Lie all you wish, slander how you like, but I know the truth of things. You and your sister are an unnatural pair and will rot in hell for what you've done—"

"Which is exactly nothing, woman!" I shouted, patience finally broken. "I know not where Mother got such a ludicrous idea, but surely you're too intelligent to believe her nonsense."

She wasn't listening. "I opened my hearth to you, and here is my repayment. I'll have the both of you arrested and put in the stocks for—"

"Oh, yes, by all means do that. I'm sure the scandal will make a most favorable impression on all your many friends."

And there it was, my killing thrust right into the great weakness she shared with Mother. I had the supreme satisfaction of seeing Aunt Fonteyn snap that foul mouth of hers shut, tighter than any clam. Though it was impossible to judge her color under the paint, it must have been very dark indeed. Had I pushed her too far? Her eyes looked quite mad.

Then, even as I watched, the madness changed to icy hatred with an alacrity that eerily reminded me of Mother's alarming changes of mood.

"You," she whispered in a voice that raised my hackles, "are no longer a part of this family. You are *dead*, the two of you. And like the dead you forfeit all right to your inheritance. You can pander in the street for your bread and your whore-sister with you. I'll see you both cast out."

"No." If she was merely icy, then I was glacial. "You. Will. Not."

From some faraway place I heard Elizabeth calling my name.

I had no mind for her, only for the hideous woman before me. I dared not spare the attention. All was in balance within me between anger and sense. Lean too far in the wrong direction . . .

Aunt Fonteyn blinked rapidly several times. She seemed short of breath or had somehow forgotten to breathe.

"You will not," I carefully repeated. "You will do nothing. The matter ends here and now. No more will be said of it. No changes of any kind will be made. No more accusations will be raised. Do you understand?"

She said nothing, but I saw the answer I wanted. I also saw, once I released her from my influence, a flat look in her eyes that I should have expected, but gave me a wrenching turn all the same.

She was afraid. Of me.

But a moment passed and she'd recovered herself and concealed it. Too late. It had been revealed. She could never take it back again. Not that I was proud of having engendered the feeling in her, but I couldn't help but think that she was more than deserving, the hateful old crow.

"Jonathan." Elizabeth was at my side, touching my arm. She'd seen and known exactly what I'd just done.

"It's all right. It's all over. We're leaving."

Aunt Fonteyn managed one last rally. "Never to return as long as I live."

As a threat it was pathetically wanting in power. If I ever saw the inside of this dungeon and its guardian dragon again, it would be too soon.

"Oliver," she snarled. "Take these two creatures out of this house. Immediately. They are no longer a part of this family."

Oliver made no move to obey. He was pale as fog and looked about as substantial, but he did not so much as shift one shoe.

"Do it, boy! Are you deaf?"

"No," he said, and there was enough force in his reply to suffice as an answer for both questions.

She turned full upon him and in an instant absorbed the fact that the mutiny had spread. "Do you know what you say?"

"Yes, and it's past time that I said it. So far past time that there's too much inside for me to get it all out. You horrify me and make me ashamed I'm your son, but no more. I'm going with them and I won't be back."

He started for the door.

"Oliver!"

And kept going.

"*Oliver!*" But there was no hint of anguish or regret in her, only fury.

Elizabeth and I hurried to follow him. I closed the door behind us, shutting Aunt Fonteyn off in mid-bellow.

The servants who had been listening were now in the process of vanishing, except for the footman who had let us in. I told him to fetch our things, which he did, moving with gratifying speed.

"Well, that's torn it," Oliver gasped. He was shivering from head to toe.

"You can apologize when she's in a cooler mind," I said. "There's no reason for you to cut yourself off just because I—"

"Apologize? I'll be damned before I apologize to that night hag. My God, the years and years I've put up with . . . Well, it's beyond further endurance and no more of it for me." He shrugged into his cloak, arms jerking every which way.

"Then I'm glad for you," said Elizabeth, pulling the hood of her wrap over her head. "Let's get away from this cursed pile of old bones."

"Yes!" he agreed, his voice rather too high and strained.

The footman rushed ahead and threw wide the big double doors of the main entrance. Elizabeth moved past me into the winter night, then Oliver, both of them in a great hurry, for which I could not blame them. Glancing back at the parlor door, I almost expected Aunt Fonteyn to emerge and renew her attack, but happily she did not.

The footman trotted off to one side to fetch the coach, for which action he was probably placing himself at risk. I would not put it past my aunt to dismiss him and the driver for assisting us, sell the horses to the knackers, then burn the coach.

I began to tremble. Reaction, of course.

"Are you all right?" Elizabeth.

"What have I done?"

"Exactly what was needed and in exactly the right way."

"But if I was wrong—"

"That's impossible or I would not feel so well off."

"Nor I," Oliver put in. "By God, I should have done this years ago. By God, by God . . ."

And then it caught up with him. His mouth shut and lines appeared all over his twisting face. He bowed forward twice, his skin gone all green.

"Oh, *hell*," he wheezed. Then he sightlessly staggered a few yards away and threw up.

The ride back was notable for its atmosphere of barely restrained hysteria. We were each pleased with the outcome of our harrowing audience, each laughing as we recalled who said what, and repeating the better points to one another, but all with an air of doom hanging overhead. This was no petty family breach, but a catastrophic rift, and we were well aware of it despite the shrill giddiness presently buoying up our hearts.

By the time we'd left the coach and mounted the steps into Oliver's house, a certain amount of sobriety had begun to manifest itself. My cousin wasted no time in dealing with it and made straight for the parlor cupboard where he kept his wine and spirits. He fumbled badly with his keys, though.

"Let me," I said, stepping in.

He relinquished them; I found the right one and used it. Wine was for celebrations, but brandy for reflection. I grabbed its decanter and two glasses. Knowing their respective capacities, I poured out four times as much for Oliver as for Elizabeth. Neither said a word until both had finished their portions. Elizabeth, not having much of a head for the stuff at the best of times, succumbed and sat down in the nearest chair, complaining that her legs felt too weak to hold her.

Jericho walked in just then. With a lifetime of finely honed perception behind him, he instantly saw that we had survived a mighty conflict and withdrew again. Not for long, I thought, and was proved right when the scullery girl appeared and began to stoke up the fire and light more candles, acting the part of the maid we did not yet have. Apparently Jericho had been instructing her in the finer points of dealing with the gentry, for she said not a word, though her expression was eloquent enough, filled as it was with excited curiosity.

Taking them away to dry in the kitchen, she stumbled out under the combined weight of our cloaks and hats, nearly running into Jericho, who was just returning. He'd known we'd not be staying for supper at Fonteyn House and had prepared accordingly. Fresh bread, a cold fowl, several kinds of cheese, and two teapots crowded the tray he carried. He put it down on a table, filled a teacup for Elizabeth, and took it straight to her.

She sipped at the steaming brew and sighed gratefully. "Jonathan, you will triple Jericho's wage as of this very moment."

"Done," I said.

Jericho paused, seeing that I was entirely serious. "But, sir . . ." he began, taken aback. I'd made legal arrangements to wrest him from the bonds of slavery soon after we'd moved from the inn, and he was still in the throes of adjusting to his newly bestowed freedom.

After this night, the same might be said for the rest of us.

"But nothing. My sister requests it and so it is done. 'Tis paltry pay for such imperial service."

He gaped and nearly let the pot slip from his fingers before his customary dignity reasserted itself.

Oliver noticed our byplay, but added no remarks, as he might have done if things had been more normal. Instead, he paced in a distracted manner, pausing in each pass before the fire to warm himself.

"Tea, Mr. Oliver?" Jericho asked, reaching for another cup.

"Oh—ah—no, thank you. Need to settle my belly first." Oliver helped himself to another brandy. The glass clinked and rattled from the tremors running through his hands.

Jericho put the first pot down and picked up the second, raising a questioning eyebrow at me. Elizabeth had apparently guessed its contents, but this time offered only a wry smile as her reaction. After a glance at Oliver, I nodded. In his present state my cousin wouldn't have noticed anything short of the roof falling on his head, but just to be safe Jericho obscured the pouring out of my own beverage by interposing his body.

"Bit of a risk, this," I murmured as he presented the cup to me. The warm bloodsmell rising from it was sweet to my senses. I felt my upper corner teeth begin to lengthen in response.

"When you left tonight, you gave me to understand that the circumstances of your visit might be exceptionally difficult. With that in mind, I thought you might be in need of reviving afterward."

"And I am grateful, but don't make a habit of it."

"Of course, sir."

I downed it in one glowing draught and had another. Drinking from a cup did have its advantage over sucking directly from a vein, being much cleaner and more comfortable, but I had some very reasonable fears against making frequent use of it. Though I could readily deal with discovery, it might not go so well for Jericho should someone notice him regularly drawing off blood from our horses.

Elizabeth ate what she'd been given, assuring me that she at least was recovering from the business, but Oliver refused an offered plate and continued pacing nervously around, rubbing his hands together as though to warm them. Elizabeth's eyes followed him for a time, then she looked at me. I raised one finger to my lips and winked to let her know all would be well.

"Oliver," I said gently. "You're making me dizzy with all this walking about to no purpose. Let's get out of here and take a little air."

"But it's freezing," he said, not meeting my eye.

"Just the tonic we want to clear our heads."

"What about Elizabeth? Can't leave her alone with all that's happened. Not right, that."

"I am going up to bed, so don't worry about me," she said. "Jericho, can you trust Lottie to ready my room? Excellent. I'll just finish this and be right up."

"Well, if you're sure . . ." Oliver said doubtfully.

"Wrap up against the chill," she advised him with a careless wave.

Jericho quickly produced dry cloaks for us to don, and with hats in place and sticks in hand, I got us out the door before Oliver could change his mind.

"There's such a thing as too much when it comes to tonics," he remarked as the first blast of wind stuck him. "Are you sure you want a walk on a night like this?"

"As long as it ends at a tavern," I said.

"But I've plenty of drink inside."

"It's not the same. Much too quiet for one thing. Elizabeth enjoys it, but I need to see that there are other people in the world right now."

He grunted a reluctant agreement to that and let me lead him away.

The cold air woke him up a bit, and he offered directions as needed to get us to The Red Swan, which he said was one of the more superior establishments of its kind in the neighborhood. It was quite different from The Oak back in Glenbriar, being much louder, smokier, and noisier. Oliver was evidently a favored patron, to judge from the boisterous greeting that was raised when we came in. Several garishly made up women squealed their hellos, but did not forsake their perches on various male customers. That was another difference. The landlord of The Oak never allowed such women into his house . . . more's the pity.

Oliver asked for a private room and got it, and though we were separate from the others, we were not completely isolated. The sounds of their current revel came right through the walls, letting us know we were most certainly not alone in the wide, lonely world.

Drinks were brought, as well as food, and an inquiry on whether additional companionship might be desired. Oliver said later perhaps, and they shut the door on us.

"You and Elizabeth worked this out, didn't you?" he asked, glowering at me, but not in a serious manner.

"It seemed for the best," I said, pouring more brandy for him. By the smell of it, it wasn't of the same quality as his own, but doubtless it would do him some good.

"Without saying a single word?"

"We understand each other very well. It's sometimes easier to talk to one friend at a time, rather than to two at once. Elizabeth knows that, so here we are."

"And if I prefer to drink instead of talk?"

"Then I make sure you come home in one piece so you don't disappoint your patients tomorrow."

"Ugh. Tomorrow. How am I going to face it after this?"

"You have regrets?"

"No, but be assured the story of what happened tonight will run through the town like an outbreak of the pox."

"Idle gossip," I murmured dismissively.

"Not with Mother doing the gossiping. She'll present herself favorably, of course, and I shall be the villain, and what she'll say about you and Elizabeth doesn't bear thinking about."

"Your mother will say nothing."

"Can you really be so sure?"

"I know it for a fact. Granted, there might be some talk of you two having a falling out, but there will be no ill rumors spread about myself and Elizabeth. Like it or not, we are still half Fonteyn and your mother would rather set fire to herself than endanger the good name of her precious father."

He finished his drink, coughed on it, then got another from the bottle. "It's horrible. Absolutely horrible what she said. Absolutely horrible."

I put my hand out, touching his arm. "Oliver."

Reluctantly he looked at me.

"It's not true."

His mouth trembled. "How can you think that I'd believe—"

"I *know* you don't believe, but you are troubled, perhaps by a doubt no larger than a pinprick. There's no reason to be ashamed of it. God knows we all have a thousand doubts bubbling up in our minds about this and that every living moment we're on this earth. It's perfectly normal. All I want is to put this one to rest forever. You have my sacred word of honor as a Barrett to you as a Marling, that Elizabeth and I are brother and sister and nothing more.

We'll leave the Fonteyns and their vile delusions right out of it." I gave his arm a quick, solid press and let go.

Oliver let his jaw hang open, then emitted a short, mirthless laugh. "Well, when you put it like that . . . I feel a fool for ever listening to the old witch."

"More fool she for listening to my mother. I'm sorry for letting my temper take hold tonight, but to hear that disgusting lie again was too much for me. I just couldn't help myself."

"Yes, probably in the same way I can't help myself when there's a boil to be lanced. The patient may howl at the time, but it's better done than ignored until it poisons his blood and kills him. No regrets, Cousin," he said, raising his glass to toast me.

"None," I responded and felt badly for not being able to return the honor, but Oliver seemed not to notice. I wondered if this might be the right time to confide to him about my changed condition.

Perhaps not. Later would suffice. He'd been through enough for one evening.

Putting his glass aside, he leaned forward across the table. "Those things you said about your mother, about the doctor and the laudanum . . ."

"All true. She goes into these fits, and Dr. Beldon and his sister are the only ones who can deal with her. The laudanum helps, but Beldon has to be sparing with it."

"Sounds like he knows his business, then."

"He's a decent fellow, all told."

"What's your mother like when she's in one of her fits?"

"About the way your mother was tonight."

"God."

"The difference being that your mother knows what she's doing when it comes to inflicting pain and mine does not."

"Grandfather Fonteyn was the same way," he said, hunching his shoulders as he leaned upon the table. "Certainly in observations I've made outside of my own family, I've seen how a nervous condition can be inherited. Let us pray to heaven that it spares us and our own children."

"Amen to that," I genially agreed.

Oliver's face went all pinched. "I . . . I don't remember

much about Grandfather, but he quite terrified me. I used to hide from him, then Mother would make my nurse whip me for being disrespectful, but better that than having to see him."

"Understandable. I've heard that he was a perfectly dreadful man."

"But you don't have all the story. Mother was always a trial, but Grandfather . . . he always treated me like—like a special pet. He'd laugh and try to play with me, gave me sweets and toys. I remember that much."

I found that difficult to believe from the tales told about him and said as much.

"I know. It makes no sense. It made no sense. But you see, children have sharp instincts, like animals sometimes when it comes to surviving a harsh life. Whenever I was with him I felt like a rabbit in a lion's den and the lion was only playing with his supper. Me. I never could fathom why until . . . until tonight."

Something cold was trying to insinuate itself in my stomach. It oozed through my guts, sending a frigid hand up to squeeze my heart.

"You think . . . ?" I had trouble recognizing my own voice, it sounded so faded and lost.

"I think that *something* must have prompted your mother's accusation in the first place—not you and Elizabeth—but something in *her* life. In her past."

My heart seemed empty itself. Making room for the welling coldness. It spread along my limbs, numbing everything, yet bringing pain.

"And in my mother's life as well," he added in a whisper.

"Oh, dear God."

"Sick making, isn't it?"

It was one thing to have the horror of incest as an abstract and untrue accusation, but quite another to be forced to face it as a ghastly probability. Oliver and I stared at each other across the table. I had no need of a mirror; I saw my own abject dismay reflecting back from his haggard face.

"But they *revere* him," I said, making a last futile protest.

"Too much, wouldn't you think?"

"But *why* should they?"

He shrugged. "Couldn't say, but I've seen dogs crawl on their bellies to lick their masters' boots after being kicked. Perhaps the same principle applies here in some way."

"It's abominable."

"I could be wrong, but growing up I heard—overheard—things from the servants. Listened to some of the adults when they thought they were alone. Didn't understand it then, but to look back on it, after this night's work, it makes a deal of sense to me now."

And to me. That time I'd sneaked into Mother's room to influence her into never hurting Father again. What she'd mumbled before she'd fully wakened . . . no wonder Oliver had thrown up. I felt like doing so myself.

"Makes you look at things differently, doesn't it?" he asked in a bitter tone.

That was true enough. It seemed to cast a disfiguring shadow upon all my past. Did Father know or suspect any of this? I couldn't recall anything that might provide an answer, but thought he did not. We had the kind of accord between us that would not allow for such secrets, no matter how ugly.

Oliver tentatively reached for the bottle again, then changed his mind, bringing his hands together. One grasping the other. Wringing away. He became conscious of it, then lay them palms flat upon the table to stop.

"It's not as though any of it were our fault, y'know," I said. "It's something that happened a long time ago. That doesn't make it less of a tragedy, but it's not *our* tragedy."

He frowned at the backs of his hands for a time, then tapped his fingers against the stained wood. "I was hoping . . ." He took in a great breath and released it as an equally great sigh. "I was hoping that you would talk sensibly to me about this. It's so hard being an ass all the time."

"You're not an ass, for God's sake."

"Yes, *I* know that, but few other people know it as well. I count myself very blessed that you're one of 'em."

"Oliver—"

"Oh, just let me say thank you."

"All right." I was a bit surprised and abashed.

He steadily met my eye. "*Thank you.*"

"You're welcome."

That achieved, his hunched posture eased, and a ghost of his more cheerful old manner showed itself. "And now, my dear Coz, I should very much like to get as drunk as a lord—if not more so."

It was an excellent idea, as far as it went, but when one is an observer rather than a participant in a drinking bout, one quickly loses a direct interest in the proceedings. It had been the same at The Oak when I'd buy drinks for all just to be sociable, then have to either pretend to drink or politely refuse to join them. The men there had eventually gotten used to my eccentricity and never failed to frequently toast my health. The difficult part was watching them gradually get louder and happier as the evening progressed, while I remained stone sober. I missed that lack of control, the guilty euphoria of doing something that was unquestionably bad for me, of surrendering myself to the heavy-limbed comfort of the bottle.

I'd done a lot of drinking at Cambridge with my cousin and our cronies. It was a wonder we got any studying done at all. Some did not. I recalled one fellow who came up for his exams in medicine full flushed with brandy. The instructors questioning him well knew it, but they'd passed him when his clever reply to a difficult inquiry set them on their heads with laughter. Ever afterward I kept his name in mind as a fellow not to go to for any doctoring no matter how dire the need.

But putting that aside, when it came down to the present, I had nothing to occupy me except to watch Oliver gradually slip into a wobbling good mood, his jokes becoming less coherent, his gestures wider and more clumsy.

"You should have some," he said for the third time over. "Do y' a world of good."

"Another time, thank you."

"Bother that, you're just thinking about the need to get

me home again, but there is no need, don't y'know. Mr. Gully takes care of that, y'see. Lots of room for us."

"The landlord here?"

"The very one, only he's a bit more 'n that, 'f y'noticed anything comin' in." Oliver gave a wink, a ponderous one employing his whole face.

"I noticed quite a bit coming in, but they all seemed to be busy."

"Hmph, should be someone free by now. Wha'd'y' say to a bit 'f fun?"

"I'd say that you were beyond such pursuits for the time being."

"*Me?* I beg to differ on that point, Coz. 'N' be more 'n' pleased to prove it t' you."

He staggered to the door and was out before I could quite make up my mind on the wisdom of his course. Just as I was to the point of getting up to follow, he returned, arms around two of the women from downstairs.

"Cousin Jonathan, you have the honor of meeting Miss Frances and Miss Jemma, who are very excellent good friends of mine, aren't you, girls?" With that he pinched or tickled each, causing them to scream and giggle. They were painted and powdered and dressed as gorgeously as peacocks, as fine a pair of London trollops as any man could wish for when he has the time and money. Neither of them looked too drunk for fun, I judged. Perhaps Oliver was on to something here. This was borne out when I found Jemma suddenly squirming on my lap.

"I think she likes you," Oliver said unnecessarily.

"Doctor Owly 'ere sez yer new 'n town, 'zat true?" Jemma asked, looking me over.

"This isn't my first visit, but I have just come from America," I politely responded.

"That means he's been on board ship for *months*, girls," Oliver put in, "so watch yourselves."

They cooed mightily over that one, and from then on the joking got much more suggestive. Jemma made it her business to ask about American men and if they were any measure against the English and so on, and I tried my best to answer, but there comes a point when talk fails and one must fall back upon demonstration.

Again, this might have been easier for me had I been drunk, for Jemma was definitely too far past the first blush of youth to be instantly thought attractive. On the other hand, she knew her business well enough and seemed pleased to find that I was in no headlong hurry to conclude things. At some point in the proceedings, Oliver and Frances disappeared, which was just as well, since Jemma and I were growing increasingly more intimate in our activity.

She had a solid figure under her gown, a little thick in the thighs, but smooth skinned and warm to the touch. I found my interest, among other things, quickening at the sight of the treasure concealed beneath her clothes and was more than happy to oblige her when it came to loosening my own. As ever, there was no real need to drop my breeches, but I found my coat to be somewhat restrictive and then my waistcoat. One was on the floor and the other unbuttoned when I came to see that though active, she was not exactly caught up in the fever of the event.

I thought of Molly Audy and her habit of saving herself up lest she be too exhausted for the work of the evening and divined that Jemma was doing the same thing. Well and good for her, but I became determined to provide this English *houri* with an equal share of delights to come. I had my pride, after all.

She noted the change in me as I began to concentrate more on her than myself, even protesting that she was fine as she was. I said I was glad to hear it and went on regardless, hands and mouth working together over her lush body. Then it was my turn to notice the change in her as she began to succumb, which only made me more eager.

When it was obvious that she was fast approaching her peak, and I found myself in a likewise state, I buried my corner teeth hard into her throat, hurtling us both over the edge. She was so far gone that pleasure, rather than pain, was her reward for this unorthodox invasion of her person. She could not have been prepared for the intensity of rapture it would engender, nor the length of it; for having finally worked things up to this point I wasn't about to abandon them after but a few seconds of fulfillment as would be the case for a normal man reaching a climax. I continued on, drawing a few drops at a time from her, relishing her writhings against me almost as much as the taste of her blood.

Here indeed was a surrender for me, to a different kind of heavy-limbed comfort, and here I intended to stay for as long as it pleased us both. I had no worries for Jemma; she seemed to be well and truly lost to it. As for myself, I knew I could continue for hours, if I was careful enough with her.

However, I had not reckoned on Cousin Oliver walking in on us.

He'd hardly been quiet about it, but I was so enmeshed in what I was doing that I paid no mind when he knocked, and none at all when he pushed the door open a crack. What he found was likely a familiar sight to him if he came to this house with any regularity—a half dressed man and woman each well occupied, this time it being myself holding Jemma tight, passionately kissing her neck.

"I say, Coz, I forgot m' brandy 'n'—"

I gave quite a start and glared up at this unwelcome intrusion. Jemma moaned at the interruption and half swooning, reached to pull me back.

Nothing unexpected for him, but that's not what made him stop cold to stare.

There was *blood* oozing from her throat. Unmistakable. Alarming.

Blood also stained my lips. Perturbing. Repellent.

And my eyes . . . by now they would be wholly suffused with blood, crimson orbs showing no trace of white, the pupils lost in the wash of what I'd just fed upon.

All highly visible to Oliver standing not two paces from us. A fearful sight to anyone, however forewarned they might be for it. My good cousin, alas, was not.

Oliver was as one petrified, frozen in mid-word and mid-movement. Only his eyes shifted, from me to Jemma and back again, his face gradually going from shock to gaping horror as he understood exactly what he was seeing.

I was frozen as well, not knowing what to do or say, and so we remained for an unguessable time, until Jemma moaned another gentle complaint.

"Why'd y' stop, luv?" she said groggily, trying to sit up.

Instinct told me that it would best to keep her ignorant of what was to come. Tearing my eyes from Oliver, I focused entirely on hers. "Hush, Jemma, hush. Go to sleep, there's a good girl." As my emotions rose in pitch, so did the strength of my influence. She promptly lay back in instantaneous slumber.

Oliver, still openmouthed, gave out with a frightened little gasp at this. "God's mercy man, wh-what are you doing to her?"

I didn't quite look at him. "She's all right, I promise you. Now come in here and close the door. Please."

He hesitated, then surprised me and did as requested.

Like it or not, the time of explanations was upon us, but for the life of me I just didn't know where to begin. Not after this infelicitous start.

Slowly he came closer. I continued to avoid his eyes. He leaned over and extended one hand toward Jemma, probing the skin close to the small wounds I'd made, studying them.

"She's all right," I repeated, a little desperately. I tasted her blood on my lips again and, turning from him, quickly wiped it away on my handkerchief. He came 'round to face me. With no small caution, he reached down and touched my chin, lifting it.

"I need to see," he said, in a strange, dark voice.

And so I looked up, and if he was afraid of what he'd find, then I was also for how he might react to it.

He pulled back, fingers to his mouth, breath rushing in and out twice as either a sob or a laugh before he got hold of himself.

"Please, Oliver, I'm not—"

What, I thought, a *Blutsäuger?* What could I tell him? What could I possibly say to ease his fear? There was a way around this awkwardness, of course. I could readily force him to acceptance. Nora had done the same for me at first. But what was right for her was not right for me, especially in this case. To even try would be enormously unfair to Oliver. Dishonorable. Cruel.

"You're like *her*," he whispered, breaking the impossible silence.

I resisted the urge to glance at Jemma. No, he was speaking not of her but—

"*She would do that . . . to me. Nora would . . .*"

Yes, he had been one of her courtiers, but she'd said he'd not been comfortable about it and she'd let him go, making sure to influence him into forgetting certain things. The influence had held firm. Until now.

His hand went to his throat, and he made a terrible mewling sound as he stumbled backward. He got as far as a chair and fell into it and stayed there. He was shivering again, not from fear of me, but from the onrush of restored memory.

"Oh, my God, my God," he groaned over and over, holding his head, giving a voice to his misery.

I swallowed my own anxieties. How unimportant they seemed. Standing, I buttoned my waistcoat, donned my coat, and put myself in order. This done, I went to Jemma and saw to her wounds. The flow from them had ceased, but the drying blood was a nuisance. Slopping some brandy on my handkerchief, I dabbed away until she was clean, then gently woke her.

"You're a lovely darling," I told her, pressing some coins into her hand. "But I need to speak with my cousin, so if you don't mind . . ."

She had no chance for argument as I smoothly bundled her and her trailing clothes out the door, shutting it. I trusted that the money would be more than sufficient compensation for my rudeness.

Oliver watched us, saying nothing. I pulled a chair from the other side of the table and sat across from him.

"Y-you've done that before," he murmured, making a vague gesture to mean Jemma.

"Not quite in the same way, but yes."

"But you . . . take from them."

"I drink their blood," I said, deciding to be as plain as possible. "Just as Nora once drank from you. And me."

He shuddered, then mastered himself. "I remember what she did to me."

"And she stopped. She knew you did not enjoy it."

"But you did?"

"I was—I am—in love with her. It makes a difference."

"So this is just some form of pleasure you've taken to like—like old Dexter and his need for birch rods?"

"No, it's not like that."

"Then what is it?" He waited for me to go on. When the pause became too lengthy, he asked, "Does it have to do with why your eyes are like that?"

At this reminder I briefly averted them. "It's everything to do with . . . this is damned difficult for me, Oliver. I'm afraid of—of losing your friendship because of what's happened to me."

He shook his head, puffing out some air in a kind of bitter laugh. "One may lose friends, but never relatives. We both know that all too well. Rely on it, if nothing else."

He'd surprised me again, God bless him. I softly matched his laugh, but with relief, not bitterness inspiring it. "Thank you."

"Right." He sat up, squaring his shoulders. "Now, *talk* to me."

And so I did. For a very long, long time.

CHAPTER
—8—

London, December 1777

"What's happened today, Jericho? Any new staff taken on?"
I asked.

"No, sir. Miss Elizabeth was too busy receiving visitors
and had no time for interviewing anyone."

"What visitors, then?"

"Miss Charlotte Bolyn called. She wanted to confirm
again for herself that you, Miss Elizabeth, and Dr. Oliver
were going to attend the Masque tonight, then she flew off
elsewhere, but was rapidly succeeded by a horde of other
young ladies and their mothers."

"Oh, dear."

"A number of them were most disappointed that you were
not available."

"Which? The young ladies or their mothers?"

"Both, sir."

"Oh, dear, oh, dear."

"Indeed, sir. Some of them had a rather . . . predatory air
about them."

"And I was hoping to be spared. Damnation, you'd think
they'd realize that not every bachelor is looking for a wife.
Can't think where they get the idea. I shall have to acquire
a horrible reputation to put them off my scent. Perhaps I

can tell the truth about my drinking habits. *That* would send them away screaming."

"I have serious doubts that such a ploy would be particularly effective as a means of avoiding matrimony, sir."

"You're right. There are some perfect rotters out there drinking far worse stuff than blood who've . . . well, I'll think of something. What else for the day? Anything?"

"Several boxes addressed to Dr. Oliver arrived in the early afternoon from Fonteyn House."

"Sounds ominous. Any idea what's in 'em?"

"None, sir. Everything was taken to his consulting room. He shut himself in with the items some time ago and has not yet emerged."

"Most mysterious. Are we done here?"

He gave me a critical look to determine whether or not I was presentable. Since no glass would ever throw back my image, I'd come to rely solely upon Jericho's fine judgment in the matter of my personal toilet. He had excellent taste, though often tending to be too much the perfectionist for my patience.

"You will do, sir," he said grudgingly. "But you really want some new shirts."

"I've already ordered some from the fellow who's done my costume for the Masque."

"Oh, sir, do you really think—"

"Not to worry, it's Oliver's tailor, a most careful and experienced man."

That mollified him. Oliver's own taste was sometimes eccentric, but he was always sensible when it came to shirts.

Released from the evening's ritual, I unhurriedly went downstairs to join the others, giving a polite nod to the new housemaid as she ducked out of my way. Her eyes were somewhat crossed, but she seemed energetic enough for the work, sober, was a devoted churchgoer, and had already had the pox. Elizabeth had only engaged her yesterday morning; that same night I'd conducted my own interview with the girl, influencing her into not being at all curious about my sleeping or eating habits. Or lack thereof. For the last week it seemed that each time I woke up there was a new servant on the premises requiring my attention. Thus far, not one of them had taken the least notice of my differences, not within Jericho's hearing, anyway. It was his job to look for any chinks in my work and give warning when reinforcement seemed required.

But for now, all was safe. My traveling trunk with its bags of earth was secreted in a remote section of Oliver's cellar, allowing me to rest undisturbed through the day. At sunset it was easy enough to make my invisible way up through the floors of the house to re-form in my bedroom and there submit to Jericho's ministrations. It wasn't quite the same as it had been back home, but the inconvenience of curling myself into the trunk each night rather than stretching out on a cot was negligible. Such totality of rest did have its advantages.

As for my excellent good cousin, well, our talk at The Red Swan had been mutually harrowing, but the experience created a more solid bond between us—something I'd badly needed and was humbly grateful to have—and all without having to impose my influence upon him. Though without doubt it was the most difficult conversation I'd been through since my first night out of the grave when I'd encountered Elizabeth. The topic was essentially the same: an explanation of myself, of the changes I'd gone through, and the desperate, unspoken plea for acceptance of the impossible.

But Oliver, my friend as well as my relative, had a large enough heart to hear that which was not said and then provide it.

Not that any of what he heard was particularly easy for *him*. It took a goodly time to persuade him that I really was not like old Dexter, one of the Cambridge administrators whose nature with women was such that he could not achieve satisfaction unless his partner birched his backside raw. We students found out about it from one of the town whores, who was not as discreet as Molly Audy when it came to gossiping about her clients. Most of us thought him a strange fellow though still very likable.

But once I'd convinced Oliver that my need to drink blood was a physical necessity equivalent in importance to his eating every day, things went a bit more smoothly.

His medical training (and curiosity) won out over his initial fear and astonishment, and he fairly hammered me with questions. Unfortunately, I could not answer them all, those being the very ones I had in store for Nora.

He had much to speak of himself, mostly of his own feelings toward her, which might best be defined as ambivalent. Certainly he'd found her to be beautiful, even bewitching, the same as many of the other men in our circle, but he'd been highly disturbed by her habits, then and now.

"She was using us—every one of us—to feed on like a wolf upon sheep," he'd said with something close to anger.

"One may look at it like that, but on the other hand, she willingly gave of herself to pleasure others."

"But that makes her a—" He cut off, realizing that I might take exception to his conclusion.

"I know what it makes her, and I'll not deny the similarities between herself and the two ladies we've enjoyed tonight. But God's death, man, I shan't begrudge her the right to make a living in whatever way that she's able. Look at the limitations our condition imposes. She can no more open a dress shop and make a profit than I can go to court to practice the law. Both require that we be up and about during the day, y'know."

He thought it over and saw the sense of it. "But I still feel . . . well, violated in some way. First by her use of me, then again by making me forget it. I'm not sure that I'd care ever to see her again after all that."

"Of course I'll not force you, but I've an idea that if I made mention of it to her, she would doubtless wish to offer an apology."

"And then there's poor Tony Warburton to think about. I can still hardly imagine him doing such a horrible thing except that that's the same time you began acting all peculiar. For three years you had this grand passion for the lady, and then you behaved as if she were no more important than any of the other women we've known."

"Only because she made me think so. She made me forget everything that was truly important between us."

"And you can do the same sort of . . . ? If you don't mind my saying so, I find that to be rather frightening."

"As do I, be assured."

"But you have . . . influenced me?"

"Yes," I admitted. "And I do humbly apologize and promise never to do so again. That's what this talk is all about, so I may be honest with you from now on."

"I can appreciate that, Coz. Apology accepted, though damn it, I've no memory of what *you've* done, either. Insidious stuff, ain't it? And Nora's used it on God knows how many of us." He gave a brief shudder.

"You must understand that she has to be secretive when it comes to certain things. As do I, now. You've only to recall your own reaction when you walked in awhile ago to see why."

"Yes, that quite woke me up. Are you sure Jemma is unharmed?"

"Quite sure. In truth, I went to some effort to see that she enjoyed herself."

"Hmph. If I'd troubled to do the same for Frances, I suppose I'd have come in much later and then we'd have not even had this talk."

"Perhaps so, but only in part. I have always intended to tell you all this, but . . . well . . ."

"Yes," he said, hooking one corner of his mouth up in a smile full tainted with irony. "Well."

And so the nights passed between that one and the present, with Oliver becoming more and more accustomed to my change—now that he'd been made aware of it. Certainly, things were much improved for my own peace of mind, for I'd taken no enjoyment whatever from the previous necessity of having to influence him. It's one thing to be compelled to use it on a paid servant, but quite another to inflict it upon so good and close a friend as he.

Never again, I promised us both.

"Oh, there you are," said Elizabeth, emerging from the kitchen to meet me as I reached the lower landing. "Thought you'd never be coming down."

"Jericho was playing the taskmaster tonight. Wanted to make sure I was properly groomed for the party."

"Did he tell you about Oliver's mysterious treasure?"

"Yes, all the boxes. Where is he? Still in his consulting room?"

She nodded. "He came home an hour ago, went in, and hasn't been out since. I decided to wait until you were up before checking on him. Wonder what they could be?"

"Probably stuffed and mounted specimens from Bedlam, knowing the bent of his studies," I said, strolling in the correct direction.

"Ugh. That's disgusting."

"I've seen worse. If you ask him, he'll arrange to take you on a tour, y'know."

"I think not."

We paused before the consulting room door, and Elizabeth knocked, calling Oliver's name. There was no immediate reply, so she repeated herself.

"Did you hear anything?" she asked, her brow puckering.

"Barely." The noise had been so low as to be impossible for even me to understand what was said, though it sounded vaguely like an invitation. I pushed the door open and peered in, making room for Elizabeth.

"Good heavens," she said, staring in astonishment at a perfect glut of disorder littering the floor. Books, papers, clothing, and toys were spread into every corner, leaving no doubt as to what had once been in the boxes, which were now gaping and empty. Cross-legged, Oliver sat in the middle of it all, a carved wooden horse in one hand, a chapbook in the other. He looked up at us, his eyes rather bleary and lost.

"Hallo, all. Pardon the mess," he said in a faint, tired voice.

"What is all this?" Elizabeth lifted her skirts and picked her way into the room.

"Mo—" He swallowed with difficulty. "Mother sent it. Her way of saying good-bye, I think."

"These are your things?"

"Every one of them. All of it. Clothes I outgrew that weren't passed on to others, letters, even some of the prizes I won at school. Here it is. My whole life. She's sent the lot of it away for good." He spoke unevenly and his eyes were red. He'd been crying, I was sure.

"Dear God," I said. The cruelty of it went right to my heart. "How could she do such a thing?"

"Actually, this was my old nurse's doing. She's working for Cousin Clarinda now, but Mother sent for her and told her to pack everything of mine up, then either burn it or give it away. Nanny couldn't bear to do either, so she sent it over to me with a note of explanation. I suppose I should be glad not to have lost it all. I hadn't even thought of the stuff for ages—I might not have even missed it—but to have it all back again in this way . . . something of a shock, that."

"Oh, poor Oliver," said Elizabeth. She gamely—and carefully—made the hazardous trek across the floor and knelt down next to him, putting an arm around his shoulder. Elizabeth knew all about the speculations Oliver and I had made to each other at The Red Swan by now and so had an understanding of the depth of the pain he was going through.

"Yes, poor me. She's a wretched mother, but the only one I've got. It's—it's so damnable to think she hates me this much."

"She hates herself, that's why she acts as she does. Like a wounded animal lashing out."

"And wounding others in turn. Well, this is it, I should think. She's got nothing else to fling at me after this, not unless she changes her mind about the inheritance money. I wouldn't put it past her."

"But you went by the solicitors, didn't you?" she asked.

"All they would tell me was that she'd not sent for them. She could, though, at any time."

"It's very difficult to alter a will," I said. "Especially one that's been in effect for so long without contest. It's also rather public, and we know she'd be extremely reluctant to carry things that far. Too much like a scandal, y'know. Besides, I can always go back, if necessary, and—"

Elizabeth shot me a warning look.

"And—well, she just won't do anything. We'll get our money every quarter, as usual. We've no need to worry."

"I suppose not." He sighed. "You know, if it hadn't been for the note Nanny put in, I'd have thought Mother had sent it today on purpose just to spoil the party for me."

"I hope she hasn't. Has she?"

"I don't think so, but I am terribly unsettled."

"What you need is your tea." Elizabeth stood and put her hand out to help him up. He accomplished this with considerable groaning, for his legs had gone to sleep. With her to lean on, he limped out of the room's chaos and into the hall.

"I'll have the new maid sort things out for you," she said, holding his arm as she led him into the parlor. "That is, if you don't mind?"

"Not a bit of it. Odd thing is, that it was rather fun seeing my old stuff again. That little wood horse was my favorite toy once upon a time. I played and played with it until the paint was worn off, but by then I was learning to ride real ones, so it was all right."

Elizabeth rang the bell for tea and encouraged him to talk about himself. Being as vulnerable as any to another's interest in the subject, he readily complied, not knowing that it was her way of cheering him. By the time they'd finished their light meal, talk had turned to the upcoming party.

"I shall have to begin dressing soon if we are to be fashionably late," she said, with a glance at the mantel clock.

"I must say that I'm looking forward to helping escort a pirate queen once again," I put in. "You're in for a treat, Oliver. She was quite the spitfire when she was 'Scarlet Bess, Scourge of the Island.' "

"I think the whole gathering at the Bolyn house is in for a treat," he said. "Think we'll frighten anyone as her 'Cutthroat Captains of the Coast'?"

"We shall certainly try."

The problem of what to costume ourselves in had been much debated until Elizabeth suggested a re-creation of our favorite childhood game. Oliver had enthusiastically fallen in with it, asserting that the three of us together would make a wonderful and memorable entrance to the Masque. Elizabeth, having since become fast friends with our future hostess, promptly took herself off to Charlotte Bolyn's highly recommended dressmaker, while Oliver and I sought help from his tailor. Colors had been agreed upon, fabrics and laces chosen, and a hasty construction was begun. I'd asked

Jericho if he wanted to join us, reenacting his role as the "Ebon Shark of Tortuga," but he'd begged to be excused from the honor. No doubt his much valued dignity would have suffered in some way.

"Are you sure you don't wish to come?" I asked him one last time as he helped me to dress. "Other people are bringing their servants. We could yet improvise something for you. I heard that Lady Musgrave was going as an Arab princess and was bringing her maid as her—uh—maid, done up in gold ropes, feathers, and a long silk scarf."

"Thank you, no, sir. I should prefer a quiet evening to organize the new staff. There are also the scattered contents of Mr. Oliver's consulting room to put in order. The new girl is in something of a state about the task and will need help sorting everything. No, sir, I am really quite sure. Now hold still that I may apply your eye patch . . ."

Obediently I held still.

"Now the mask . . ." He tied it firmly in place, concealing me from forehead to nose.

"How do I look?" I asked anxiously.

"Most formidable, sir."

"Trouble is I can't see a damned thing. This patch throws off the eyeholes on the mask."

"Do you wish the patch removed or the mask?"

"The patch. I've been anticipating this gathering too much to end up missing half of it by keeping one eye shut."

He worked for a moment to adjust things. Sans patch, with the mask properly in place, I was able to see excellently and said so. A pity I could not provide myself with the satisfaction of admiring the final results in the mirror, for it seemed a very superior costume. Though the tailor's idea of pirate clothing was probably lacking in accuracy, I did feel that I cut a fine figure in my bloodred coat, gold satin cloak, and sinister black velvet mask. Once the wide baldric had been secured over one shoulder and my cutlass sheathed, Jericho finished it off by presenting me with a hat matching the coat's color, lavishly trimmed with gold lace.

"Have a very good time, Mr. Jonathan. You won't forget to keep track of the hour?"

The Bolyn's Masque would likely not conclude itself until well into the next morning. "I shall be home before dawn, I do promise you. If nothing else, Elizabeth will see to it."

Assured, he finally gave me leave to go.

Oliver's estimation of our reception had been conservative. The three of us sweeping into the entry caused a happy stirring in the crowd that had already arrived, and we were even honored with applause. Though we were indeed resplendent in our black, red, and gold colors, Elizabeth was the best of the lot. She'd found some crimson powder from an unknown source and had used it for dressing her hair, making a fiery difference between herself and the other ladies who were present. Woven into her coiffure were a number of red and black ribbons long enough to trail down to her shoulders. Her gown—and I was thinking as her protective brother in this—was short enough to reveal her legs to a shocking extent, had they not been modestly encased in high boots. The rest of her costume was a wonder in gold lace and rustling red satin. Even her mask was trimmed with lace, the gold showing off well against the black velvet.

Oliver's costume was identical to mine, but the colors were reversed, giving him a gold coat and a red cloak, and he looked very fine in them. A few people recognized him, though; his long chin, left visible below the half-mask, was unmistakable. With his identity discovered, our own was also given away, but only to those who had already met us and could guess that we would be with our cousin.

Charlotte Bolyn immediately came over to give welcome and proclaim her pleasure at the success of our apparel. She was very fetching herself as the Queen of Hearts, and dragged her brother Brinsley over, who was dressed as the Knave of Spades. Someone in the crowd called out that all the reds and blacks together were too much for his bewildered eyes, and Brinsley waved his sword at him in mock threat.

"He may have an idea in that," said Oliver. "Think we should break things up a bit?"

"Refreshments are over there," Brinsley laconically informed him, pointing to a large, well-supplied table.

"Heavens, man, are you a playing card or a reader of minds?"

Oliver excused himself, Brinsley asked Elizabeth if she would honor him with the next dance, and Charlotte had to see to the next group of guests coming in. This suited me, for I was well occupied with study of the mob, trying to guess who this one or that one was under the rainbow of disguises. I wandered from room to room and out into the garden, my eye running over each and every woman of a certain specific height and figure.

I was looking for Nora, of course.

My hope was that she might, just might be here at this, the party of the season. She had been most fond of the Bolyns, never failing to come to any of their gatherings. Brinsley had once been one of her courtiers. I had already asked the Bolyns, particularly Brinsley, if they had any idea of Nora's whereabouts, but got only the speculation that she'd gone to Italy, or so their friends the Warburtons had told them.

Several times during my search my dormant heart gave a sharp upward leap as I spied a woman who matched my memory of Nora. But each closer investigation proved me to be mistaken. As the evening passed, I became frustrated and morose with the constant failure. The worst part was going through the garden when I braved the twistings of its shrubbery maze, for it was here that we'd shared our first kisses. It was here that I had once and for all time fallen in love. Now this magical place with its paper lanterns shedding their fairy lights over other couples seemed a bleak and blasted vanity to my disappointed soul.

I doggedly found the center of the thing, which was a large courtyard decorated by marble statues set 'round a large marble fountain. Its water had been drained from the supply pipes, lest the winter weather freeze and crack them. Without the splashing from the fountain, this was now a strangely desolate spot. No one was here at the moment, probably because of the wind. Outside the shelter of the maze's living walls, it was very bad, a feature that would certainly drive any sightseers to more temperate areas. The cold air was tolerable, but not when combined with so fresh a breeze. The ends of my light satin cloak snapped like flags, and a gust threatened to send my hat flying. I gladly quit the place and hurried back to the house.

The noise, costumes, and lights dazzled me, but there was really no quiet retreat to hide in. Not that I wanted to conceal myself, but I did long for a few moments of solitude. None were to be had, though. A group of the younger men, friends from my previous visit, recognized and hailed me. It proved to be something of a blessing since they took my mind off my inner sorrows for a time.

As ever, the talk was on politics, and I was closely questioned about the war. There was dismay amongst them about General Burgoyne's unfortunate surrender at Saratoga. The first dispatches of the disaster had arrived that week, and though the news was supposed to remain secret, it had escaped, causing no end of speculation on how England might recover her honor from such a setback.

"Mind you, the Frenchies will start pouring themselves across the sea after this," said a short Harlequin. "Once they're in we'll be set for a real war right here and now. We won't have to go to America to fight, just hop across the Channel."

"They wouldn't dare," opined another, taller Harlequin.

"They would, sir. We gave them a thrashing the last time about Canada and they want revenge. You mark me."

This reminded me of all the things Father had said on my last night at home. It had been only a couple of weeks since I'd seen him—at least how I reckoned the time in light of my singular hibernation—but I missed him terribly just then and had to leave or make a fool of myself.

"But you're a fool already, Johnny Boy," I muttered. To be at so fabulous a celebration and in such a dark mood was ridiculous. I was here for distraction from my woes, to sample and enjoy the myriad delights whirling and laughing about me, not to impersonate a waker at a funeral.

As if to help draw me out of the depths, some sprightly music started up nearby, drowning out the nearby conversations. I followed the sounds to the great ballroom, where all the dancers had gathered to indulge themselves in festive exercise. The combinations of partners were astonishing and amusing as I spied a lion dancing with Columbine and a Roman soldier bowing over the hand of an Indian maiden. One lady's costume, what there was of it, caught my eye for some goodly time, for the short skirt was so transparent one could see the supporting panniers, not to mention her very shapely legs and the flash of the silver garters holding up her stockings. Her silver mask covered too much of her face for me to readily identify her, but she was not Nora and that was all that really mattered in the end.

The only thing to distract me from her was a fellow in deep black stalking past holding a skull. His Hamlet might have been more striking had he not been drunk and trying to get the skull to share a sip from his glass. Still, he seemed to be having a fine time providing entertainment for others. He also reminded me that I had not yet bought any plays to send to Cousin Ann as I'd promised. Tomorrow I'd see about making an expedition to Paternoster Row and explore its book stalls. Surely *some* of them would still be open after dark.

Familiar laughter, slightly breathless, came to me over the music, and I saw Elizabeth dancing past, partnered by a big fellow in a Russian coat and tall fur hat. He grinned back at her from behind a vast false beard. For all that covering, he seemed familiar. Probably one of my old schoolmates. If so, then I'd better stay handy to make sure he behaved himself with her.

"Enjoying yourself, Coz?" asked Oliver, who suddenly bumped into me from pushing his way through the press at the edge of the dancing.

"I am. I can see that you are, too."

He had a wineglass in hand. Not his first, to judge by his flushed face and wandering eyes. "Indeed, indeed. Having a marvelous good time in spite of the old hag."

"What do you mean?"

He jerked his head back the way he'd come. "Mother's here, don't you know. Saw her in one of the rooms with some of her cronies, the lot of 'em passing sentence against every pretty girl who happened to walk through. She's not in costume, just has a mask on a stick to hide behind, like the others. Ask me and I tell you I think they need 'em. Nothing like a bit of papier-mâché and paint to improve their sour old faces, the harpies. Hic! 'Scuse me, I'm sure."

"It doesn't seem to have soured you, though."

"Not a bit of it. I'm too drunk to care. In fact, I made a point to stagger right through the room so she could see that her cast-off son is alive, well, and having a devil of a good time."

"You think that was wise?"

" 'Course not, but then I'm too drunk for wisdom. Besides, all her friends saw me, too. Probably embarrassed her to no end, especially when I gave such a loud hail to Cousins Clarinda and Edmond."

"My God, they're here, too?"

"I just said so, din' I? Amazing, ain't it, that Clarinda got Edmond-the-stick out of the house for this. He was even in costume, a Harlequin, no less. Should say more, rather. There must be a dozen of 'em drifting around here tonight. Just shows he hasn't much imagination. Cheap, too. Looked as if it'd been made for someone else and he inherited it. Clarinda is very jaunty, though. Came as a Gypsy. You should see her. Very lively!"

No doubt, I thought, looking around but noticing no Gypsies, lively or otherwise, and feeling absurdly thankful about it. Though my one encounter with her was enchanting, I had no desire to try for a second, particularly in a strange house with her husband lurking about. He'd seemed the jealous type, or so I'd convinced myself from the single look I'd had of him across the dim hallway of Fonteyn House.

The dance ended and the couples bowed to one another. A different fellow came up to claim Elizabeth's attention, smaller than the Russian, but not lacking in verve.

"Hallo," I said, giving Oliver a nudge. "Is that Lord Harvey trying to partner Elizabeth for the next one?"

He gave a wobbly stare, "I think so. No one else has such spindles for legs that I know of."

"Did he ever take care of his creditors?"

"No, had to fly the country to avoid 'em. Heard he got into a card game in France, won a fortune, and returned in triumph to pay off everything. Still, I understand he's not given up looking for a rich wife. Bad luck for Elizabeth if he—no . . . she's too smart for him, and after that bad business she's been through, she won't be much impressed by a title."

"Maybe I should go out and interrupt him before—"

"Too late, the music's already started. Don't worry, old lad, it's just one dance. She can take care of herself."

On that I could only tentatively agree; but once they're stirred up, it's hard to put one's protective instincts aside.

The dancers fell into the patterns required of them and the stragglers cleared themselves from the floor. The Russian, who was heading in another direction, changed course when he spotted Oliver and apparently recognized him. He sauntered over to us.

"Is that you, Marling? Thought so. Grand party, what?"

"Very grand. Ridley, isn't it? Can't mistake you, two yards tall and then some, you great giant. You need to meet my cousin from America, Jonathan Barrett. Jonathan, this is Thomas Ridley."

We bowed to each other. Ridley, red from the dance and sweating, untied his beard and stuffed it into a pocket.

"He was a couple of years ahead of us at Cambridge, weren't you?"

"At Oxford, Marling," he said in a near patronizing drawl.

"Yes, of course. Haven't seen you in ages. Back from the Tour?" Oliver asked, referring to the popular fashion the gentry followed of exploring the Continent.

"Something like that. London gets too small for me, y'see." He grandly stretched his arms wide as if to illustrate.

That was when the now nagging familiarity I felt about him changed instantly to utter certainty. Ridley was the leader of the Mohocks that I'd bedeviled on my first night in London.

Good God.

"And how is America, these days?" he asked me, again with that almost, but not quite, patronizing tone. It was finely balanced, just enough so that he was unpleasant, but not to the point where anyone could take exception to it.

"Fine, very fine," I answered, not really thinking.

"Fine? You're not one of those damned rebels, are you?"

"Absolutely not!" cried Oliver. "My God, but Jonathan's done his share of the fighting for our king. How many have you killed, Coz? Half a dozen?"

"You exaggerate, Oliver." I had no wish to dwell on that part of my past.

"Blazed away at a roomful of 'em, at least, only this summer."

"How interesting," said Ridley, giving me a narrow stare.

Damnation. Had he recognized me as the victim he and his gang had tried to sweat? Hard to tell if it was that or his reaction to Oliver's tipsy boasting.

"Not very," I countered. "Just defending my family. Any man would do the same. Are you enjoying the Masque? That coat must be very warm." God, but I was babbling, too. Really, now, there was nothing to fear. It was unlikely that he'd remember me; it had been dark and he very drunk. Besides, half my face was obscured by my mask. The music and the great press of people were simply making me nervous.

"Rather," he said, a lazy amusement creeping over his heavy features. Neither handsome nor ugly, but possessing distinct enough looks to make him stand out, he seemed to know how to use them to his best advantage. But moments ago he'd almost seemed dashing as he squired Elizabeth 'round the dance floor. Now he was decidedly base as he spoke more loudly than necessary to be heard over the music and other speakers. "There's plenty of other things here to make a man warm, though."

"Yes, all the dancing. I may try a turn or two myself, later."

"It'd be well worth the trying, I can guarantee you, Barrett. The ladies here tonight are of superior stock. Very lively."

"I have noticed."

"Now," he said, pointing out at the couples on the floor. "See that pirate wench with the red hair? There's a pretty slut who knows what's best for a man. It's the way she walks and moves is how you can tell. I'll give you seven to five that I'll be pounding her backside into the floor within the hour. What do you say?" He grinned down at me.

Oliver, for all the wine he'd taken, was just quick enough
to get between us. I heard him shouting my name, trying to
get through the blast of white-hot rage roaring between my
ears. I fought to push him to one side to strike at Ridley,
but our violent activity seized the instant attention of some
of the other men present who had overheard, and they all
leaped in to hold me back.

"Have a care, sir!"

"Calm yourself, sir!"

"For God's sake, Jonathan, don't!"

Through it all, Ridley stood with his hands on his hips,
grinning. I wanted to smash his face to a pulp and knew
perfectly well that I could do it with ease if only these fools
would just let go my arms.

"You heard the bastard!" I shouted. "You heard him!"

"Aye, we did, an' there're ways for gentlemen to settle
such things," said an older man with an Irish accent.

"Let them be settled, then. I'm issuing challenge here
and now."

"First cool yourself, young sir."

I stopped fighting them, falling back on my heels, but
still searing inside and ready to tear Ridley in two at his
next word. But he said nothing and just walked away with
that ass's grin fixed in place.

"That was a rare harsh insult to you, sir," said the older
man with dark sympathy.

"To my sister, sir," I corrected. "And thus making it a
greater offense."

"Then you're familiar with the Clonmel Summer As-
sizes?"

"I am." Oliver had acquired a copy of the Irish Code
Duello that autumn, and I'd studied it with interest, hardly
dreaming I'd find so quick a use for its rules.

"Are you cooled enough to properly deal with it?"

I could not take my eyes from Ridley's retreating back.

"Jonathan?" Oliver, looking sober, yet held my arm.

"Yes," I snarled. "You heard him? You all heard?"

Some three or four of them said they had. All looked
grim.

"I need a second," I heard myself saying. "Oliver, would you—?"

"Need you ask? Of course I will."

"Hold now," said the Irishman. " 'Tis contrary to the rules to deliver a challenge at night. No need for being a hothead. It can wait till the morrow."

"I must beg your pardon, sir, and disagree. If anything I shall be even more angry tomorrow. His insult was too great. We will settle things tonight."

And with those words, a change went over the men around us, a kind of drawing together, as though they'd erected an invisible wall between us and the rest of the crowd. Those outside the wall seemed to sense it. Other men nodded; women whispered behind their fans to each other. Something Had Happened. And even better, Something Was About To Happen. I felt their eyes burning through me as our group left the ballroom.

The older man, whose name was Dennehy, took charge of things, having appointed himself to the position of seeing that all was done according to the strict rules of the Code. He'd heard everything that Ridley had said and been shocked by it, but was no less determined to stick to the rules of gentlemanly behavior, though Ridley had already proved himself to be no gentleman.

I was swept along by the others to a more secluded room. Brinsley Bolyn was sent for, rather than his father, for it was thought the elder Bolyn might have tried to postpone things. Once arrived, he was told what had happened and asked if there was a place nearby where a meeting might be arranged. This put him rather in the middle, being host to both myself and Ridley, but he promptly named an orchard just west of the house as a likely site. He promised to have lanterns brought to shed adequate light for the proceedings and said we could choose whatever was needed from his own collection of arms.

With those important points covered, Oliver was dispatched to speak with Ridley's second. He was back quickly enough. Ridley had decided on the smallsword as his weapon, which was not surprising considering the use he'd tried to make of it at our first meeting. In premeditated encounters like this, pistols were usually more favored than blades, since they tended to level any physical inequalities between opponents, but it made no difference to me. I knew how to use either one.

Though at the center of all their attention, I was also strangely apart from them. Even Oliver, who trudged close by my side on our way to the orchard, was silent, as if afraid to speak with me, yet wanting to very badly. A quarter hour from now, for all he knew, I might be dead.

For all I knew as well.

I'd survived pistol bullets, musket balls, and even a cudgeling hard enough to kill an ordinary man; perhaps because of my change I would survive the sword, but I did not know, nor did it matter one way or another to me. Words had been said, ephemeral words, yet they could not be forgiven or forgotten. That foul-mouthed bastard had grossly insulted my sister, and I was going to kill him for it or die in the trying.

"Oliver, you'll be sure to tell Elizabeth all that happens, should things . . . not go well? She'll not appreciate it if you try to spare her feelings."

"You've the right on your side. Everything will be fine," he said, trying to sound hearty for my sake.

I let him hold on to that. He needed it.

We arrived at the orchard. Apple trees they were, and under Brinsley's direction servants began hanging paper lanterns from the bare limbs. The wind was a nuisance; some of the lanterns went out and could not be relit. Ridley and I were questioned on whether we wanted to proceed under such conditions. We each said yes.

Ridley shed his gaudy coat and fur hat, handing them to someone, then stretched himself this way and that to loosen his muscles. He had a very long reach and obvious strength. Perhaps he thought that might give him the advantage over me, yet another reason for blades over pistols.

Following his example, I did a few stretches after getting rid of my now ludicrous pirate disguise. Stripping away the mask, I took care to study his reaction, but he gave none that could be construed as recognition . . . not right away, that is.

He was inspecting the sets of blades that Brinsley had brought, plucked one up, and swung it around to get the feel of it. Then he briefly leveled it in my direction, looking down its length. Satisfied, he handed it back, but continued favoring me with that same annoying smile.

" 'Fore God, I'll need some beer in me soon for the thirst that's coming. Have you any with you, Barrett?"

No one else understood what he was talking about, only I. Mr. Dennehy told Ridley's second to ask him to refrain from speaking to me unless he was ready to offer apology for his insult.

Ridley laughed, but did not pursue the issue. His point had been made.

"What's behind that?" asked Oliver, leaning close to speak quietly in my ear.

"He's letting me know that we've met before."

"Indeed? When?"

"I'll tell you later, God willing. Let it suffice that his insult to Elizabeth was on purpose in order to provoke me. He knew we all of us were together because of our costumes. He wanted this duel."

"My God."

"I must ask a promise of you should anything adverse happen."

"Whatever I can," he said, too caught up to gainsay my doubts.

"First, to take care of Elizabeth, and second, not to challenge Ridley. If he should better me, the matter ends here, to go no further. Understand?"

He was very white in the lantern light. "But—"

"No further. I won't have your blood shed to disturb my rest."

It ground at him, that was plain, but he finally nodded. "I promise, but for God's sake, be careful. The way he keeps smiling at you like that, he doesn't look right in the head."

"The fool's only trying to unman me."

Then the time was upon us. Swords were presented, the distance marked, and I found myself but a few paces from Ridley preparing to go *en garde*. Again, Ridley was asked if he was prepared to apologize. He said he was not.

"Gentlemen, *en garde . . .*"

Dropping slightly with legs bent in the prescribed manner, I got my blade up and at an angle across my body, its point even with Ridley's head. He mirrored me exactly, but from a higher level because of his height. I found myself noticing small things: how he placed his feet, the pattern of embroidery on his waistcoat, the strange way his sand-colored brows hooked down on the outsides.

"*Allez!*"

I let him make the first pass. As I'd expected, he was relying on his reach and strength. He swatted my blade aside with a powerful slap and lunged, but I backed off in plenty of time, and countered with a feint to the right. He was smart, backing in his turn, and was fast enough to block my true attack to the left. I drove in again on the same side, hoping he'd take it for another feint, but he seemed to know my mind and was ready for it. Damnation, but he was fast. I didn't see his blade so much as his movements.

Some say to watch the other's eyes or his blade or his arm, but the best fencing masters advise their students to watch everything at once. This had seemed an impossibility until my training had advanced to such a degree that I abruptly understood their meaning. To fix upon any single point put you in danger of missing another, more vital one. By focusing only on the blade, I could overlook some telltale shift of an adversary's body as he prepared a fresh attack. Instead, I found myself moving into a strange area of non-thought, where I could see all of my opponent as a single coordinated threat, rather than a haphazard collection of parts, each requiring a separate reaction.

Ridley had apparently followed the same school of training, to judge by his look of serene concentration. I took this in and left it at the door, so to speak. It was important, but only as part of the whole. My mind was empty of thought and emotion; having either cluttering up my actions could be fatal. As great as my anger was toward this man, I could not allow its intrusion, for it would only give him the advantage.

We danced and lunged and parried, playing now, taking each other's measure and comparing it to our own best skills. He was surprisingly fast for so large a man, but I knew myself to be considerably faster. I was also much stronger than he, though this was mitigated by the swords. Had we been grappling in the mud like common street brawlers, I'd have had the better of him without question.

Fencing is like a physical form of chess, requiring similar strategies, but executing them with one's body rather than the board pieces. Ridley knew his business and twice tried a gambit of beating my blade, feinting once, twice, thrice, retreating a step, then simply extending his arm to catch me on my advance. It worked the first time, but all he did was snag and rip my sleeve. No blooding, therefore no pause. The second time I was wise to it, but on the third attempt, he retreated an extra step, leading me to think he'd given up the ploy.

Not so. He grinned, caught my blade, and flicked his wrist 'round in such a way as to disarm me. Even as he began the move, I divined his intent and backed off at the last instant. If I hadn't frozen my hand to the grip, my sword would have gone flying out into the darkness.

He must have fully expected it to work; there was a flash of frustration on his face. He was sweating. It must have felt like a coat of ice on his skin what with the wind. I'd grown warm enough; it would be awhile before any cold could get through to me, and by then we would be long finished.

He had an excellent defense; time and again I'd tried to break past it and failed, but he was starting to breathe hard. My mouth was open, but more for the sake of appearance than any need of air. If nothing else, I could wear him down to the point of exhaustion. As he began to show early signs of it, I played with him more, subtly trying to provoke him into a mistake. Not that I was resorting to anything dishonorable; all I had to do was prevent him from wounding me. For him that was quite sufficient as an annoyance. He was probably very used to winning, and as each moment went by without making progress, his initial frustration looked to be getting the better of him. When that happened, he'd defeat himself.

But in turn, my own great weakness must have been overconfidence. Or underestimation.

The wind tore the plume of his breath right from his lips, and he looked hard-pressed to recover it. The pause between attacks grew perceptively longer; he was slowing down. In another few minutes I'd have him.

I beat him back to tire him that much more. He retreated five or six steps, rapidly, with me following. Then he abruptly halted, beat my blade once, very hard, and as my arm shot wide, he used his long reach and drove in.

Catching me flat.

The first I noticed of it was a damned odd push and tug on my body. I looked down and gaped stupidly. His blade was firmly thrust into my chest, just left of my breast bone. Sickening sight. I also could not move, and so we stood as if frozen for a few seconds, long enough for the shocked groans of the witnesses to reach me. Then he whipped the thing out and stood back, waiting for my fall.

I stumbled drunkenly to both knees. Couldn't help it. The crashing impact of pain was overwhelming. It felt like he'd struck me with a tree trunk, not a slim V-shaped blade of no larger width than my finger. I let go my sword and clutched at my chest, coughed, gagged on what came up, then coughed once more.

Bloodsmell on the winter air.

Taste of blood in my mouth.

My blood.

CHAPTER
~9~

Oliver was suddenly there, his arm supporting me.

"It's all right," he was saying over and over in a terribly thin, choking voice. Lying to himself. He'd seen. He knew that it was most certainly not all right. He called for Brinsley and for more light to be brought. The others crowded close to see.

The agony was stunning; I wanted only for him to let me alone. I gasped, feebly pushing him off. He would not budge. Instead, he tried to hold me down, just as Beldon had done before him when I'd fallen into that soft sleep one stifling summer day, my last day. Not again. Never again.

Panic tore through me. "*No!* Let me up!"

But he was not listening and told me not to move, to let him help. To get at the wound, he pulled at my hand. It came away covered with blood. The stuff was all over my shirt and waistcoat.

"You must hold still, Jonathan," he pleaded. I heard the tears in his words. Tears for me, for my death.

"*No!*" I couldn't say if I was shouting at him or myself. It wasn't even much of a shout. I had little enough air left to spare for it. To breathe in meant more pain. I doubled over— Oliver kept me from falling altogether—and coughed.

More blood in my mouth. I spat, making a dark stain upon

the dead grass, then the grass begin to fade away before my fluttering vision.

Good God, *no*. I couldn't . . . not here . . .

I clung to Oliver, *willing* myself to stay solid in spite of every instinct wanting to release me from the fire tearing at my chest. It would have been so easy to surrender to the sanctuary of a noncorporeal state, to its soothing silence, its sweet healing. So easy . . .

I struggled to right myself, ignoring Oliver's protests.

"We'll take him back to the house," Brinsley was saying. "I'll have them fetch a cart."

"No," I said, raising a hand. The bloodied one. "A moment. Wait."

A pause. God knows what they expected of me. Momentous last words? They'd have a hard time of it, for my mind was quite bereft of anything like that. Still, they hovered close in hope.

The seconds passed in disappointing silence . . . and I became aware that my devastating hurt was not as bad as before.

Movement was easier now. Pain. Ebbing. I was able to suck in a draught of air and not forcibly cough it out again.

All I'd wanted was the time to recover myself.

Recover?

God's death, what was I on about?

Then as swift as Ridley's attack the comprehension came to me that I was not going to die. Too occupied by the present, I'd forgotten the past. Flashing through my mind was the memory of another dreadful night. I saw Nora once more, heard again her gasp of surprise when a similar blade had pierced her heart. I'd watched in helpless despair as she slid to the floor, thinking her dead—and so she was with neither breath or heartbeat to say otherwise.

But she had come back.

Somehow she had survived that mortal injury.

And by that, I knew I would as well.

With the very thought's occurrence, the raw burning in my chest eased considerably. I even heard myself laugh, though it threatened to become a cough. At least I was in no danger of vanishing in front of—

There they stood about me. Dozens of them. All to bear witness that I'd been run through and had bled like a pig at the butcher's.

And there was poor Oliver, tears on his face as he held me.

What in God's name was I to say to them?

If one lies often enough and loud enough, the lie eventually becomes the truth.

But for something like this? It seemed a bit much to expect of them.

On the other hand, there were few other options. I could play the wounded duelist and let them carry me back for a suitably long convalescence, or I could brazen it out right here and hope for the best.

The latter, then, and get it over with.

"Some brandy?" I called, summoning a strong voice from heaven knows where.

Brandy was offered from several different sources, all of them extremely sympathetic. Oliver grabbed at the nearest flask and held it to my lips. So caught up was he in the crisis that he'd forgotten my inability to swallow anything other than blood, but it was of no matter. I'd only asked for brandy for the show of it.

"I can manage, thank you," I told him and reached up to take the flask.

This caused some startled murmuring. Oliver nearly dropped me, but I straightened myself in time. It was difficult not to sneak a look at him, but I had to act as though nothing were seriously amiss. With my clean left hand, I raised the thing to my lips and pretended to drink.

"Much better," I said. "I am most obliged to you, sir."

"Jonathan?" A hundred questions were all over Oliver's strained face, and not one of them could get out.

"I'm fine, Cousin. No need to fear."

"But—you . . . your wound . . ."

"It's nothing. Hurts like blazes. Sweet God, man, I pray I did not worry you over a scratch."

"*A scratch!*" he yelped.

I might have laughed, but for knowing the true depth of what he was going through. "You thought me hurt? But

I'm fine or will be. It just scraped the bone, looks worse than it is. Fair knocked the wind from me, though."

This was said loudly enough for the others to hear and pass it along. Those who had not seen the incident clearly took it as the happy truth, but the ones who had been closer were doubtful. Perhaps even fearful.

I noticed this, apparently, for the first time. "Gentlemen, thank you for your concern, but I am much improved." There, that at least was the absolute truth. Not giving anyone time to think and thus dispute the statement, I slowly stood.

Oliver came up with me, mouth hanging, eyes wide with shock. They dropped to my chest and the stains there, but I could do nothing about that for now. The effect on the witnesses was gratifying. The near ones fell back, the far ones leaned closer, but none of them could say that I was even remotely near death.

"Jonathan, in God's name what—?" came my cousin's fierce whisper.

I lowered my head and matched his tone. "It's to do with my changed state. Trust me on this, I am all right."

His mouth opened and shut several times, and his eyes took on the flat cast of fear. "Dear God, you mean—"

"Just play along and I'll explain later. Please!"

The poor fellow looked as if he'd been the one to take the wound, but he bit his lip and nodded. He understood my urgency, if little else.

That settled for the moment, I gave back the flask, then asked to have my sword.

Dennehy came forward, holding it. "Mr. Barrett, are you sure you—"

"I've business to finish, sir. If Mr. Ridley is up to the task, then so am I."

The man in question was not ten paces from me and, if one could tell anything by his expression, was the most dumbfounded of the lot. He had every right to be since he'd certainly *felt* the blade go in and had had to pull it out again. From the twinges still echoing through me, I got the idea the bastard had turned his wrist at the time, just to increase the damage.

He said nothing at first, his gaze going from me to his sword. The end of it was smeared with red for the length of a handspan. He murmured something to the white-faced dandy who was his second. The young man came over to speak to Dennehy and Oliver. I couldn't help but overhear.

"Mr. Ridley has no wish to take the advantage over a wounded man," he said.

"Does Mr. Ridley offer a full and contrite apology for his insult?" I asked.

He glanced back to his friend. Ridley shook his head.

"Then let things proceed as before. He has no advantage over me."

He hesitantly returned, backing all the way.

"Are you sure?" asked Oliver. He was regaining some of his composure, I was glad to see.

"Exceedingly so." Though I'd been very shaken, my unnatural state was such that I was feeling near-normal again.

Or rather extranormal. It was true that Ridley had no advantage on me, but I had a hellish one over him. Unpleasant as it was, he could stab me as much as he liked, but sooner or later I would shrug it off and return to the fray. Not that I planned to give him the chance. I'd learned my lesson and would be more careful than before.

As had he, it seemed. Our next bout was slower, more measured, more cautious, each seeking to find an opening or to make one. I beat him back twice but did not fall for his favorite stratagem, instead pulling away well before he could strike again with his reach. When he saw that was not going to work, he tried to use his strength and speed, and found himself surprisingly outmatched.

I made a rapid high cut, was blocked, got under it, flicked left, right, left, caught his blade, beat it hard to my right, and lunged. It seemed fast enough to me, to him it must have been bewildering. He barely made his defense in time for the first attack; the last one—and it was the last—took him out of the reckoning. He gave a guttural roar of rage and pain and dropped his sword to clutch at his right arm.

Bloodsmell on the air.

His second rushed forward. Dennehy joined them. Then

Oliver. I dropped back and silently looked on.

"Mr. Ridley is sore wounded, sir," reported his second to mine.

"Well blooded and disabled," added Dennehy.

But not dead, I thought. I stalked forward to see for myself. Ridley wasn't going to fight any more this night or any other in the near future. With luck he'd be laid up for weeks.

I raised my blade and touched it to Ridley's shoulder. "I spare your life," I declared loud enough for all to hear. By ancient custom I could have killed him then and there, but the Code had stated once and for all that that was not strictly necessary. With my supreme advantage over him it hardly seemed fair to hold to such a tradition, and besides, to a man like Ridley, this was much more humiliating.

The dandy scrambled to present me with Ridley's dropped sword, and by rights I was entitled to break it. However, since it belonged to Brinsley, I was reluctant to do so. Instead, I handed both blades to him as he came up. "Thank you for the loan of 'em, sir. Uncommonly kind of you."

He began stammering something, but I had no ear for it, feeling suddenly awash with fatigue. My own blood loss was catching me up. There was no rest for me, though, for I found myself abruptly in the center of a cheering, backslapping mob determined to whisk me away and drink to my very good health.

"Best damned fight I've ever seen!"

"A real fire-eater!"

"By God, no one will believe it, but they'll have to or face my challenge!"

"Gentlemen! If you please!"

This last half-strangled cry was from Oliver, who had fought his way to me and seized my arm. I groaned—in gratitude this time—and leaned on him. With the immediate needs of the duel no more, my legs were going all weak.

"Back to the house, if you don't mind?" I asked him.

"Damned right, sir," he promised, an ominous tone in his voice. He threw my cloak over me, and I pulled it tight to conceal the alarming state of my shirtfront. We made a slow parade, but others ran ahead with the news, and as we neared the house, more came out to greet us and hear the story. Unfortunately, it grew in the telling, and nothing I said could stop it. As it was fantastic to begin with, it hardly seemed worth the trouble to try.

Enlisting Brinsley's aid to speed things along, we were soon in the relative peace of a small chamber. I allowed myself to be stretched upon a comfortable settee and disdained all offers of help as being too much fuss. What I wanted was solitude, but my earnest admirers took it as evidence of modest bravery. They held true to their promise and began toasting my health then and there, creating another problem for me since I could not join in their celebration.

Just as things were starting to become unbearable, Elizabeth appeared, pushing her way through the others to get to me.

"Jonathan, someone just told me that you—" She interrupted herself by giving forth a heartfelt shriek. My cloak had slipped open a little, revealing the alarming bloodstains.

"He's in no danger," Oliver hastened to assure her. "He just needs a bit of quiet. Gentlemen, would you please allow me to attend my patient?"

Easier said than done, what with all the crowd. I asked for them to leave, though it was a sore disappointment to my well-wishers. Brinsley, with his authority as host, stepped forward and persuaded them to be herded outside.

Throughout all this, Elizabeth pounded us both with angry questions.

"A duel? How in God's name did you get into a duel?" she demanded.

"That blasted fellow in the Russian costume insulted you," said Oliver. "If Jonathan hadn't challenged him, I certainly would have, the filthy bounder."

"Insulted—what on earth did he say? Jonathan, are you all right? Oh, why did you *do* such a thing?"

And so on. She said quite a lot in a very short time, torn as she was between rage and relief. I had to tell her over and over that I was fine, while keeping one eye on Oliver . . . who was keeping one eye on me.

Once the door was closed and we were blessedly alone, Oliver pulled a chair up next to me, and I did not relish the sick worry that so obviously troubled him. He reached toward me, saying he needed to see my wound.

I tried to wave him off. "This is not necessary. I'm fine. I just need a little rest."

Blinking and swallowing hard, he looked as if I'd slapped him. "I—I know what I saw, Jonathan. Please don't make light of me."

"What does he mean?" asked Elizabeth. "Just how bad is that scratch?"

"Bad enough," I muttered.

Oliver bowed his head, raised it, then quickly moved, and opened my shirt. He gave a kind of gasping sob, full of fear. Just to the right of my breastbone was a fierce-looking red welt, like a fresh scar, about as large around as my thumb. There was drying blood all around it, but the wound itself was cleanly closed. The rest of the area was tender like a bruise and about as troubling.

"It's not possible," he said, as miserable as any man can be on this side of hell. "Not . . . possible."

Elizabeth leaned close. "My God, Jonathan, what happened? What *really* happened?"

"I was careless. Ridley got through. A palpable hit, it was."

"You—"

"Should have killed me, but didn't. Thought I had been killed . . . then I was better. It hurt, though." My voice sounded rather hollow—little wonder when death comes so close. Even a mocking touch from the Reaper is enough to melt one's bones.

"How can this be?" Oliver pleaded. Fear again. Fear sufficient for all of us to have a share.

No more for me. I was weary of that dismal load. I straightened as though to shake it from my back. "Remember what I told you about Nora?"

Elizabeth knew the full story on that and understood of what I was speaking. It took poor Oliver a little longer. To be fair, he'd been rather drunk when we'd had our talk; he might not have possessed a clear recollection of everything.

Besides, being told something and actually witnessing it are two very different things.

"You were run right through the heart," he insisted. "I saw it. So did the others, then you—"

"Others?" Elizabeth froze me with a look. "How many others?"

"Most of the lot that Brinsley chased out for us."

"And they saw everything?"

"It was very fast and dark. They've already convinced themselves that they didn't see what they thought they saw."

While she sorted that out, I turned back to Oliver.

"There's no need to be upset about this. It's all part of my changed nature, and I can no more explain why it is than you can tell me what causes the flying gout."

"But for you to survive such a—for you to heal so quickly . . ."

"I know. It's one of the things that puzzles me as well. It's why I have to see Nora and talk to her."

"But it's just not *natural*!" he insisted.

The little room went very silent, with none of us moving. Finally I asked, "What do you want me to do about it?"

"I didn't know you could do anything about it."

"I can't."

"Oh." He sat back, a dull red blush creeping up his long face as the point came home. "Um—well, that is."

"Agreed," I said.

"Guess I'm being an ass again," he mumbled.

"No more than myself for forgetting all about what happened to Nora until after the fact. I was so damned angry at Ridley I couldn't think of anything except smashing his face in."

Elizabeth scowled. "Just what *did* he say about me?"

My turn to blush.

"It was that terrible?"

"Let it suffice that I doubt he will ever be invited to one of the Bolyns' gatherings ever again. He's a genuine rotter—and a Mohock."

"No!" said Oliver, aghast.

"Saw him myself on my first night here. He was leading a pack of 'em, drunk as Davy's sow—"

"And you said nothing of it?" Elizabeth's eyes were fairly blazing.

"Well . . ."

Oliver leaned close once more. "I think you should very quickly tell us about this business."

"There's not that much to tell."

"Nevertheless . . ." He glanced at Elizabeth's eloquent face.

"Nevertheless," I faintly echoed, needing no more prompting, but I was tired and in want of refreshment, so my recounting of my initial meeting with Ridley was straightforward and as brief as I could make it. I thought longingly of Jericho and his clever juggling with teapots, but that was not a luxury I could enjoy just now.

Just as I finished, someone knocked at the door, and Brinsley hesitantly put his head in.

"I say, won't you be wanting some bandaging or water or something?" he asked of Oliver.

It took a moment for my cousin to adjust his attention from my past exploit to his present dilemma. He gave me a wide-eyed look, a mute inquiry of what to do. I answered with a short nod, and he told Brinsley that he had use for those very items, if it would not be too much trouble.

"None at all, old chap. How are you doing, Barrett?"

"Very well. I'll be up and about soon."

"What a relief! Can I get you anything?"

"Perhaps you can spare an old shirt for me? Mine's a bit—"

"Heavens, man, I can do better than that!" He bobbed out again, eager to get things moving.

"It seems to be working," said Oliver. "Brinsley was right next to me and saw the blade go in, and look how he is now. He *believes* you."

I sighed. "Thank heavens for that."

God have mercy, if I'd had to influence the lot of them into denying the evidence of their own eyes, I'd have burst my own head from the effort. As things stood, the witnesses were apparently doing a much better job of it on their own.

"Incredible." Oliver was shaking his head. "And all this because you curtailed Ridley's drunken sport. If he was that far gone in drink, I'm surprised he was able to remember you."

"No more than I was to find how he moves so easily from the gutter to polite company. He's a very dangerous fellow, and you must do all you can to avoid him."

"He's got no quarrel with me, but we two are blood kin—I'll do my best, Coz, but I doubt that he'll be much of a problem for now. You skewered him properly, though killing him would have been better."

"I've had enough of killing, thank you very much." Yes, now. Now that I was cooled enough to think again.

"Still, he's a spiteful type, you can see that. It might be over for tonight, but he's just the sort to come after you later, though. According to the Code, he cannot reopen the argument, but that won't stop him from beginning a new one."

"I'll keep my eyes open, not to fear," I promised.

"I wonder how he's doing, anyway?"

"If you really want to go find out . . ." I began doubtfully.

"Not a bit of it! Just wondered is all. I suppose they've turned up another doctor to attend him or I'd have been called in by now. Just as well, I suppose."

Some of the Bolyn servants appeared, bearing the promised washing water, bandaging, and a clean shirt of very fine silk. Brinsley—it seemed—was in the midst of a very severe bout of hero worship with myself being the object of adulation. I was rather nonplussed to be in such a position, feeling neither worthy of the honor nor comfortable, but it could not be helped.

The room was cleared again, and this time Elizabeth went out to deliver a report to the waiting throng about my condition and to order Oliver's carriage to be brought 'round. It would have been too much to expect us to remain and participate in the rest of the evening's festivities after all this.

I cleaned the dried blood away, donned Brinsley's shirt, and bundled up my torn and stained costume shirt and waistcoat for Jericho to deal with. Perhaps he could work a miracle and salvage them in some way. Oliver, seeing that the bandages were unnecessary, stuffed them away in one of his pockets.

For the sake of appearance and to discourage questions, I leaned heavily on his arm on our way out, keeping my head down. Not all of my weakness was a pose; I was very enervated by the blood loss and would soon need to replace it. My energy came in fits and spurts; I'd have some lively moments, then sink into an abrupt lethargy as if my body was trying to conserve strength.

Though our concerned hosts were disappointed that I would not remain with them for my mending, they got us all to the carriage without too much delay and we piled gratefully in.

"I'm sorry to have spoiled the party for you," I said to Elizabeth as we settled ourselves.

She snorted. "After this kind of excitement a masqued ball, no matter how elaborate, is but a tame occupation by comparison. I shall be in need of rest, anyway, for there will be a hundred callers coming 'round to the house tomorrow to see how things are with you. I hope Jericho and the staff will be up to the invasion. I'll wager that most of them will be young ladies with their mothers, all hoping for a glimpse of you."

My heart plummeted. "You can't mean it?"

"I saw it in their faces before we left. There's nothing so stirring to the feminine heart as watching a wounded duelist stoically dragging himself away from the field of battle."

"That's ridiculous."

"Indeed, many of the girls expressed disdain for any man unless he's blazed away at another in the name of honor— or in your case taken up the sword to—"

"Enough, for heaven's sake!" I moaned.

"No, little brother, I think this is but the beginning. Like it or not, you've become a hero. . . ."

"Oh, my God."

Oliver's eyes had flicked back and forth between us and now came to rest on me. His mobile face twitched and heaved mightily with suppressed emotion for all of two seconds, then he burst forth with a roar of laughter.

Had Oliver not been in sore need of the distraction, I'd have objected to his finding humor in my situation, but I held my peace and endured until he'd quite worked through it. By then we were home and trudging up to our respective rooms to prepare for bed, myself excepted, of course. I went to the parlor to rest a little while, until Jericho came in. Elizabeth had apparently told him about tonight's adventure, for he raised no question concerning the bloodied bundle of clothes I handed him.

"Don't know if you can salvage 'em, but it might be a good idea not to let the others see this lot. Might alarm them or something, and I've no wish to add to the gossip about this incident."

"I shall be discreet, Mr. Jonathan. You're certain that you are all right?"

"I think so, but for being wretchedly weak, and that will soon be remedied. Has the coachman finished with the horses?"

"He just came back from the stables and is having tea in the kitchen. The way is quite clear for you . . . unless you wish me to see to things?" he asked, referring obliquely to fetching the blood himself.

Tempting, but that would involve an additional wait. No, I was tired, but not that far gone. I told him as much and thanked him for the offer.

After he'd gone away to the kitchen, I traded the inadequate pirate cloak for my own heavy woolen one and slipped out the front door to walk unhurriedly around the house. The grounds of Oliver's property were limited, with barely room for a small vegetable garden, now dormant, and the stables, but at least he had no need to board his carriage animals and hunter elsewhere. With Rolly added to this little herd, I had a more than adequate supply of nourishment for my needs, though other sources were available. London was positively bursting with horses, and should it become necessary, I'd be able to feed from them easily enough.

It was Rolly's turn tonight. He'd filled out somewhat now that he was done with ocean voyaging. I'd been generous with his oats and had him groomed every day, and the extra care showed in his bright eyes and shining coat. We'd lately been out for a turn or two around the town when the weather wasn't too wet, so he wasn't snappish for lack of exercise.

I offered him a lump of sugar as a bribe, soothed him down, and got on with my business. He held perfectly still even after I'd finished and was wiping my lips clean. For that he got more sugar. Intelligent beast.

The blood did its usual miracle of restoration on my battered body. I felt its heat spreading from the inside out, though it seemed particularly concentrated on my chest this night. The skin over my heart was starting to itch. Opening Brinsley's shirt, I found the angry red patch around the fresh scar had faded somewhat. Very reassuring, that.

Since I was finally alone, though, I was free to take a shortcut to speed up my healing. I vanished.

Rolly didn't like it much. Perhaps he could sense my presence in some way; perhaps it had to do with the cold I generated in this form. He stirred in his box, shying away in protest. To ease things for him, I quit the stables and floated through the doors into the yard, using memory to find the path leading to the house. Despite the buffeting of the wind, I was able to make my way back again to materialize in the parlor right before the fireplace.

Jericho, being extremely familiar with my habits, had built the fire up into a fine big blaze during my absence and set out my slippers and dressing gown. I listened intently for a moment to the sounds of the house. Jericho was in the kitchen exchanging light conversation with the coachman and the cook. I couldn't quite make out the words, but the voices were calm, ordinary in tone, indicating that all was peaceful belowstairs. Just as well.

The itch in my chest was no more. A second look at the place of my wounding both assured and astonished me. All trace of red was gone, and the scar appeared to be weeks old. In time, most probably after my next vanishing, it would disappear altogether.

Suddenly shivering, I pulled a chair closer to the fire and sat miserably huddled in my cloak.

I thought of Father, missing him and his sensible, comforting manner with me whenever life became troubling.

"You should be glad that you still have a life to be troubled about," I muttered aloud. God knows with the times being what they were, had I not been cut down by that fool at the Captain's Kettle over a year ago, I'd have met a bad fate soon after.

And recovered from it. Because of my change.

A nasty sort of unease oozed through my belly as I pondered on how things might have been had I not met Nora. Without her, I'd have certainly stayed in my early grave; Elizabeth would be dead as well, foully and horribly murdered. That would have shattered Father, to lose us both.

I shivered again and told myself to stop being so morbid. It was all because of that damned duel and that damned Thomas Ridley. The thought of him filled me with fury and disgust, the former for his picking the fight, the latter for his stupidity in continuing it. Blooding aside, I'd not enjoyed my revenge against him. My hand could still feel how my blade had stabbed into the tough resistance of his fleshy arm until it grated upon and was stopped by the bone beneath. A singularly unpleasant sensation, that. He'd be weeks healing, unless it became fevered, and then he'd either lose the arm or die.

Well, as with everything else, it was in God's hands. No need for me to wallow in guilt for something not my fault. Yes, I had wanted to kill him for his insult to Elizabeth, but that desire had gone out of me after the first shock of my own wound had worn off. It was as if I'd seen just how foolish he was, like a child trying to threaten an adult. To be sure, he was a very dangerous child, but he'd no earthly idea of just how overmatched he'd been with me. And I . . . I'd forgotten the extent of my own capabilities, which made me a fool as well.

No more of that, Johnny Boy, I thought, shaking my head.

Warmer, I threw off the cloak, exchanging it for the dressing gown, and struggled to remove my boots. I'd just gotten my left heel lifted free, ready to slip the rest of the way out, when someone began knocking at the front door.

Damnation, what now? Slamming my foot back into the

boot, I made my frustrated way to the central hall and peered through one of the windows flanking the entrance.

A man wrapped in a dark cloak stood outside. For a mad second I thought he might be Ridley because of his size, but the set of his shoulders was more squared and there was nothing amiss with his right arm. He turned and raised it now to knock again and I caught his profile.

Cousin Edmond Fonteyn? What on earth did he want?

Probably come to berate me about the duel. He was something of a dogsbody to Aunt Fonteyn—and to her only—and if she wasn't of a mind to vent her doubtless acid opinion of the matter herself, she'd have sent him in her stead. Not that I had a care for the substitution or even his presence. So much had happened tonight that I was simply unable to raise my usual twinge of guilt from having hung the cuckold's horns on him that Christmas years past.

"I'll get it, sir," said Jericho, emerging from the back.

"I'm already here, no need." Obligingly, I unbolted and opened the door, and Edmond swept in, seeming to fill the hall. It was not his size alone that did it, so much as his manner. Stick-in-the-mud he might be, according to Oliver, but when he entered a room, people noticed.

"Hallo, Edmond," I began. "If it's about the duel, I can tell you—"

"Bother that," he said, his brown eyes taking in the hall, noting Jericho's presence, then fastening on me. "Where's Oliver?"

"In bed by now."

"Have him fetched without delay."

Edmond always looked serious, but there was a dark urgency to him now that made my flesh creep with alarm. I signed to Jericho. He'd already started up the stairs.

"There's a fire going in the parlor," I said, gesturing him in the right direction.

He frowned at me briefly, then accepted the invitation, striding ahead without hurry. Under the cloak he still wore his Harlequin guise, though he'd traded the white skullcap for a normal hat. He wore no wig, revealing his close-cropped, graying hair. It should have made him seem vulnerable, half-dressed in some way, but did not.

"What's all this about?" I asked.

His eyes raked me up and down, caught mine, then turned toward the fire. "Duel," he said. There was derision in his tone, like that of a schoolmaster for an especially backward student.

"What about it?"

"Never mind, it's of no importance."

"Then tell me what's going on."

"You'll know soon enough," he growled.

Very well, then, I'd not press things. It seemed forever, though, waiting for Oliver to come down. Edmond was throwing off tension like a fire throws off heat; I could almost feel myself starting to scorch from it. Relief flooded me when Oliver finally appeared, clad also in a dressing gown, but wearing slippers, not boots.

Sleepily he glanced past Edmond to me, as if asking for an explanation. I could only shrug.

"Oliver—" Edmond paused to brace himself. "Look, I'm very sorry, but something terrible has happened, and I don't quite know how to tell you."

All vestige of sleep fell away from Oliver's face at these alarming words. "What's happened?" he demanded.

"What?" I said at the same time.

"Your mother . . . there's been an accident."

"An acci—what sort of—where is she?"

"At the Bolyns'. She had a fall. We think she slipped on some ice."

"Is she all right?" Oliver stepped forward, his voice rising.

"She struck her head in the fall. I'm very sorry, Oliver, but she's dead."

CHAPTER
–10–

In England, for those in high enough and wealthy enough circles, funerals were customarily held at night, which was just as well for me as it would have raised some comment had I not attended, but then I only wanted to be there for Oliver's sake and not my own.

The weather was atrocious, all bitterly cold wind and cutting sleet—most appropriate, considering Aunt Fonteyn's temperament. Her final chance to inflict one last blast of misery upon her family, I thought, cowering with the rest of the family as we followed the coffin to its final destination. I walked on one side of Oliver, Elizabeth on the other, offering what support we could with the bleak knowledge that it was not enough. For days since the delivery of the bad news, the color had drained right out of his face and had yet to return. He was as gray and fragile as an old man; his eyes were disturbingly empty, as if he'd gone to sleep but forgotten to close them.

I hoped that once the horror of the interment was over, he might begin to recover himself. The ties are strong between a mother and child, whether they love each other or not; when those ties are irreparably severed, the survivor is going to have a strong reaction of some kind. For all his years of abuse from her, for all his mutterings against her, she was, as he'd said, the only mother he'd got. Even if he'd come to hate her, she'd still been a major influence in his life, unpleasant, but at least familiar. Her sudden absence would bring change, and changes are frightening when one is utterly unprepared for them. Certainly I could attest to the absolute truth of that in light of my past experience with death and the profound change it had delivered to my family.

The memory of my demise came forcibly back as we shivered here in the family mausoleum a quarter mile from Fonteyn House. No mixing with other folk in the church-yard for this family; the Fonteyns would share eternity with their own kind, thank you very much; and no muddy graves, either, but a spacious and magnificent sepulcher fit for royalty, large enough to hold many future generations of their ilk.

The huge structure had been built by Grandfather Fonteyn, who was presently moldering in a carved marble sarcopha-gus a few yards from where I stood. His eldest daughter's coffin was even now being pushed into its nearby niche by the pallbearers. Tomorrow its stone cover with a brass plate bearing her name would be mortared into place on the wall.

As depressing as it was to stand here surrounded by the Fonteyn dead, it was preferable to standing 'round a gaping hole in the ground with the sleet stinging the backs of our necks. The cloying scent of freshly turned earth might have been too much for me, though being at a funeral, period, was bad enough. The same went for Elizabeth, for she not only had memories of my burial to wrestle with, but those of James Norwood's, too.

I glanced over to see how she was holding up, and she gave me a thin but confident smile meant to reassure. Much of her attention was concentrated on Oliver, which was probably why she was able to get through this at all.

Sheet white and shaking miserably with the cold, he looked ready to fall over. He wasn't drunk, and he should have been; he was in sore need of some muzzy-headed insulation from what was happening. He stared unfocused at his mother's coffin as they pushed it into place, and I had no doubt that every detail was searing itself forever into his battered mind.

He must have help, I thought, and wondered what I could possibly do for him. No shred of an idea presented itself, though. Perhaps later, after we were out of this damned death house, I could come up with something.

The service finally concluded. Since I'd not listened to one word of it, I knew only by the last *amens* and general stir about me. No mourners lingered in this torch-lit tomb. As one, we left Elizabeth Therese Fonteyn Marling to God's mercy and all but galloped back through the crusty mud and snow to the lights and warmth of Fonteyn House.

The servants had set up a proper feast for the occasion, and the family set to it with an unseemly gusto. Soon the gigantic collection of cold joints, pies, sweets, hams, and lord knows what else began to steadily disappear from the serving trays. The drink also suffered a similar swift depletion, but no one became unduly loud or merry from all the flowing Madeira. Oliver, I noted, never went near the groaning tables.

Very bad, that, I thought.

There had been an inquiry about Aunt Fonteyn's death, but only a brief one, since it was obvious to all that it had been an accident. She'd been found in the center of the Bolyns' shrubbery maze, having had the bad luck of somehow slipping on a patch of ice and striking her head on the edge of the marble fountain there. Some servant had found her and raised the alarm. A doctor was sent for, but her skull had been well and truly broken; nothing could be done. At least it had been quick and relatively painless, people had said; that should be something of a comfort to her family. After all, there were worse ways to die.

Of the talk I overheard or participated in, it was universally agreed how unfair and awful it was, but then God's will was bound to be a mystery to those who still lived. Thankfully, Cousin Edmond assumed the duties of making arrangements for the funeral. A lawyer himself, he moved things quickly along out of deference for Oliver's condition, and three nights later most of the family had gathered at Fonteyn House to pay their last respects.

If everyone had not been garbed in black, it might have been another Fonteyn Christmas. All the usual crowd was present, and one by one they expressed their sympathy to Oliver. Some of them, being sensitive to his downcast countenance, were even sincere.

One or two latecomers were ushered in by the sad-faced mute hired for the task. Gloves and rings had been distributed to the closest relatives; I'd gotten a silk hat hand and chamois gloves, all black. God knows what I'd do with them, being unable to truly hold any grief in my heart for the foul-minded old hag, but I was expected to put on a show of it, nonetheless. Hypocritical to be sure, but I took comfort from the fact that I could hardly be the only member in this gathering with such feelings. Aunt Fonteyn had not been the sort of person to inspire deep and sincere mourning from anyone in their right senses . . . then I suddenly thought of Mother and just in time whipped out a handkerchief to cover my painfully twitching mouth before betraying a highly improper grin to the room.

The only thing that settled me was the knowledge that I'd have to write home with the news. Father wouldn't have an easy time of it—not that he ever did—once Mother learned about the demise of the sister she doted upon. With that in mind I was just able to play my part, nodding at the right times and murmuring the right things and trying to keep my eye on Oliver as much as possible.

He was still hemmed in by a pack of relatives and not too responsive to whatever they were saying. Elizabeth was with him, doing her best to make up for his lack. Oh, well, no one would think badly of him for it and only put it off to grief.

My lovely cousin Clarinda moved in and out through the crowds, having assumed the duties of hostess for him. I could not honestly say that black suited her; tonight she looked almost as drawn as Oliver. Though far more animated than he, her natural liveliness was well dampened owing to the circumstances. We'd exchanged formal greetings earlier, neither of us giving any sign of having a shared secret. I suspected, given Clarinda's obvious appetite for willing young men, that our particular encounter had faded quite a bit in her memory. Not that I felt slighted in any way; relief would best describe my reaction if this proved to be so.

I moved among the various relatives as well, shaking a hand here, bowing to a lady there, but inevitably ending up with a group of the men as they spoke in low tones about the tragedy. As there was actually very little one could say about it, and since it was considered bad taste to speak ill of the departed, no matter how deserving, the topics of talk soon shifted from things funereal to things political. The dispiriting details of General Burgoyne's surrender were now in the papers, and the men here had formed the idea that I could somehow tell them more than what had appeared in print. But with my mind on Oliver's problems, I had no interest in discussing the situation in the Colonies tonight.

"Forgive me, gentlemen, but I know only as much as you do from your reading," I said, trying to put them off.

"But you're from the area, from New York," insisted one of my many Fonteyn cousins.

"I'm from Long Island, and it's as far away from Saratoga as London is from Plymouth—and with far worse roads in between."

This garnered some discreet laughter.

"But you weren't so very far from the general fighting yourself if Oliver is to be believed."

"I've been close enough, sir. There have been some incidents near our village concerning the rebels, but the King's army has things well in hand now." *I hope*, I silently added, feeling the usual stab of worry for Father whenever I thought of home.

"You're being too modest, Mr. Barrett," said another young man, one of the many in the crowd. I had a strong idea he was here more for the feasting than to pay his respects. He was a handsome fellow and familiar, since I'd seen him before at other gatherings, but nameless like dozens of others. "I believe by now all of you know that your cousin here is a rare fire-eater when it comes to battle," he added. "Perhaps some of you were there at the Bolyns' party and saw him in action."

I didn't like his manner much or the fact he'd brought up

the subject of the duel. Unfortunately, the other men were highly interested and wanted a full recounting of the event.

"Gentlemen, this is hardly an appropriate time or place," I said, being as firmly discouraging as possible.

"Oh, but we may never have another opportunity," the young man drawled with expansive insistence. "I think we'd all like to hear how you defeated Mr. Thomas Ridley after he'd so grievously wounded you."

"Hardly so grievous or I'd not be here, sir."

More suppressed expressions of good humor.

"Do you call me a liar, sir?" he said slowly, deliberately, and worst of all, with no alteration in his pleasant expression.

Great heavens, I'd dreaded that some idiot might turn up and make a nuisance of himself by wanting to provoke a duel with me, but I hadn't expected it to happen so soon and leastwise not at Aunt Fonteyn's funeral. Those around us went very still waiting for my answer.

I could have found a graceful way of getting out of it, but the man's obvious insult was too annoying to disregard. "Your name, sir?" I asked, keeping my own voice and expression as bland as possible.

"Arthur Tyne, sir. Thomas Ridley's cousin."

If he expected me to blanch in terror at this revelation, he was in for a vast disappointment. "Indeed? I trust and pray that the man is recovering from his own wound."

"You have not answered me, Mr. Barrett," he said, putting an edge into his tone that was meant to be menacing.

"Only because I thought you were making a jest, sir. It seemed polite that I should overlook it, since we are all here to pay our solemn respects to the memory of my aunt."

"That was no jest, sir, but a most earnest inquiry. Are you prepared to answer?"

"You astound me, Mr. Tyne. Of course I did not call you a liar."

"I find you to be most insolent, sir."

"Which is not too surprising; poor Aunt Fonteyn often made the same complaint against me." If some of those around us were shocked by my honesty, then more were struggling not to show their amusement.

"Are you deaf? I said you are most insolent, Mr. Barrett."

"Not deaf, only agreeing with you, dear fellow." I fixed my eyes and full concentration upon him. "Certainly you can find no exception to that."

In actuality, Arthur Tyne found himself unable to say anything at all.

"This is a most sad occasion for me," I went on. "I should be sadder still if I've caused you any distress. Come along with me, sir. I am very interested in hearing how things are with your cousin."

So saying, I linked my arm with his and led him out of earshot of the rest. Tyne was just starting to blink himself awake when I fixed him again with my gaze.

"Now, you listen to me, you little toad," I whispered. "I don't care if the idea to have a fight with me was yours or your cousin's, but you can put it right out of your head. You're to leave me and mine alone. Understand? Now get out of my sight and stay out of my way."

And so I had the pleasure of seeing Arthur Tyne's back as he made a hasty retreat. He was visibly shaken, and the other men noticed, but I kept my pretense of a smile and easily ignored them. What I could not ignore was Edmond Fonteyn's sudden presence next to me. Unlike his wife, black suited him well, made him look larger, more powerful, more intimidating.

"What the devil are you up to?" he demanded.

"Just trying to avoid an embarrassing scene, Cousin," I said tiredly, hoping he would go away.

He gave me a stony glare. "More dueling?"

"Just the opposite, as a matter of fact."

He pushed past me and went in pursuit of Arthur. I could trust that Edmond would find things in order. If Arthur was typical of the others I'd influenced, he'd not remember much of it; if not, and Edmond returned with questions . . . well, I could deal with him if necessary. It might even be amusing to see *his* grim face going all blank and vulnerable for a change.

But there were more pressing things for me to deal with tonight than fools and irate cousins, and it was past time I

got on with them. Putting Edmond and Arthur firmly from
mind, I searched the ranks of the servants, at last spotted
the one I wanted, and drifted over.

"Radcliff?"

"Yes, sir?" He was busy supervising the sherry and
Madeira, making sure most of it went into the guests, not
the servers.

"I should like two bottles of good brandy sent along to
the blue drawing room, please. Put some food with it, breads
and sweets, some ham if there's any left."

He raised one eyebrow, but offered no more comment,
and went to order things for me. I now drifted over to Oliver
and Elizabeth. As she looked pale and strained from the
effort she was putting forth, her gaze fell on me and she
grasped my arm convulsively.

"Here now, you're not planning to faint, are you?" I
asked, concerned that this was becoming all too much for
her.

"Don't be an ass," she whispered back. "I'm just tired.
All these people . . ." There were quite a lot of them, and
dealing with each and every one while looking after Oliver
had put her teeth dangerously on edge.

"Well, I'm taking over for you and no arguing. See that
fellow by the wine table? Go ask him for anything you like
and have him send it to some quiet room. Make sure you
eat. You look ready to drop in your tracks."

She needed no more persuasion, and I took her place at
Oliver's side. I made sure the person who was presently
trying to speak with him understood that my interruption
had some urgent purpose behind it. He gracefully excused
himself and I slipped a hand 'round Oliver's arm.

"Come along with me, old man, something's come up
that wants your attention."

He passively allowed himself to be led away. We reached
the blue drawing room just as one of Radcliff's efficient
minions was leaving. I got Oliver inside, firmly closed the
door, then steered him toward the warmth of the fireplace.

"Beastly night for a burying, what?" I asked, pouring
brandy for him. There were two glasses; I slopped a few
drops into the second one for the sake of appearance.

Oliver shrugged and decorously sat in the chair, rather than resorting to his usual careless fall. One of his hands was closed into a fist. He wore a mourning ring on that one, a ring made from his mother's hair.

I picked up the brandy glass and offered it to him. He listlessly took it, but did not drink.

"Go on, then, do yourself some good," I said encouragingly.

He gave no sign that he'd heard.

"You'll have to sometime, you know damned well I can't touch the stuff. Come on, then."

Casting an indifferent glance at me, he finally raised it to his lips and sipped, then put it aside on a table. "I'd really like to be alone," he mumbled.

He wasn't the only one who could ape deafness. "Radcliff seems to have provided the choicer bits of food for you, so it's pity on me for missing out on the feast." In actuality, the cooked meats smelled nauseating, but I stoutly ignored the sensation.

"Not hungry," he said, still mumbling.

"I can hardly believe that."

"Believe what you like, but please let me alone."

"All right, whatever you say." I started to turn. "Half a minute, there's something on your hand. . . ."

I caught the mourning ring and suddenly pulled it free from his finger, pretending to examine it. "Now, here's a grisly relic. Wonder if it's her own hair or from one of her wigs?"

"What the devil are you—give that to me!" He started to lurch from his chair.

"Not just yet." I shoved him back into place.

He knocked my arm away. "How dare you!"

"It's easy enough."

"Have you gone mad? Give that—" He started up again, and I backed away, holding the ring high. He lunged for it, and I let him catch my arm, but wouldn't allow him to take the ring. I dragged us toward the middle of the room where there was no furniture to trip over, and we wrestled around like boys having a schoolyard scuffle.

"I'm sure your mother . . . would be delighted . . . to

know," I said between all the activity, "the depth of . . . your regard for her."

Oliver had grown red-faced with anger. "You bastard . . . why are you . . . I hated her!"

Now I showed some of my real strength, getting behind him and pinning his arms back as if he were a small child. Half-lifted from the floor, he struggled futilely, trying to kick my shins and sometimes succeeding; not that it bothered me much, I was too busy taking care not to hurt him.

"You hated her?" I said in his ear, sounding astonished.

"Damn you—let me go!" He wriggled with all his might but was quickly wearing out. His self-imposed fasting for the last few days had done him little good.

"You're sure you hated her?" I taunted.

"*Damn you!*" he bellowed and landed a properly vicious one on my kneecap with the edge of his heel. I felt it, grunted, and released him. He staggered a step to get his balance and whirled around. His face was so twisted with rage, I hardly knew him. Had I pushed too far?

Apparently so, for he charged at me, fists ready, and made use of them willy-nilly on any portion of me that I was foolish enough to leave within range. I blundered into tables and other furnishings trying to keep away from him. Ornaments fell and shattered, and we managed to knock a portrait from the wall; the worst was when a chair went right over and I went with it—backward. My head struck the wooden floor with a thud, and the candlelight flared and flashed dizzyingly for me.

This is really too wretchedly stupid, I thought as my arms bonelessly flopped at my sides. I was too stunned for the moment to offer further defense and expected Oliver to take advantage of it to really pummel me . . . but nothing happened.

After a minute I cracked an eyelid open in his direction and saw his legs. Traveling upward, I made out his hands— fists no longer, thank God—then his heaving chest, then his mottled face. He hiccupped twice, and that's when I noticed his streaming tears.

"You are. A bastard." He swiped at the tears with the back of one arm.

I felt like one, too. I also felt pretty badly from the fall and took my time getting untangled from the chair and standing. Jericho would be appalled when he saw my clothes; I'd have to assure him that the damage—buttons torn from the waistcoat, a coat sleeve partly ripped from its shoulder, shredded lace, and dirtied stockings with gaping holes over the shins—had all been in a good cause.

"Here," I said shakily, holding the ring out.

He grabbed it away and tried to thrust it back on again, but was trembling and half blinded by tears; he just couldn't do it.

"Damn you, damn you, damn you," he said throughout his efforts.

"And damn you for an idiot, dear Cousin," I growled back.

"You dare? How can you—"

"You hated her, so why do you even bother with that?" I gestured at the ring.

He took another swing at me. A halfhearted attempt. I successfully dodged it.

"You think anyone here cares whether you're in mourning or not? Or are you worried about what they might think?"

"I don't give a bloody damn what they think!" The next time he swung, I caught his arm and, after more scuffling, dragged him to the chair and more or less got him to sit.

"I'll kill you for this!" he roared.

"I don't think so. Now shut up or—"

"Or what? You'll use your unholy influence on me?"

"If I'd planned that, I'd have done it sooner and spared myself a beating. You'll behave now or I'll slap your poxy face until you're silly."

He must have decided that I was serious, for he slumped a bit. "My face isn't poxy," he muttered.

This was said with such pouting sincerity that I stopped short to stare at him. He returned with a stubborn look of his own for a full ten seconds, then both our faces began crumbling, first with a sharp pulling at the mouth corners, then suppressed snickers, then full-blown laughter. His was short-lived, though, quickly devolving back to tears. Once started, he kept going, head bowed as he sobbed away his inner agony. Putting an arm around his shoulders, I wept myself, not for any grief of my own, but out of sympathy for his.

Then some oaf knocked at the door.

I wearily moved toward it, wiping my nose and eyes, and when I'd put myself in order, opened it an inch. "Yes?"

Radcliff was there, along with a few other servants, all seeming very worried. "Sir, we heard something break . . . is there a problem?"

They'd heard more than that from the looks I was getting. I gave them an easy and innocent smile. "No, just had a bit of a mishap. Nothing to worry about. Mr. Marling and I are having a private talk and would appreciate it if we could be left undisturbed for the time being."

"If you're sure, sir . . ."

"Quite sure, thank you. You may all return to your duties."

With considerable reluctance and much doubt, they dispersed, and I shut the door, putting my back to it and leaning against it with a heartfelt sigh. My head ached where it had struck the floor, and I half debated on vanishing for a moment to heal, then dismissed the idea for now. Though Oliver knew about that particular talent of mine, an unexpected exhibition would likely alarm and upset him; he had more than sufficient things to worry about.

He was presently sniffing and yawning and showing evidence of pulling himself together. His eyes were very red, and the white skin above and below them was all puffed, but a spark of life seemed to be returning to them.

He held up the mourning ring. "Did that on purpose, did you?"

"I plead guilty, m'lord."

"Humph."

In deference to my head and bruised shins, I crept slowly from the door, taking a chair opposite him. The table with the food and brandy bottles was between us, and he gestured at it.

"I suppose the next step is to make me eat or get me stinking drunk or both."

"That's exactly right, dear Coz."

"Humph." He turned the mourning ring over and over. "Y'know, this is the closest I ever got to touching her. She wouldn't allow it. Messed up her dress or hair, I suppose, though now when I think about how Grandfather Fonteyn might have treated her . . ."

"There's no need to do so."

"I have, anyway. Because of him I really had no mother, just a woman who filled the position in name only. My God, the only woman who was a real mother to me was my old nanny. Even if she didn't exactly spoil me, she didn't mind getting or giving a hug now and then. I'll weep at *her* funeral—and for the right reason. I wept tonight because . . . because . . . I don't know." He rubbed his face, fingers digging at his inflamed eyes.

I waited until he'd finished and was able to listen. "My father says that guilt is a useless and wasteful thing to carry in one's heart, and it's even worse to feel sorry for oneself for having it."

"I'm guilty?"

"No, but you *have* guilt, which is something else again. It's not your fault you came to hate your mother. What is, is your feeling badly about it."

"Sorry, but I can't seem to help that," he said dryly.

I shrugged. "It'll go away if you let it."

"Oh? And just how might this miracle be accomplished?"

"I'm not really sure, but sooner or later you wake up and it doesn't bother you so much."

"How do you know?"

"It has to do with forgiveness. All this heartache I've felt for Nora . . . she hurt me terribly by making me forget everything. Even when I came to understand that she must have had a good reason for it, I was still hurting. But over the last few weeks . . . well, it's faded. All I want now is to see her again. I suppose I've forgiven her."

"Very fine for you, but then you've said you love her. Besides, Mother had no good reason for how she treated me."

"True, but the similarity is that you were hurt—"

"And the difference is that I can't forgive her," he finished. "I still hate her for what she did to me."

"Which is the source of your guilt. You want to live with that pain the rest of your life?"

"Of course not, but I know of no way past it, do you?"

He had me there . . . until a mad thought popped into my mind. "Maybe if you talked to her."

Incredulity mixed with disdain washed over his face. "I think it's just a bit late for that."

"Not really. Not for you. Have some of that brandy, I'll be back shortly." I limped from the room, pausing once in the thankfully deserted hall to vanish for a few moments. My head was wrenchingly tender, making the process more difficult, but when I returned, my body was much restored. The headache was fading, and I could walk unimpeded by bruises.

I took myself quickly off to find a suitable lackey and sent him to fetch dry cloaks and hats and a couple of thick woolen mufflers. Despite my disheveled appearance, he hurried to obey and got a penny vale for his effort, which impressed him to the point that he wanted to continue his service by carrying the things to my destination. I pleasantly damned his eyes and told him to see to the other guests. When he was gone, I went back to the blue drawing room.

Oliver had drained away a good portion of the brandy I'd poured earlier and had wolfed down some bread and ham. I hated to interrupt the feasting and particularly the drinking, and so slipped one of the brandy bottles into the pocket of my coat.

"Put this lot on and no questions," I said, tossing him half of my woolly burden.

"But—"

I held up a warning hand. "No questions."

Exasperated, but intrigued, he garbed himself and followed me. I took us out one of the back entries, managing to avoid any of the other family members as we quit the house and slogged over the grounds.

Our sudden isolation made the sleet seem worse than before. It cruelly gouged our skin and clung heavily to our clothes, soaking through in spots. The unrelenting wind magnified the glacial chill, clawing at our cloaks. The scarves, which we'd used to tie our hats in place, were scant protection against its frigid force. Someone had opened the door to hell tonight and forgotten to close it again.

"This is bloody cold," Oliver commented, with high disapproval.

I gave him the brandy. "Then warm yourself."

He accepted and drank. Good. The stuff would hit his near-empty stomach like a pistol ball.

Ugh. My hand went to my chest. Wish I hadn't thought of that.

"What's the matter with you?" he demanded, unknowingly pulling me out of my thoughts about black smothering graves.

"No questions," I said, plowing forward through the wind with him in my wake.

It was a devilish thick night, but Oliver's eyes had adjusted to the point where he could see where we were headed.

He balked. "We can't go there!"

"We have to."

"But it's . . . it's . . ."

"What, a little scary?"

"Yes. And I feel like we're being watched."

"So do I, but it's just the wind in the trees."

"You're sure?"

I cast a quick look around. "This is like daylight to me, right? Well, I can't see anyone. We're quite alone."

"*That's* hardly a comfort," he wailed.

"Come *on*, Oliver."

I took his arm and we continued forward until once more we stood in the mausoleum before his mother's coffin. Two lighted torches had been left behind in this house of stone to burn themselves out.

"Now what?" He sounded tremulous and lost, for which I could not blame him. Out here in the dark menace of the cemetery with the wind roaring around the tomb as if to give an icy voice to those departed, I felt my own bravado preparing to pack up and decamp like a vagrant.

I cleared my throat rather more loudly than was needed. "Now you're going to talk to her."

His mouth sagged. "You *have* gone mad."

"True enough, but there's a purpose to it. Talk to her. Tell her exactly how you feel on her treatment of you. I guarantee that she won't object this time."

"I couldn't do that! It's foolish."

"Is it? Hallo there! Aunt Fonteyn! Are you home?" I shouted at the end of the coffin that was visible to us. I thumped at it with a fist. "Are you in there, you horrible old woman? We've come to call on you and we're drunk— Oliver is, anyway—"

"I'm *not* drunk!" he protested, looking around fearfully.

"Yes, you are." I addressed the coffin again. "See? Your son's drunk and your least favorite nephew's gone mad and we're here to disturb your eternal rest. How do you like *that*, you bloody harpy?"

Oliver gaped, horrified. I grinned back, then shocked him further by bounding up on Grandfather Fonteyn's sarcophagus and jumping down the other side. "How about that, Grandfather? Did that wake you up? Come on, Oliver, have a bit of exercise."

He took a deep draught of brandy, coughing a bit. "I couldn't," he gasped. It was but a faint protest, though.

"You most certainly can. What's it to him? He can't feel it. But you will." I hopped up, capered on the carved marble, and dropped lightly next to him. "Right, if you don't want to dance, it's all one with me, but you are going to talk to *her*. Scream at her if you like, no one's going to hear a word."

He shot me a dark look. "You will."

"Hardly. I'm going back to the house." So saying, I turned and started away. "Best get on with it. The sooner you begin, the sooner you can enjoy the fire and food waiting there."

He returned about half an hour later, teeth chattering, and skin gone both red and white with the cold, but with a sharp gleam of triumph in his eyes. Not all of it had been inspired by the brandy.

He'd talked to his mother.

He'd also shouted, bellowed, and cursed her in a most splendid and inspired manner. I knew, because I'd hung back out of sight, just close enough to hear his voice but not understand the words. Once I was sure he was truly into the business, I hared off to have some hot broth waiting for him in the drawing room. Radcliff brought it himself, clucking unhappily over the breakage there, but hurriedly leaving at my impatient gesture when Oliver walked in. The talk in the servants' hall would doubtless be quite entertaining tonight.

Oliver flopped into the chair with his familiar abandon and declared that he was ready to perish from the cold.

"Feels like the devil's grabbed my ears and won't let go," he cheerfully complained. He held his hands out to the fire to warm them, then gingerly cupped his palms over his ears. "Ouch! Well, if I lose them, I lose them. I'll just have a wig made to cover my unadorned ear holes and no one'll be the wiser. What's this? Broth? Just the thing, but I'd like more brandy if you don't mind. And some ham, no, that thick slice over there. Gone cold, has it? Just let me catch it with the fire tongs and toast it a bit. . . . there, that'll hot it up nicely. Y'know she would *never* have allowed this. Dining's to be done in the dining room and nowhere else, but to hell with the old ways. This is my house now and there will be changes made, just you wait and see! And see this, too!"

He held up the mourning ring in his long white fingers.

"Are you watching, Coz? Are you? There!" He tossed the ring into the fire. It landed softly and Oliver was silent as the flames crept up and quickly consumed it.

"There," he repeated more softly. "No more hypocrisy. No more damned guilt. Dear me, but the ham's scorching. Hand that plate over, will you? Mind the brandy, precious stuff, that."

I stayed with him, listening with a glad heart to his chatter as he made inroads on the food. He was drunk and getting drunker. Tomorrow he would have a very bad head, but that would give him something else to think about than his guilt—if any remained. I rather thought there might be, for the stuff has a tenacious grip on certain souls and Oliver had already shown his vulnerability to it. But I was also thinking that the next time he felt its talons digging in, he'd go out to shout in the mausoleum again, now that he knew to do so.

Soon Oliver, replete and bone tired, asked if I could take him upstairs and put him to bed.

"Don' think I cou' manage on m' own 'n' tha's God's own truth, Coz." He confessed this woeful tiding with a wobbling head.

I told him that I'd be pleased to assist him. After getting him to his nerveless feet, we staggered into the hall and found a stairway to stumble up. He was not exactly quiet, giggling and declaring that I was the best damned cousin in the world and he'd give challenge to any man who said otherwise. This brought out some servants to investigate the row, one of whom was an older woman that Oliver greeted with tipsy joy.

"Nanny! You won'erful ol' darling! How 'bout a nice hug for your bad lad?" He flailed out with one arm, but I kept him from toppling over and falling on the poor woman.

"Mr. Oliver, you need to be in bed," she in a scolding tone, putting her hands on her hips. She was tiny, but I got the impression her authority in the nursery was never questioned.

Oliver smiled, beatific. " 'Xactly where 'm goin', Nanny. May I please have a good night choc'late, like ol' times?"

"Have you a room we can put him in?" I asked her.

"His old one's just here—no, that might not be a good choice, being bare as a dog's bone. This way, sir."

She took us along to one that had been made up for the use of guests who would stay overnight. A small chamber for the new master of the house, but the fire was laid and the bed turned down and ready. I eased him onto it and let her fuss over him, taking his shoes off and stripping away his outer clothes as though he were still four years old. Oliver, for what little he was aware of it, seemed to be enjoying every minute. As soon as his head struck the pillow, he was asleep, snoring mightily.

The nanny dutifully tucked him in, then paused to make a curtsy to me on her way out. We got a good look at each other. I saw a cautious but kindly face, not pretty, but certainly intelligent. What she saw I wasn't sure of, but her expression was strangely reminiscent of Oliver's own

version of pop-eyed surprise. Then I remembered that my
clothes were still in need of repair. No doubt torn sleeves
and missing buttons were a rare sight in this house. I made
a polite nod to her and sailed from the room as if utterly
unaware of my dishevelment.

Unfortunately, I sailed smack into Cousin Edmond, collid-
ing heavily with his sturdy frame. He snarled a justifiable
objection to my clumsiness.

"I do beg your pardon," I said, having all but bounced
off him. He was about as solid and forgiving as any brick
wall.

"What? Are you drunk as well?"

"No, but poor Oliver needed some help finding his way
up."

"I'm sure he did. Half the house heard his disgraceful
carrying on." Edmond pushed past me for a look into the
room to grunt at Oliver's sleeping form and growl at the
nanny. "Mrs. Howard, what the devil are you doing here?
Get yourself along and see to the other brats. The one in
here is long past your help."

Apparently well used to his rough ways, Mrs. Howard
plucked her skirts up with underplayed dignity and left. She
quickly covered a fair amount of the hall without seeming
to hurry and turned a corner without looking back.

Edmond glared after her, then focused the force of it on
me for an instant. His lips curled as if he wanted to speak.
I waited, but nothing came forth. He thinned the set of
his mouth into a tough line of contempt, but after all that
had happened, I was utterly immune to intimidation from
him. When one has gone to a cemetery in the dark of a
winter night to dance with the dead, it takes more than a
bad-tempered cousin to shake one's inner esteem. Perhaps
he sensed that. Without another word, he pushed past me
to go below.

"Edmond?"

He stopped halfway down and did not quite turn to look.
"What?"

"Just wanted to let you know that your work making the
arrangements was excellent and much appreciated. Oliver
is very grateful, y'know."

He said nothing for a moment, then grunted. Then he moved on.

Even as he descended, my sister ascended, glancing after him pensively.

"You look much improved," I commented, happy to see her again.

She reached the landing, her eyes wide as they raked me up and down. "What on earth have you been *doing?*"

"Oh, nothing much. Just had a nice little chat with Oliver. He feels all the better for it."

"You must have been chatting in a cockfighting pit. What's happened to you?"

I gave her a brief explanation for my condition.

"And Oliver's all right?" she asked with justifiable disbelief.

"Right as rain—at least until he wakes up."

Now she took her own opportunity to look in on him. "God, what a row," she said, in reaction to his snores. "I suppose he must be better if he can make that much noise. So what was troubling Cousin Edmond? He seemed more broody than normal."

"He had some objection to Oliver's carrying on is all." Poor old stick-in-the-mud Edmond, I thought. "Maybe his temper will improve with Aunt Fonteyn's absence."

"Jonathan!"

"Or is that too much to hope for?"

"If I didn't know better, I'd say you were drunk. So will anyone else."

"Bother them. They're probably thinking the same as I about her, but they'd just never admit it. Oliver is now the new head of the family, and he's bound to be more congenial in his duties than she, so everyone ought to be celebrating tonight. Things are looking up for the Fonteyns."

"Unless Mother decides to take things over when she comes to England," Elizabeth pointed out.

"She can't. It may have been Aunt Fonteyn's will, but hers was mostly a continuation of Grandfather Fonteyn's testament. Except for a few special bequests and such it stays the same, and his eldest daughter's eldest son inherits the lot."

"What? Nothing for his own sons?"

"That's already covered, as in the case of our incomes. The old man had his favorites—and they were his daughters."

Elizabeth briefly shut her eyes and shook her head. "In light of your speculations about—about how things were with them . . . well . . ." She spread her hands, unhappy with the ugly idea.

"It explains much about Mother and why she is the way she is," I said in a small voice, starting to feel a cold emptiness stealing over me. It was a kind of black helplessness that settled on my heart whenever this subject was mentioned. Perhaps if we had *known*, if any of us had had the least inkling of what her young life might have been like, then things might have been different for our mother. I wondered if we had a similar night like this awaiting us in the nebulous future, requiring that we shout at her coffin to exorcise our guilt.

"God forbid," I whispered.

"What?" Elizabeth gave a little start, having perhaps also been in the thrall of dismal thoughts. "Forbid what?"

"Just thinking aloud. It's nothing. Well-a-day, I wish I could get drunk, but I expect if I mixed brandy with my usual beverage it would just send me to sleep."

She straightened her shoulders. "Yes, and we all know how alarming *that* is."

"Nothing for it, then, I shall have to brave the family sans defenses."

"You've plenty of better ones to make up for that lack, little brother. What was the problem you had with the young man who left you so fast? I saw how you were speaking to him. Who was he?"

"Thomas Ridley's loving cousin Arthur Tyne, and he was either hoping for revenge or to make a name for himself as a duelist. He tried to provoke me tonight."

"Good God! You're not—"

"I've had enough of fire-eating, dear sister. I sent him off for good."

"But if he insulted you and you allowed him to get away with it—"

"He didn't, my honor is unsullied. Not that I give hang for him, but I'm just not in a hurry to send the dolt to hell for just being a dolt. Now, if he'd said anything against *you*, funeral or not, he'd be wishing he hadn't."

"You'd kill him?"

"No, but I'd serve him as well as I served his poxy-faced cousin."

"But Thomas wasn't poxy," she said thoughtfully. "In fact he's . . . Jonathan, what *are* you laughing about?"

CHAPTER
–11–

Even the most entertaining funeral must end sometime.

Those mourners who were not staying the night began to take themselves home, causing much bustling for the servants as they prepared things. New torches were lighted, carriages were brought around, farewells were exchanged, and one by one the relatives departed, leaving Fonteyn House a bit roomier than before. Those who remained behind, either because of their reluctance to face the weather or the fact that they lived too far away, were lodged in every likely and unlikely corner of the house.

Clarinda and Elizabeth oversaw things, each bringing her own expertise in organization to the problems that arose, from a shortage of blankets to what would be served to break the morning fast. My talents for such matters were sadly undeveloped, but I made myself useful directing people to this room or that, according to the list I'd been given.

After all were settled, I planned to return to Oliver's house as usual, since my bed of earth was there. Thus would I be spared the task of having to influence a veritable army of servants into ignoring my peculiar sleeping arrangements. Elizabeth had been staying at Fonteyn House since the day after Aunt Fonteyn's death and would yet be lodging here, this time with a roomful of other young women.

"How enviable," I said lightly.

"You may think so, but they're bound to talk until dawn, wanting to know all about you."

"Well, try to be as discouraging as you can. The ones I've met always seem to think that any stray unmarried male is only interested in finding a wife."

"I know, that's been made abundantly clear to me since we moved into Oliver's and started getting callers. The ladies coming by to see you outnumber the gentlemen paying respects to me by nine to four. Perhaps I should be jealous of you."

"Rather blame it on the shortsightedness of the London men. There's also the possibility that they may feel the same about marriage as I."

"I think not, little brother, I've already gotten three proposals."

"What?"

She laughed at my stricken expression. "One was from a mature lad of ten who was pleased with my face."

"And the others?"

"Fortune-hunting cousins on the Fonteyn side of the family."

Now didn't that sound familiar? "What did you say?"

"I told them that my aunt's funeral was hardly the place to be making marriage proposals."

"But that's not a proper refusal," I said, worried. "They might be back."

"Indeed they might," she agreed. "One of them was rather handsome in a horsy sort of way. I wonder if he is descended from Cousin Bucephalus?"

"Good God, Elizabeth, you're not seriously—"

"Certainly not, but I want to have some enjoyment of life while it's still mine to enjoy. When I think of what a cheerless, bitter existence Aunt Fonteyn made for herself, I could just weep at the waste and sadness of it."

"After the awful things she's said and done you can feel sorry for her?"

"Wounded animals, Jonathan," she reminded me. "It's not their fault that someone's been cruel to them. With that in mind, it's easy to understand how they might lash out at those who stray too close."

"Does this mean you'll form a more lenient attitude toward Mother?"

She made a wry face. "You do ask a lot, don't you? I suppose I must then say yes, but then again, it's easy for one to be tolerant when one's source of irritation is several thousand miles away."

"Very well, I'll ask you again when she's closer."

"I'm sure you will." Humor lurked in her dry tone, but I sensed that it was meant to cover some well-concealed low spirits.

"Are you going to be all right here?" I lifted a hand to indicate the vast house. "I mean after the funeral and all. I can take you home, y'know."

She shook her head decisively. "I'm fine. It's not what I'm used to, but I don't mind a little change now and then. Besides, I'm needed here. Poor Oliver's going to be feeling the torments of hell when he wakes tomorrow, and I thought I'd try one of Dr. Beldon's remedies on him."

"And what would that be?"

"Tea with honey and mint. Better than moss snuff for his head, I'm sure." She wilted a little. "I hope that they're all right, too. Father and the others, I mean."

"As do I, but I'm sure they are, so please don't worry. You've had more than your share of it already. Getting on well with Clarinda?"

"Very well, thank you. She's quite different from Edmond. I wonder how they ever got together."

"Who knows?" I said with a shrug, not really caring.

We said good night, and I promised to be back soon after sunset tomorrow. Oliver's new status as master of Fonteyn House required that he remain in it for some time longer before returning to his own home. As I put on my cloak and wrapped up against the wind, I speculated on whether he would forsake his other household and move back. For all the gloomy corners, it was still a fine big place, and he had promised changes. Heavens, he might even open the shutters and put in some more windows. That would make Grandfather Fonteyn spin in his coffin, and I could think of no one more deserving of the disturbance, unless it might be his eldest daughter. Unlike Elizabeth, I found it difficult to summon compassion for the wretched woman even if she was dead.

On my way out I saw Edmond and the unpleasant Arthur Tyne with their heads together by the main door. I hung back, wanting to avoid both of them. They were garbed for the weather, ready to leave; Edmond was probably headed home, the same as I. Perhaps he didn't mind abandoning Clarinda to her own devices for now, not that anyone remained in the house to tempt her to an indiscretion. The guests were either too young or old, too married or the wrong gender for her—unless one wished to count Oliver. She might find him attractive, I knew, but on the other hand he was dead drunk and not likely to be of much use to her.

I fidgeted, wishing Edmond and Arthur would get on with themselves so I could go. Perhaps I could just vanish and float past them. I'd planned to exercise myself in that manner on the trip home, anyway, providing the wind wasn't too much of a nuisance.

"Jonathan?" A woman whispered from the darkness of the hall behind me, giving me a start.

I squinted against the shadows and made out her figure, then her face. "Clarinda?"

She remained in place, partially hidden, so I went to her. Reluctantly. Edmond had only to look over and see me, and if he somehow recognized his wife's form in the—

"What is it?" I whispered back, my neck hairs rising.

"I must talk with you."

Oh, dear. Was this the prelude to another seduction to be consummated in some deserted room? "Well, I was just leaving, y'see—"

"This is important. I want only a minute. Please come away."

Her tense tone hardly seemed appropriate for so delicate a thing as a carnal interlude. Perhaps the nearby threat of Edmond was providing a cooling mitigation for her normally ardent nature.

With him discouragingly in mind—not to mention uncomfortably close—I cast a fearful look 'round, then followed her into the deeper darkness of the hall.

She made her way with frequent glances behind to make sure I was there. She tiptoed, swiftly, with her skirts barely making a whisper over the floor. Reluctant to draw any attention as well—especially Cousin Edmond's—I imitated her example of being quiet.

We passed a number of rooms, heading for the far reaches of the house, ultimately ending up in what for me was a most familiar chamber. There was the same settee; the same bust of Aristotle (or one of the Caesars) rested on the mantel as before. The draperies were drawn owing to mourning, and this time the fireplace warmly blazed, but otherwise all was the same as it had been that Christmas when we'd shared a most happy and vigorous encounter here.

Johnny Boy, whatever are you letting yourself in for? I thought, but it took no real effort on my part to guess what she had in mind. Heavens, but this would be a serious exercise in diplomacy to make an escape without causing her offense.

She shut the door, turning to face me. Her manner was very nervous, quite different from the randy, confident woman I'd known before. Something was wrong.

"What is it?" I asked.

Her eyes were fixed on mine. "I must ask if Edmond has said anything to you."

"About what?"

She gestured at the room. "What do you think? You do know why he hates you so, don't you?"

"I assumed it was because he was aware of our—ah—past liaison."

"Has he spoken to you about it?"

"No. Not one word."

She seemed extremely relieved to hear it, slumping a bit. "That's good. I saw him glaring so at you earlier, and then when he went upstairs to find out why Oliver was making such a row . . . well, I wasn't sure what to think."

"I've gotten nothing more than some hard looks from him. It's obvious he doesn't care for my company. Not that it really matters."

"But it does," she hissed. "He can be very dangerous, Jonathan."

"I don't doubt it, but he doesn't worry me. Is that what troubles you? You think he might try to harm me?"

"Yes. He's a difficult man and has a particular hatred for you over the other—the other young men I've known." She watched my reaction. "Good. I'm glad you're not going to go all gallant and pretend you weren't aware of them."

She'd made mention of them herself once upon a time, but it seemed more politic to say nothing. "I can only think that they are most fortunate that you should choose to grace them with your company."

The flattery that worked so well on Molly Audy had a similar effect on Clarinda; she broke into a most charming smile. "You have a pleasant memory of me, then?"

"It is one of my treasures. I recall every moment of your most generous gift to me."

"And to myself," she added. "God, but you make me remember it all afresh even now. You've grown even more handsome since. More muscle, too." She gave herself a shake, rolling her eyes. "Back to business, Clarinda."

"What business?" I asked. "A warning to stay out of Edmond's way? I'm already keen to do just that, so you needn't be troubled. But why does he hate me more than the others?"

She looked long at me, studying my face before finally giving an answer. "He hates you because I took a fancy to you that Christmas right here in this house, right under his nose. But I couldn't help myself. He'd been perfectly beastly to me that day, and you were so sweet and kind and *different*. Oh, damn, this must sound like I was with you just to spite him, but that's not true. I wanted to be with someone I *liked*, who liked me in return, as you seemed to."

"Believe me, my affection was quite genuine. It's not something a man can falsify."

She arched a brow. "You'd be surprised, my dear, but bless you for saying so. As for your affection for me now . . . well, I sense that you're somewhat more cautious these days."

"It's because of your being married."

"Married to Edmond?"

"No, just married, period. It's not in my nature to . . ."

"Ah, I see. Fornication's one thing, but adultery's quite another?"

I had to laugh a little, she said it so prettily. "That's it, exactly."

"You are such a sweet fellow. I see no real distinction between the two, myself, but can respect that you do." She pushed from the door, going to the settee, sitting wearily. "Such a ghastly day it's been. This is the first time I've had a bit of quiet for myself and enjoyable conversation with another. I hope I wasn't too alarming when I lured you back here."

"A bit mysterious, nothing more."

"I had to be, what with Edmond in plain sight, but you were about to leave, and I wanted a word with you on this before you got away."

"It couldn't wait until a better time?"

"When might that be with this houseful? I had to act while the chance existed, while you were alone and no one else about to see and tell tales. Please say that you will be careful around him."

"Very careful. He's not likely to give challenge, is he?"

"No. Not that he's a coward to dueling, but the scandal involved would be abhorrent to him. He's very proper, y'know."

That sparked a question in me. "Clarinda, if you would not mind my asking you something personal . . ."

"After what we've shared here? What have I to hide? Ask away."

"I was only wondering why you did . . . why you . . . that is, does Edmond not fulfill his duty toward you?"

She stared blankly a moment, then softly laughed. "Goodness, that is personal—but easily answered. The fact is that Edmond cares for me in his own fashion and I care for him in mine, but we are two extremely different people with different tastes and appetites. To be perfectly honest, the main reason we married was that he wanted a stronger connection within the family by fostering Aunt Fonteyn's pet nephew, and I very much wanted security and a father for my boy. Boys," she corrected, flashing me a rueful look.

"We've had a child since, y'know."

"Yes, Oliver mentioned something of it, congratulations. But I thought your children were taken care of by Grandfather's estate."

"To a degree, but Edmond has friends throughout London that will help them when they're older. It's not enough to have money, one must have influence as well, but being in law yourself, you understand that."

"Yes, I do have an idea on the importance of influence," I said, smiling at my unnatural talent in that area.

"As for the interest I have in handsome young men, well, I just can't seem to help myself. Edmond knew about it before our marriage, and we talked about how we would conduct things afterward. He said he wouldn't mind as long as I was discreet, but that didn't last long. He tries not to be jealous, but sometimes he . . ."

"He what? He doesn't mistreat you, I hope?"

Her eyes suddenly dropped and she primly laced her fingers together. "No more than many other husbands with their wives."

"What do you mean by that?"

"Now, Jonathan, I must insist you stop there, as what goes on between us is really not your business. He can be churlish, but I know how to handle him." She still wasn't looking at me.

After her warnings, I could only assume them to have been inspired by her direct experience with his temper. The idea of him harming her in any way was sickening. Perhaps I could arrange an interview with Edmond on the subject. A private little talk to spare Clarinda from future harm . . . Yes, that was very appealing to me. On the other hand, if an alternative presented itself, it should also be explored. My influence, unless regularly reinforced, had its limitations.

"Can you not leave him? I mean, that is, if you don't love him—"

She sighed and shook her head. "God have mercy, but you are so young and dear. You have no idea how complicated life can be for a woman."

"I'm not entirely ignorant. If you need a place to go, Oliver will gladly put you up here and protect you."

She was shaking her head again. "No, no, no, it's impossible or I'd have done that ages ago with Aunt Fonteyn. I have to live the life I've got, but that's all right, I'm happy enough. Besides, it's not as bad as you seem to be imagining. He's very decent most of the time, but the funeral has upset him greatly. I was thinking that with you here he might be tempted to do something rash."

I again reassured her of my intent to avoid all trouble with Edmond.

"Then I shall be relieved on your account. I should feel awful if anything happened to you because of him."

"You flatter me with your concern."

"Flatter? It's more than flattery on my part. My dear, you have no idea of the depth of pleasure you've given me."

"It was so brief, though."

"But treasured, as you've said. Of course, we can always make another happy memory for ourselves . . . if you like."

Oh, but did she not have a bewitching smile? I couldn't help but feel that delightful stirring through all my body as I looked at her. She'd not altered much, a little fuller of figure, but that just made more of her to explore. I wondered if her thighs were as white and silken as I remembered. . . .

Don't be a fool, Johnny Boy.

It wasn't just that she was married, though that was a major detraction; it was my change that made me hesitate over her invitation.

I could surge upon her here and now like a tide and bring her to a point where she wouldn't notice my biting in and drinking from her until it was all over. But then she'd want an explanation, and I wasn't about to sit down and tell her my life's story concerning Nora. Enough people knew already. No more.

Or I could make her forget about the blood-drinking part, but Clarinda deserved better treatment than that. It was different when I was with women like Jemma at The Red Swan; their favors were for sale and well paid for, but to treat Clarinda in the same cavalier manner smacked of theft in a way. Or rape. Certainly *I* was not comfortable with either idea.

Perhaps if there was a possibility of having a lengthy

liaison with her as I'd had with Molly, I might then . . .

No, that wouldn't be right, either. Not with Edmond lurking around any given corner as we arranged trysts for ourselves. I liked Clarinda, but not that much.

Then there was Elizabeth to consider.

And Oliver.

One look at Clarinda's throat and they'd know what was going on.

No, it was simply too embarrassing. I couldn't possibly . . .

Still, I could go in, leaving my mark on an area not readily visible to others. Her soft belly or the inside of one of those wondrous thighs suggested themselves readily to my hot imagination. The very thought made my mouth dry and my corner teeth begin to extend. I put a hasty hand to my upper lip, trying to push them back.

But even with that caution taken I'd have the same problem as before, having to explain everything about myself to her.

Then again, I *could* just pleasure Clarinda in the more acceptable fashion. I was yet capable of that, but how frustrating since it denied me any kind of a consummation. And if, in the throes of the event, I lost control and took from her anyway . . . I knew myself well enough. Once started it was hard for me to stop, for once the passions are aroused, it's all too easy to forget solemn promises made when the mind is cool and capable of sensible thought.

No. Not this time, sweet Cousin.

Damnation.

"Is something wrong, Jonathan?"

My debate was much like the other I'd held with myself in this room, running through my head in the blink of an eye. Only this time I would have to steel myself and hold to my decision. "I wish things—circumstances—could be other than what they are."

"Such as my being married?"

I nodded, grateful to have her taking that as the most obvious excuse for my refusal. "You are a most beautiful, desirable lady, and it is with the greatest reluctance that I must decline your gift."

Another rueful smile. "Then I shall have to be satisfied with a memory?"

"I fear you must, as I must. I do apologize."

"Oh, nonsense. You've not lost your manners, anyway. Yours is the most polite refusal I've ever gotten. Besides, I can hardly force you to bed me—not that I wouldn't like to *try*—but I've no wish to impose upon your honor."

I thanked her for her consideration, then begged to take my leave. "It's a bit of a walk home for me—"

"Walking? You're going to *walk* in this weather?"

"The sleet's stopped and the wind is down. The cold air should be most reviving after the press of tonight's gathering."

"You are perfectly mad," she said, with something between admiration and alarm.

I waved a careless hand. "You are not the first who has made that observation, madam. Nor, I think, the last, but I enjoy a good walk and—"

"No doubt," she interrupted, standing. "Well, my dear cousin, if you are sure of your decision—you are?—then I shall have to wish you Godspeed home. It is very late, after all. . . ."

With that broad a hint placed before me, it would have been rude not to take it. I bowed over her hand, wished her a very good evening, and let myself out.

Apparently that was her room for the night, for she did not follow as I made my way back to the entry hall. I wondered if she'd arranged to have it for her use with a mind to sharing it with me. Now, there was an interesting thought. Instead of a hasty and surreptitious coupling, we could have had hours and hours to—

None of that, Johnny Boy. You've made your bed, and you will *sleep in it—even if it is empty.*

Damnation.

Again.

Out the front doors and down along the long drive I went, moving briskly.

The sleet had indeed stopped and the wind had lessened, but that which remained was still knife-sharp and unfor-

giving. Though I possessed a degree of immunity to the
cold, I was not going to unduly strain it. Halfway between
Fonteyn House and Oliver's home lay The Red Swan, and
there I planned to stop for a time and warm myself by
taking full advantage of its hospitality. Clarinda had gotten
me quite thoroughly stirred up, and I had a mind to settle
those stirrings in the company of the lovely Jemma or one
of her sisters in the trade.

Dour Cousin Edmond was also in my mind. If he was
treating Clarinda roughly, I wanted to do something about
it. We'd likely be running into each other again soon, and
it would be the work of a moment to take him to one side
to deliver a firm speech on the subject of treating his wife
gently from now on. I'd done similar work with Lieutenant
Nash often enough to curb his greed; why not again with
Edmond for his temper?

Then the thought of Nash reminded me of home and of
Father and all the others. I hoped that he was all right, as
I'd so quickly assured Elizabeth. We had no letters from
him yet, but it was getting on into winter, and the crossing
was bound to be more difficult for the ships that followed
ours. The war would cause additional delays . . . wretched
business, that. As if there weren't enough troubles in the
world, those fools and their congress were wanting to add
to them. Nothing like a bit of war, famine, and death to provide
entertainment for those who would not be directly involved
with such horrors.

Death . . .

I'd have to write something tonight on it, or at least begin
writing. It had been several days since the accident and
past time that I sent off the bad news about Aunt Fonteyn,
though it could hardly be called bad from Oliver's point of
view now. (I'd not mention *that* in my missive.) I'd enclose
a mourning ring for Mother in the packet and hope she
wouldn't make life too hellish for Father. God, she might
even find a way to blame him for the business. I wouldn't
put it past her.

Worry, worry, worry.

So sounded my footsteps as I paced carefully down the
drive, avoiding patches of ice. The ground was hard, prob-

ably frozen. The tip of my cane made no impression in it. Just as well Aunt Fonteyn went into her niche in the mausoleum instead of a grave; it'd be much too much work for the sexton and his fellows to chop their way down through this stuff. It was probably one of the only times in her existence that she'd done anything for the convenience of another person.

Wicked thought, Jonathan.

I grinned. Not all that capering in the mausoleum had been for Oliver's benefit. I'd thoroughly enjoyed myself— once I'd gotten over the unease of being there in the first place. Nasty spot, all cold stone and so far from everything and probably just as cold in the summer. A pity it wasn't summer; then she wouldn't have had any ice to slip on. What had the old crow been doing out in the middle of the maze for, anyway?

An assignation with some man? Not likely with her supremely bad temperament and acidic nature. She'd ever been very clear in her views on carnal exchanges, being so strongly opposed to the act that I wondered just how Oliver had ever come to be conceived.

It was also unlikely that she'd been enjoying the innocent folly of the maze for its own sake. Again, her temperament forbade it.

Also, the wind that night had been almost as keen and cutting as it was now. She would have needed some strong reason to give up the comfort of a fire to be out there.

To meet someone for a private talk? But why go to the maze when there were any number of warm rooms in the Bolyns' house to accommodate a discreet conversation? And what had she to talk about? Whom would she talk with?

My speculations were nothing new; many others both before and after the funeral had asked as much from one another, but without forming any satisfactory answer. The gossips in Fonteyn House could only conclude that It Was Very Mysterious.

But it had all been investigated. No one at the Masque had particularly noticed her leaving the house for the garden that night. They'd been too involved with their own pleasures to pay attention to one disagreeable old woman. Those

friends as she'd been with at the ball had likewise nothing
to contribute; besides, if she'd been meeting anyone, they'd
have come forward by now, wouldn't they? But if not, then
why not?

Heavens, I was getting as bad as the gossips.

It was easy for them to speculate, easy to wonder and
whisper, but so hard to—

Now who the devil was that?

Well ahead of me were the gates to the property, wide
open with torches on either side to mark the entry. Their
flames were nearly burned out by now. Had my eyes not
been so well suited to the dark, I'd have missed seeing
the figure entirely. A man it was, made anonymous by the
masking shroud of his cape. He stood in the shadows—or
what should have been shadows to anyone else—and his
posture suggested that he was waiting for someone.

A footpad? They usually operated within the warrens of
the city, where the harvest was more abundant, not away
here on the West End, where the grand houses stood on
their own spacious grounds.

Then it jumped into my head that he might be a medical
student come to steal a body for study. Oliver had filled me
with plenty of grisly tales on the difficulties of mastering
anatomy. So desperate were some for specimens that if they
couldn't get a corpse from Tyburn, then they resorted to
theft for their needs. Good God, but that would be the worst,
for Aunt Fonteyn to end up as a subject on a dissection
table somewhere. I hadn't liked her, but she deserved better
than that.

Having come to this conclusion—and it seemed likely,
given the late hour and the fact the funeral had hardly been
a secret—I debated how best to deal with the situation.
Only one man was visible to me, and though one alone
could easily bear away her corpse, I could not discount
the possibility of his having allies present. The macabre
nature of such a dark errand as grave robbing must dictate
that the thief bring along at least one friend to bolster his
courage.

I held to the same pace, pretending not to see the fellow.
He must have been aware of me by now, but made no move

to further conceal himself. I'd fully expected him to do so as I got closer, and that's when I'd planned to spring upon him for a reckoning on his intrusion here.

He continued to wait, though. Perhaps he was a footpad, after all, or some highwayman sheltering behind the gates, hoping for a late traveler on the road outside to prey upon. I worked the catch on my cane, readying to draw forth its hidden blade. There's nothing like a yard of Spanish steel for discouraging a man from breaking the law—unless it's a six-shot flintlock revolver by Powell of Dublin. Unfortunately, I'd left that most useful weapon at Oliver's house in the mistaken belief I would not need it while attending a funeral.

He'd not moved yet. I was nearly to the gate, close enough so that even ordinary eyes could see him. As it seemed pointless to extend the fraud of being ignorant of his presence, I slowed and stopped, looking right at him.

"Who are you, sir, and what business have you to be here?" I demanded, half expecting him to run like a startled cat at my hail.

He made no reply.

His lower face was covered by the wide scarf wrapped 'round his head and hat; the brim of the hat was pushed well forward to further obscure things.

"I'm addressing you, sir. I expect an answer." I stepped toward him and pulled the blade free of the cane.

That got a reaction. He slipped away suddenly from the gate, moving to my right, where some trees offered a greater darkness to hide in. Because of the wind battering my ears, I couldn't hear his progress, so he seemed to glide along very fast in preternatural silence. Well, he wasn't the only one who could show a bit of heel. I hurried after, almost catching him up until he reached a particularly fat tree and darted sideways. It was a feint, though. Instead of waiting to ambush me from there, he sprinted ahead, perhaps thinking its intervening trunk would conceal his progress. All it did was speed me up. I lengthened my stride, blurring past the tree—

And on the edge of vision glimpsed something scything down in a fearful rush. Instinct made me throw my right arm high to shield my head. The thing, whatever it was, crashed solidly into my forearm, sending a stunning shock through my whole body. My headlong pursuit immediately ceased as I dropped straight onto the frozen earth like a block of stone.

I was aware of a terrible pain along my arm, as if a giant had seized me there and was pinching it between finger and thumb. The agonizing pressure changed to an agonizing burning so great that the force of it left me immobile for several terrible moments. I could see and hear nothing, taste and smell nothing; the only sense I had was for the grinding torment that had fastened itself to my flesh.

What had they done to me?

They. On the dim borders of the mind between sense and nonsense, I was aware of at least two of them. Footpads or grave robbers, it mattered not. Whoever had struck me might do so again. The panicked thought whipped through my mind.

Helpless. I was utterly *helpless*.

I must get *away* . . . vanish . . .

But the pain continued, and I lay there wholly susceptible to its reality, quite horribly solid.

Couldn't move. Whatever the damage, it must be very bad to paralyze me like this. As bad as I'd ever known before. Worse.

I tried again to take myself out of the world. This effort made the burning hotter than it already was, as if someone had stabbed a fiery brand into my arm. I instantly ceased trying and cursed instead.

"He's alive," a man above me said.

"Good," said another a little breathlessly. The one I'd been chasing apparently.

Bloodsmell. My own.

It was all over me.

Ice mixed with the fire as the wind struck the red flow of my life, chilling it. The simple knowledge that I must have been bleeding freely was enough to raise another panic-inspired attempt to vanish.

Another flare of pain. I stopped and cursed again.

"How does it *feel*, Mr. Barrett?" the breathless man

taunted. "That's more than a scratch from the look of it. You'll not jump up so fast this time, I'm sure."

I knew his voice now. Thomas Ridley.

"He'll bleed to death," his companion pointed out. Arthur Tyne.

"He's going to die one way or another, but I'd rather it be me that dispatches him."

Sweet God.

I was on my left side, exactly as I'd fallen. I saw their boots and little else. Couldn't really move. Not at all. Just softly curse.

"Listen to him whine," said Ridley, enjoying himself.

"You would, too, with something like that in you."

"Then pull it free and see what other noise he can make."

"We don't want to wake anyone, Tom."

"Who's to hear? Come on and do it."

Arthur bent and worked at something, and I madly thought he was tearing my arm from its socket. The fire plaguing me before seemed like cold ashes compared to this. I couldn't help but cry out. The sound itself was frightening, as if it had come from someone else. I did not know my own voice.

Ridley was laughing, giggling like a young child.

No breath left in me to curse. Could only lie there and feel as if my arm had been thrust into a furnace.

"I think I've killed him," said Arthur. He did not seem unduly worried over the possibility.

Ridley crouched next to me, turning me over. He was still swathed in his scarf and cloak; the latter had slipped open enough to reveal his right arm in a sling. He moved carefully so as not to jar it. He put his left hand on my chest, but withdrew it when he saw me glaring at him, very much alive.

"Not yet," he said, grinning. "He'll last a bit longer, I think. Though I'll lay good odds he'll wish otherwise. Here's a pretty souvenir." He reached over to pick up my blade and scabbard.

"You won't want to keep that. Someone'll know it."

"I'm not planning to keep it, but I will put it to good use." He rose slowly. "Stand him up and let's get on from here."

Stand? He must have been mad.

"Right, take this, then." Arthur gave Ridley a sword he'd been holding. Blood was all along its blade. My blood. My God, he'd hit me with *that?* It should have taken my arm right off. Maybe it would have, too, had I been an ordinary man.

Arthur was a strong lad. He had no trouble shifting me around like a sack of grain to hook my left arm 'round his shoulders. It didn't matter to him whether I could walk or not, he'd drag me along regardless. It didn't matter to me, either. As soon as he'd hauled me upright, the agony blasted through my body again. I bit out a grunt of protest, which was ignored.

With a heave, he boosted himself straight, taking me with him. The sudden shift from lying down to fully upright had its effect. My vision flickered, then was lost altogether. Myself, the world, everything . . . simply ceased to be.

CHAPTER

–12–

The god-awful pain in my arm drew me out of the comfort of nothingness.

I woke aware only of the hurt, lying on something hard and brutally cold. With no understanding of what had happened, I moved not a muscle. It seemed . . . safer.

Some battered portion of sense that was not wholly consumed by the distraction of pain whimpered, feebly protesting something I was unable to comprehend.

It was afraid.

Things had gotten bad.

They could get worse.

They will *get worse. That's why you're afraid.*

The thought seemed to take weight and size in my skull. I didn't want it there, but hadn't the strength to get rid of it. No other thoughts could raise themselves against it.

You have to get up. You have to get away.

But I was hurt. I could not move. To move meant more pain.

To not move means death.

Very well, but something small first. Like opening my eyes.

High overhead, thick with shadows, stretched a broad slice of marble ceiling. Walls of the same pale stone seemed to rush straight toward me. The hard and cold thing I lay upon . . . also marble, but not part of the floor; I was somewhat higher, as if floating above it. Where . . . ?

Down and away to one side was a rectangle of stone leaning against the wall, and propped near it a brass plate with engraved lettering spelling out Aunt Fonteyn's name. Above them was an open niche and just visible within was one end of her coffin.

The *mausoleum?* How had I come to be here?

They'd taken me . . . one of them had . . .

First I'd been hurt, then helped—no, that wasn't right. One of them had struck me . . .

Had struck my *arm*.

Struck to kill.

Yes.

The whimpering increased, became a full throated howl of terror, its echoes battering upon my ears from within.

Ridley and Arthur.

There, I'd put names to the shapes that had attacked, had taken me to this house of death.

They weren't here. That was good.

I was quite alone.

And lying on Grandfather Fonteyn's sarcophagus.

Already frightened and not thinking straight, I lurched up—and instantly regretted the action. The fire in my arm blazed high, and at the same time the top of my head felt as if it was coming off. I fell back the way I'd been, breathless, though I had no need of breath.

Lying quietly did not aggravate the hurts, so I lay quietly and tried to reason away the superstitious dread that had seized me. After all, the silent residents here were long past doing harm to anyone. It had just been a shock to realize I was on the old devil's last resting place. It's one thing to dance on it when one is in full control, and very much another to waken on so harsh a bed, injured and frightened and too confused to understand what was going on.

I listened and watched, wanting very much to find some understanding. Ridley and Arthur, if they were still nearby, were out of sight of the mausoleum door and either keeping quiet or too far away to be heard. Nothing outside the structure moved, except the wind shivering against the trees. I hated the sound they made, the loneliness of it, as if God had abandoned us and the dead together forever in this bleak spot.

Steady, Johnny Boy. No need for that, you're scared enough.

Right. Back to the problem at hand.

That Ridley was determined to avenge himself for the humiliation of losing the duel was obvious. He'd recruited a cousin to be his ally; for all I knew Arthur might even have been one of the Mohocks who had plagued me on my first night in London. I hadn't seen all their faces, since I'd been incorporeal part of the . . .

Refuge. Healing. Mine, if I could but *vanish.*

Cursing myself for a dolt for not thinking of it sooner, I tried to summon the nothingness back again, this time on my terms.

This was not my usual swift, effortless leaving, though, but an imperfect and prolonged striving. My vision clouded, very slowly, and did not quite depart, which meant that I did not quite depart.

Raising my left hand to judge my progress, I saw that it was only partially transparent and, no matter how hard I tried, stubbornly remained in that halfway state. Disturbed, I ceased and became solid again.

Much too solid. My poor body seemed to weigh a thousand pounds. I was as weak as an infant. My guts felt as if they'd been scraped out, jumbled, and dropped carelessly back, not quite into place. For several bad moments I thought I might faint once more.

Lie still, still, still. Let it pass.

Thus did I obey the soft dictate of instinct, not that I was remotely able to ignore it.

Bit by bit, my strength returned, a ghost of it, anyway. At least I was able to move a little and not lie flaccid as a corpse.

Ugh.

Must have been my surroundings.

For all this, my arm . . . was improved. The furnace still raged, still seared my flesh, but its heat was focused on a single area rather than the whole limb. Healing had begun.

Very cautiously I lifted up on my left elbow to take a look at myself. The right sleeve of my coat had been cut through; it and much of the rest of my clothing on that side was soaked with blood. I'd lost a terrifying amount of it. No wonder I was so wretchedly enervated.

And with that knowledge came the *hunger*.

Now it awakened and surged, washing over me, colder than sea spray. My mouth sagged with need. My corner teeth budded, lengthened, fixing themselves hard into place. I absolutely had to feed. Feed immediately.

But how? I barely had the strength to sit, much less walk, much less seek out food. But to lie here starving like a sick dog in the gutter . . .

No. Not for me. I had to get up and would. The hunger would not let me do otherwise.

Stiffly I pushed myself away from the freezing stone slab, twisting at the hips to drag my legs around. They dangled off the edge of the sarcophagus. I shifted again and dropped, jolting as my feet struck the floor.

Swaying. God, but I was *dizzy*.

I slapped a hand on the stone, desperately trying to steady myself. Falling would only complicate things further, and I had more than enough difficult tasks to occupy me.

Like getting to the doorway.

One step, another, teetering like a drunk. Two more steps and I was at the door, left hand flailing to grab for its iron gate. I caught it just in time, saving myself from dropping on my face.

None of this activity made me feel better. I paused to get a look at the agony in my arm. The coat sleeve gaped wide over a fearful wound. Arthur's blade had cut through the thick part of my forearm right down to the bone. The flesh was well parted here, revealing details about the layers of skin and muscle that I would much rather not have known. I looked away, belly churning, ready to turn itself out.

At least I wasn't bleeding. My body probably had nothing more to spare.

Cold. Colder than before. Cloak useless against it.

Then *move*.

It was a quarter mile to the house. A quarter mile to the stables. All the blood I'd ever need waited there. I had only to walk to get it.

Walk.

Or crawl.

Shut up and move.

I pushed on the gate, following its outward swing. The hinges squawked.

"Here! What's this?"

God have mercy. Arthur was standing hardly five paces away. I'd given him a start. Fair enough, for he'd done the same and more for me. I couldn't budge. What would be the point?

"Thought you'd gone and died on us," he said, hurrying toward me. "Not that it matters, but Tom'll be more than pleased. Come along with you."

From this I got the impression that we were alone. Well and good, though if we'd been in the middle of Covent Garden on a theater night, I'd not have been able to stop myself. With a last burst of hunger-inspired strength I lunged at him, reaching.

Instinct is a strange thing. Much of the time we ignore it, but in certain select and extreme moments, it can completely take us over, causing us to do extraordinary things in the name of survival that we would never otherwise attempt. Had I been in my right mind I'd have known it to be impossible to tackle Arthur the way I did. Nor would I have been able to knock him senseless, rip away his neckcloth, and tear into his throat as I did.

But then . . . I was not in my right mind.

I was hurt and hungry and terrified and desperate and this was my enemy.

And his body flowed with life. My life.

The stuff crashed into my mouth, the first swallow gone before I was aware of the act. This was not a leisurely feeding for refreshment, but a frantic gorging for existence itself. I drank deeply, not tasting, aware of little else other than the overwhelming necessity to keep on drinking until the hurt ended and the vast hollow within was filled.

I woke out of it as quickly as I'd succumbed. One second I was a mindless thing of raw need and appetite, the next, a man again, suddenly realizing what I was doing.

Dear God, I was *killing* him.

I broke away. Blood on my lips. Blood seeping from the wounds in his throat.

He was deathly white and very still, but I put an ear to his chest and detected the fluttering of his heart. Its beating was too fast, I thought, for all to be well, but as long as he was yet alive . . . In truth, I was less concerned with the prospect of his death than the possibility of my being blamed for it. Callous? Perhaps, but I placed a higher value on my skin than his, and it would have been a damned shame to hang at Tyburn for the likes of him.

I found my feet and stood, the horrible dizziness fading. The burning in my arm was less pronounced than it'd been only moments ago. I'd have looked to see how far the healing had progressed, but decided to spare myself. Instead, I shut my eyes, concentrated, and felt the glad lightness slipping 'round me like a soft blanket as I vanished.

No burning. No pain at all. I felt the tug of wind, nothing more. How tempting it would be to let it carry me away through the woods and far from this place and its problems. So wonderfully, sweetly tempting.

But not the best thing to do, especially for Arthur. Like it or not, I would have to take care of him, which meant resuming form again and deciding how best to go about it.

The next time I felt the wind, it seemed as solid as myself, catching my cloak as if to sweep it from my shoulders. I grabbed the ends and pulled them close. Using both hands. Now I braved a glance at my wound and found it to be no more than a thick red welt of a scar halfway circling my arm, which was sore to the touch, but workable. Overall, I was yet extremely shaky. The blood had saved me, but much of its good had gone toward my healing. I'd want more before the night was out, and this time from a source that could spare it in abundance. A trip to the Fonteyn stables was in order, but before that I had to decide what to do about Arthur Tyne.

He'd freeze to death out here. He'd need warmth and care, though God knows what Oliver could do for him. I winced at the thought of Oliver, of having to try to explain this. Elizabeth would understand, but then she'd had a lot longer to get used to certain facts about my condition.

Later. I'd worry on it later.

Had I been at my full strength I could have carried him back to the house, but I was not, being hard pressed even to get him into the mausoleum. As he'd done before with me, now did I lay him out on the sarcophagus. I noticed I'd left some bloodstains on the marble from my occupation of the same spot and wondered if they might prove permanent, then concluded I didn't really care to know.

I further noticed my hat, lost when Arthur had attacked me, was at the foot of the thing, along with someone's sword and my own swordstick. The former's presence puzzled me, the latter I gladly repossessed. It was still in two pieces, which I remedied, slipping the blade into the stick and engaging the catch. I'd find a good use for it as a simple cane again, until I could bolster myself with more blood.

The wounds I'd made on Arthur's neck had stopped bleeding, but his skin had taken on a bluish cast. Whether from the cold or the damage I'd inflicted by draining him mattered not; with a grimace, I stripped off my cloak and drew it over him. It would be only a five-minute walk to the house, and I could stand up to the chill better than he for that long. As an afterthought, I pulled his neckcloth back and more or less knotted it into place, thus ensuring a bit more protection as well as covering the evidence of my madness.

"I'll be seeing you shortly," I muttered to him and turned to leave.

And alas, did not get far. Only to the gate. In time to see Ridley hurrying down the path from Fonteyn House with another figure behind him. A woman. What the—?

I would have liked to quit the business then and there, to vanish and pass them by and let them find Arthur and do as they pleased, but tired as I was, I was also damned curious.

And angry. I'd paid Arthur back for my injury, but not Ridley.

He and the woman were closer, heading purposefully toward the mausoleum. Melting into the shadows beyond the gate, I slipped behind the far side of the huge sarcophagus, and lay flat on the floor between it and the wall. If it looked as if one of them might come 'round, then would I vanish, but not before. I was of a mind to hear their talk.

"Arthur!" Ridley called impatiently for his cousin. He pushed the gate open and came in.

"*Arthur!*" called the woman in turn.

I recognized her voice, and the sheer surprise of it nearly made me raise up. As it was, all my skin seemed to leap from the shock. What in God's name was Clarinda doing out here with Thomas Ridley?

"Where is he?" she demanded of him.

"How the devil should I know?"

"Then find him. I'm freezing here."

Well-a-day. Wrapped in my cloak and in the darkness, it seemed that they'd mistaken Arthur's body for mine. I wondered how long that would last.

"You could have stayed in the house," Ridley pointed out.

"No. I want to see it done."

He snorted. "You're already missed the best part."

She moved closer to the sarcophagus, but not too close, thank heaven. "You're sure he's—"

"Arthur took care of him, you needn't worry."

"But he was supposed to be shot," she said peevishly. *What?*

"Too late now. I'll just put swords in their hands and leave it at that."

"But if it doesn't look right . . ."

"It will, and even if anyone should raise a question, you and your precious Oliver can easily hush it up."

Oliver? My God, how was he involved in this? It was hard enough to believe that Clarinda was here and up to heaven knows what, but *Oliver?* I felt a sickening shift in the depths of my belly, ten times worse than any illness I'd ever known. Betrayal. Pale, ugly, unforgivable betrayal. I'd faced it before from Caroline Norwood, but for it to come from my good cousin, my dearest friend . . .

"Have you a candle and tinderbox?" Ridley asked her. "Good, then be useful and make some light. It's black as Hades in here."

"Afraid of the dark, are you?" she countered good-naturedly.

"No, but I can't work in it—not unless it's the right kind of work."

"Time for that afterward. Now get you along and find Arthur."

With a grunt of disappointment, Ridley went out, calling Arthur's name.

I waited with a patience I'd not been aware of possessing as she played with the tinderbox and coaxed sufficient flame from it to transfer to the candle. Its light was unsteady because of the air flowing in from the entry, but it served.

She placed the candle on one corner of the sarcophagus, then paced up and down to keep warm. When the sound of her steps indicated that she was walking away from me, I put a hand on the stone lid and boosted myself up. Damnation, but I was so insidiously weak, shaking from the exertion, but the look on Clarinda's face when she turned and saw me made the effort worth it.

An instant's surprise, an instinctive falling back, and then unhappy recognition.

"Good evening, Cousin," I said calmly.

Oh, but she was clever. Her eyes swept from me to Arthur Tyne and returned. She divined who was really wrapped in the cloak just that fast. Her gaze next fastened on my cut sleeve. In the dim light she'd not be able to see the blood against the black cloth, but the stains had crept as far as my waistcoat and shirt.

She made a step forward, one hand out as though to help. "You're hurt," she observed, putting a convincing tone of concern into her voice.

"But not dead." My own tone was such as to let her understand I was impervious to further attempts at deception.

She let her hand drop to rest on her skirts and suppressed a shiver. She was wrapped well for the weather, but I fancied any chill she felt now was not connected to the cold. "What went wrong?" she asked evenly, abandoning her playacting for a more sober demeanor. She pointed at Arthur.

"Does it matter?"

She made no reply.

"Why, Clarinda?" I whispered. "Tell me *why*."

More silence.

"Ridley I can understand, he wants revenge for the duel, but why are you involved in this? How?"

I waited in vain.

"Is he one of your lovers, then? Is he doing it for you because of that? Did he force a fight on me because of what happened with us four years past?" It sounded ludicrous even as I spoke it, but I couldn't imagine any other reason.

A smile twitched at the corners of her mouth. A singularly unpleasant smile. "You're remarkably close to the truth, Jonathan, but are too flattering to yourself."

"Then why? Why are you a part of this? What have you against me?" I moved closer, fully intending to force an answer from her, but in the blink of an eye she drew a dueling pistol from the pocket of her skirt and aimed it right at my chest. I stopped hardly two paces from its muzzle. Even an inexperienced shooter could not miss at that distance, and Clarinda appeared to be well acquainted with the workings of her gun.

"I've nothing against you, dear lad," she said, "but it's better for all concerned that you not be around Fonteyn House any longer."

"But *why*? And how is Oliver involved? Where is he?"

"Drunk in his room where you left him, I'm sure."

"How is he a part of this?"

She seemed startled. "He's not. Not yet."

Yet? "What do you mean? Answer me!"

But she held her peace and edged toward the entrance. "*Thomas!*"

There wasn't enough light, but I had to try. "Listen to me, Clarinda. I want you to hear me and—"

Perhaps she sensed the danger, somehow. She could not have known what I was trying to do, only that it was a threat.

She sighted along the muzzle and fired, just like that.

My only warning was the tiny pause as she aimed. Without hesitation, I made myself fade away—and just barely in time. I glimpsed the explosion and roar, but thank God did not feel the ball scorching through the space where I stood. Floated. For but an instant. A half second later and I was solid again.

Weak. I was so *weak*. Drained. Hollow. Swaying.

Clarinda watched me avidly. The powder flash in this dim chamber must have blinded her to my brief disappearance. She couldn't see that I was untouched. She was waiting for me to fall.

And fall I might. I'd used myself up, pushed myself too far, more of this and I might not—

Ridley appeared at the entrance. The mate to Clarinda's dueler was in his hand.

Damnation. Another vanishing would finish me. And if he fired, the shot might also finish me. I hadn't the strength to handle either.

I should have gone on to the stables, I thought, crumpling forward and letting myself gradually slip to the floor. Shutting my eyes, I held very still. Waiting. Hoping.

"What the devil's happened?" Ridley snarled. "Where did he come from?"

Clarinda's voice was high with the strain. "See if he's dead. Go on!"

"You—"

"*Go on!*"

Cautiously Ridley stepped past her and knelt by me, putting a hand on my heart. "Done for," he pronounced.

Thank God for that. Now if they'd only *leave*.

"You're sure?" My, but wasn't she anxious.

"He's gone, I say. What happened?"

Excited as she was, she managed to explain everything to him in a few short rushing words. He seemed caught between admiration for her nerve at being able to kill a man and anger that he'd been cheated of the task.

The winter cold was seeping up from the marble floor and into my very bones. I'd be shivering soon, giving myself away. *No, Johnny Boy, that would be a very bad idea. Let*

*them get on with their work, get out, and then you can
stagger to the stables and fill yourself.*

"Why'd you have to shoot him?" Ridley complained.
"Now how will it look? A sword cut *and* a pistol ball in
one—"

"It will seem as if they'd fired, wounding each other, then
finished themselves off with swords."

"But it won't lo—"

"I can't help that! We use what we have and make the
best of it. Now see to Arthur. Quickly."

Ridley abandoned me to look at his cousin. Arthur was
still with the living, which I found to be something of a
relief.

"Wake him," said Clarinda.

But alas for them, Arthur was quite unconscious. "What'd
the bastard do to him?" Ridley wanted to know, but I was
not planning to answer, having cares of my own.

"Never mind him, then," she said. "We'll manage without."

"The slab's too heavy. It was all we could do to move it
earlier. I need Arthur to—"

"Who's not going to wake until spring. I'll help you. Just
put your back into it."

With ill-grace, and grumbling, he acquiesced. I cracked
an eye open to see what they were about.

Using his good arm and with Clarinda's assistance, Ridley
dragged Arthur's body from the lid of the sarcophagus and
away to one side. He groaned and complained and favored
his wound, but Clarinda had little sympathy for him.

"You should have killed Jonathan outright at that bloody
Masque, not played with him," she reproved, catching her
breath.

"I thought I had. I *know* I—"

"Yes, you ran him through, so you've told me."

"Right through—and dropped him."

"Except that he got back up again to return the favor."

"Then perhaps you should have fought him yourself."

"I was busy elsewhere."

He gave a mirthless laugh.

"Come along," she said. "I can't be out here all night."

He sighed. "Very well, take that end and push, and I'll pull on the corner."

She did as directed, placing her hands against the edge of the slab covering the sarcophagus. After a bit of Herculean effort on their part, the thing budged. I saw then that the lid was divided into two great squares and that they were trying to move one of them. What devilry was this? Were they planning to hide me away in *there?*

They paused, panting awhile, then tried again, shifting it even more. Perhaps while they were busy with it, I could creep out, lose myself in the woods . . .

Someone *inside* the sarcophagus cursed. Clarinda and Ridley dodged back as a hand shot up from the opening they'd made. Ridley clawed hastily for his dueler and held it ready.

"Awake are you?" he said. "Out, then, and save us some trouble."

My hackles went up. A man began to emerge, a large man, moving slowly as though injured. He sucked air in and all but sobbed it out again. His mourning clothes were much disarrayed, and there was blood on his hands where he'd beaten them against the confines of his ghastly prison.

Edmond Fonteyn.

"Damn you to hell," he grated at them. His eyes were blazing. I could feel the hate, the sheer *fury* rolling from him, filling the room.

"We'll see you there first," said Ridley, showing his teeth. "All the way, now, there's a good fellow."

Edmond painfully struggled to haul his big frame free of the small opening. Clarinda watched from a safe distance behind Ridley. Both were between me and the door.

Finally out, Edmond leaned exhaustedly on the great stone box. He first saw Arthur, then me. I made my eyes fix sightless on nothing at all.

"My God. How many more, Clarinda?" he asked.

"Just you, husband," she softly answered.

"And you think you'll not swing for it?"

"I know I won't. It will seem as though you and Jonathan had your own private duel and killed each other." She smiled. "Over me, of course."

"No one will believe that."

"I'll make certain they do, never you worry. You've already helped things along. All that glaring at Jonathan—anyone with eyes could see how you despised him."

"And then what? You'll marry that fool?" He nodded at Ridley, whose eyes narrowed at the name-calling.

"No . . . not yet, anyway. But dear Cousin Oliver, now—"

"*Oliver?*" Edmond laughed.

"He likes me well enough, and I'll see to it that he has every chance to comfort this grieving widow."

"Oh, yes, you're good at that, aren't you?"

"Excellent good, Edmond." She smirked. "Well do you know yourself."

He started toward her, but Ridley told him to be still, using the gun to enforce his direction. "Let's finish this, Clarinda," he said. "I thought you were in such a hurry."

"All right, but I want to put things properly in order. Where are the swords?"

"There." Ridley indicated the end of the sarcophagus where I lay. She glided over, picking up the sword I'd found earlier.

"Where's the other?"

"In Barrett's cane. There's a trick catch—"

She bent and got it. "Oh, one of those things. How do I . . . yes, there it is." She drew the blade free, discarding the stick. She placed the blade on the floor near my hand, then put her empty pistol next to it. I watched through cracked lids.

"Come on," Ridley urged.

"Never you mind me, just make sure you hit Edmond properly."

"Do you want to do it?" he asked, exasperated.

She gasped a little. It sounded like a laugh. "Yes, I do."

"You've the devil in you, woman, and no mistake."

"Sure you want to marry her later?" Edmond queried. "I assume that's the final plan to all of this. First she marries Oliver, then she inherits his money. How do you plan to kill him, hey?"

I opened my eyes a bit more. None were paying attention to me. The hilt of my sword was only inches from my hand.

I moved enough to close my fingers around it.

Now what, Johnny Boy? Charge Ridley, waving and yelling, and hope he misses?

Possibly. If I could just stand up.

Edmond continued. "Will you arrange another duel? That is, if she doesn't kill you to keep you quiet."

Ridley laughed in his turn.

"Just look at her. Go ahead. Trust her. She'll soon serve you as you're serving me. See if she doesn't."

"She already *has*, Edmond. And what a marvelous fine piece she is to be sure."

"Joke if you like, but after tonight she won't need your help, you know. She'll soon have what she wants, the Fonteyn money and a protector she can twist round her finger. She won't need you at all."

"It's not working, husband," Clarinda put in. "Thomas and I understand each other too well for you to put doubts between us."

That seemed true enough, though it had been a good argument.

"Give me the pistol," she said.

"Not so close to him," Ridley cautioned. "Don't want him to grab it away from you, do you?"

They stepped back. Clarinda's skirts brushed against me.

Ridley handed over the dueler, swiftly, smoothly. The barrel wavered but a quarter inch, then she fixed it on Edmond. "Don't hit him to kill," he advised. "Remember he's supposed to last long enough for some sword play afterward."

"I know, I know. Where, then? His leg, shoulder—?"

"The stomach, my dear. Will you want to put the sword in yourself, too? To finish him?"

Edmond was dead white, but held his ground. Brave man.

"Yes," she answered. "I think I want to do that, as well."

There were Clarinda's feet peeking from under the hem of her gown. Not quite within reach, but if I let go my sword and . . .

"What will it feel like?" she wondered.

I twisted and dug my knees against the floor, reaching with both hands. Suddenly engulfed in a drift of black fabric and petticoats, I blundered heavily into her. She screeched in surprise as I tried to take hold of her legs. She kicked once and began to fall, overbalanced.

Ridley cursed and I had an impression of him starting for me until something large slammed into him. Edmond, probably. I left them to it, being busy myself.

Clarinda kicked again, viciously, catching me on the forehead with the sharp edge of her heel. I yelped and held fast to the one leg I had. Her vast skirts hampered us both, she for movement and me for sight as I tried to see what was going on. She screamed Ridley's name, fighting to break free. Her heel next caught me on the shoulder. This time I got hold of it while breathlessly damning her to perdition.

I could hear some commotion going on between Edmond and Ridley. Clarinda also seemed aware of them and abruptly ceased trying to get away from me.

Oh, my God.

Letting go of her legs, I surged up and glimpsed her taking aim at Edmond's broad back with the pistol.

"*No!*" I cried, throwing myself bodily forward.

The explosion deafened me. Too late. Too late. In panic as much as anger, I cracked a hand against her jaw. She slumped instantly. Behind and above me I heard more commotion, grunts and thumps ending with a soft but sickening thud. Someone made a gagging sound, then a body fell on the floor next to me.

I pushed and turned away from Clarinda, fearful of an attack from Ridley; I need not have worried. It had been his body that had fallen. Edmond towered over us, chest heaving as he struggled to regain his breath, his eyes dark pinpoints in a white sea, not quite sane. For a second I thought his mad stare was for me, then realized it was Clarinda that held his attention. I was glad she was unconscious. What he might have done had she been awake did not bear imagining.

Neither of us moved. I was too tired, and he, well, his mind was in the grip of the shadows. Having been in their thrall myself more than once, I knew it would take a bit of time for him to break loose. I remained quiet for his sake.

Bloodsmell in the air. Edmond's. Fresh.

There was a long tear on the outside of his left arm. The ball from Clarinda's pistol had come that close. It might have been closer, had I not—

My teeth were out again.

Ignore it, Johnny Boy. Now's not the time or place.

God, but I was hungry. Thankfully not to the point of losing control. I wasn't on the edge of starving survival this time. I could wait a little longer.

But not too long.

Edmond stalked around us to sit on the defiled sarcophagus. He pressed one hand to his wound, bowing his head. There were lots of new lines on his face, but the old ones had settled back into something resembling their previous order.

"Let's get some help for that, shall we?" I suggested, my voice so thin and shaken I hardly knew it.

Edmond raised his eyes to stare at me. His expression rippled as the muscles beneath the skin convulsed. Not a pleasant sight, that. Even worse when I realized he was starting to laugh. Was laughing. With only the slightest of changes it might also be weeping. I fell quiet again. To offer a comforting arm as I'd done for Oliver would not have been welcome in this case. Edmond shook with laughter, was racked by it, sobbed with it, the sounds reverberating against the shocked walls of the mausoleum until the last of it dribbled away and he was utterly emptied.

In the thick silence that followed, I strove to remove myself from the floor and, after a bit of struggle, succeeded. Like Edmond, I half sat, half leaned on the sarcophagus. Unlike him, I had no laughter in me, only a vast fatigue that would have to be answered for very soon.

Ridley was alive, I noticed, and I was somewhat surprised by the fact. Edmond had thoroughly pulped him from what I could see of the fellow. His face was well bloodied, and there was more blood on the wall that may have come from a nasty-looking patch on one side of his shaved scalp. He'd lost his wig sometime during the battle, else it might have provided a bit of protection. Then again, perhaps not. Edmond had been terrifically incensed.

Now he appeared to have regained a measure of self-possession. He was looking at his unconscious wife.

"I . . . I really thought she loved me, once upon a time," he said softly. "Didn't last long. But it was nice for a while."

"I'm sorry."

He puffed some air out. Almost a laugh. "You've no idea."

I thought I had, but said nothing. I shut my eyes and thanked God that Oliver had not been involved, after all. I let myself feel ashamed for having believed it even for a moment. Ridley's talk had been too vague on the point, and I'd suspected the worst. *Bad, Johnny Boy, very bad of you.*

Yes. Very bad, indeed.

Then there was one other thing that had been said . . .

"Edmond?"

He grunted.

"Did Clarinda kill Aunt Fonteyn?"

His great head swung in my direction. "Why do you think that?"

"Because she reminded Ridley that she'd been busy elsewhere during the duel. It's bothered everyone on why Aunt Fonteyn had gone to the center of the maze that night, but Clarinda might have managed to get her there."

He was quiet for a very long time, head bowed, shoulders down. He took in a draught of air and let it out slowly, shuddering. "I think you're right," he whispered. "Clarinda was somewhat . . . nervous that night. Very bright, she was. I thought it was because of the party, because she may have been going to meet someone. Another man. Always another man in the past. We'd long passed the point where I didn't give a damn what she did anymore and separated at the party soon after arrival. She must have—"

"She killed Aunt Fonteyn so Oliver would inherit everything. Then we were to die tonight so she could be free to marry again. To marry the money."

"With enough scandal involved so that the family would hush the worst of it up."

"But why kill me?" I asked.

"Eh?"

"They wanted me to die at the Masque. Both of them." Yes, I had a separate quarrel with Ridley over that street brawl with him and his Mohocks, but why had Clarinda wanted me dead?

"You really don't know?" He seemed bitterly amused at my ignorance.

"Do you? What is it, then?"

"I'll have to show you. At the house. These three can keep themselves until we can send someone for them. Come along, boy."

He ponderously moved toward the door. I got my cloak back from Arthur, and put my swordstick together to use as a cane. Tired as I was, I needed its support just to hobble. Edmond was in better fettle and walked up the path toward the house more easily. He paused to wait for me, but I waved at him to go on ahead. As soon as he was out of sight, I veered away on a course that would take me directly to the Fonteyn stables and their red promise of swift revival.

Afterward, of course, I took care not to show myself to be too lively when I made it back to the house. The cloak covered the alarming state of my blood-soaked clothing, and while Edmond was busy rousing certain members of the staff and household and giving them orders, I managed to avoid drawing undue attention to myself.

Elizabeth was the one exception to this ploy. The instant she saw me, she knew something was wrong. The next instant she was whisking me away to a room where we could have the privacy necessary to talk.

That talk was both lengthy and brutally truthful. I told her all.

All that I *knew*, that is.

It was just an hour short of dawn when Edmond had sorted things to his satisfaction and Fonteyn House settled a bit.

Won't last, I thought, dreading the gossip to come. Not for my sake, but for Oliver's.

He had been awakened early on but had proved too befuddled to make much sense of the business. Elizabeth stayed behind trying to coax some *café noir* into him in the hope that it would help.

Clarinda had recovered very fast from the blow I'd dealt her. At first she'd tried to run, then endeavored to convince Edmond she'd been under duress from Ridley, then attempted to bribe the servants guarding her. Under orders from her husband she was locked into a small upper room usually reserved for storage. He kept the only key. After a time she gave up shouting her outrage to the walls and fell into sullen silence.

Ridley and Arthur, both still unconscious, were being cared for by a closemouthed doctor from the Fonteyn side of the family. He pronounced both to be concussed and not likely to wake anytime soon. He totally missed the wounds on Arthur's neck. Just as well.

"What will you do with them?" I asked Edmond, who was glaring at the two as if to burn them to cinders.

"Nothing," he rumbled.

"Nothing?"

"What would be accomplished in a court of law? They'd be let off with a five-shilling fine and advised to behave themselves in the future. Their fathers are too important in the Town for them to get what they really deserve. They didn't actually kill us, y'know."

"It wasn't for lack of trying."

"Yes, but since they failed, what they've done can be put down to the high spirits of youth. They knocked you about and shut me in that damned pit, nothing more. Pranks."

He was right about that. For my own sake I'd had to conceal the true extent of my injury, which was now considerably better. Without such visible evidence of their intent to kill it would be nearly impossible to see any justice done—at least through the courts. However, I had some very firm ideas of my own and planned to act upon them at the earliest opportunity. In the near future both men would have to endure a late night visit from me that neither would remember, but which would have a profound effect on their lives. By God, I might even make churchgoers of them.

"And Clarinda?" I asked.

"Oh, she's mad, Cousin," he informed me matter-of-factly.

"What?"

"Quite, quite mad. I fear she will have to be confined for the rest of her life because of it." He fastened me with a dangerous look. "Any objections?"

I pursed my lips and shook my head.

"She did do murder," he went on softly, "of that I'm now certain. And she planned to do murder, of that we both know, but there's no way in which it might be proven."

"Unless she confesses," I mused.

"Not bloody likely, and even if she should, what then? Better this than watching her dance a jig at Tyburn."

Probably.

"No good would come of it to the family. We have to think of them," he added.

"Oh, yes, certainly the family must be considered first."

I half expected a sharp reproach for my sarcasm, but he only lifted his chin a bit. "Come along with me," he said, starting off without waiting to see if I'd follow.

I caught up. "Why?"

"You wanted to know why she was going to kill you. Still interested?"

I was. He went upstairs and down one of the halls. I worried how long this might take. Brought back to strength again by means of the horse blood I'd lately fed upon, I could float home if pressed for time, but preferred to ride safe in a coach if possible. Before pushing myself further, I wanted a solid day's rest on my earth first.

Edmond stopped before a closed door and gently opened it. The room beyond was lighted by several candles standing in bowls of water. Many cots had been set out, each bearing a small sleeping occupant. When I saw Nanny Howard, I came to the reasonable conclusion that we were in the nursery.

"All's quiet, Mr. Fonteyn," she said in a low voice. I think she meant it as a warning for him not to disturb the children. She gave me a piercing stare, but I'd since borrowed some of Oliver's clothing and was secure that I was more respectable appearing than at our last meeting.

Edmond brushed past her, picking up a candle along the way, and headed for one of the cots, pausing before it. The child lying in it was young, not more than three or four. He was very pretty, with pale clear skin and a headful of thick black hair.

"Clarinda's boy," Edmond told me. "His name is Richard."

Yes, I could see that he'd want to protect his son from the stigma of Clarinda's crimes, but what had this to do with . . .

A cold fist seemed to close upon my belly, tighten its grip, and twist.

"Oh, my God," I breathed.

"Oh, yes, by God," Edmond growled.

"It can't be."

"It *is*. When he opens his eyes, you'll find them to be as blue as your own."

The next few minutes were a dreadful haze as my poor brain tried to keep up with things and failed. I eventually found myself drooping on a settee out in the hall with Edmond looming over me, telling me to pull myself together and not be such a damned fool.

"Too late for that," I muttered, still in the throes of shock.

The Christmas party. My God, my God, my God . . .

"I knew he wasn't mine," Edmond was saying. "And she wouldn't name the father, but when I saw you that night, I understood whose whelp he was right enough. You can be sure that Aunt Fonteyn would have seen as well had she been given the chance. Clarinda was always careful to keep the boy out of her sight. Easy to do when they're young. Must have given her quite a turn for you to come back to England."

"But—"

"She couldn't afford to have you around, y'know. Anyone seeing you and Richard would make the connection, but with you dead and buried, memories would soon fade, and she'd lie her head off, as always, to cover herself. Not with Aunt Fonteyn, though. The old woman was too sharp for such tricks. She'd have cut Clarinda out of the family money quick as thought. Another reason to kill."

"Wh-what's to be done?" I felt as if a giant had stepped on me. I couldn't think, couldn't move. Was this what all men feel when fatherhood is suddenly thrust upon them?

"Done? What do you mean?"

"You can't introduce me to the child and expect me just to walk away. I'd like to get to know him . . . if it's all right with you." That was the problem. Would Edmond allow even that much?

Edmond studied me, and for the first time there seemed to be a kind of sympathetic pity mixed into his normally grim expression. "You—what about the gossip?"

"I don't give a damn about gossip. Nor do you, I think. After all this, people are going to know or guess anyway. Let them do so and be damned for all I care."

A long silence. Then, "You're all in, boy. Time enough to think about such things tomorrow."

"But I—"

"Tomorrow," he said firmly, taking my arm and helping me up. "Now get out of here, before I forget myself and pound your face into porridge for being a better man than I."

EPILOGUE

But I could not bring myself to leave Fonteyn House. Not after this. The rapid approach of dawn was as nothing to me. When the time came I'd find some dark and distant corner in one of the ancient cellars and shelter there for the duration of the short winter day. There would be bad dreams awaiting me since I'd be separated from my home soil, but I'd survived them before and would do so again. Compared to what I'd just learned, the prospect of facing a week's worth of them hardly seemed worth my notice.

After Edmond had left and under Nanny Howard's eye, I crept back into the nursery to look again at the sleeping child. *My* sleeping child. Richard.

My God, but he was beautiful. Had my heart been beating, surely it would now be pounding fit to burst. As it was, my hands were shaking so much from a heady mixture of excitement, uncertainty, joy, and sheer terror that I didn't dare touch him for fear of waking him.

Questions and speculations stabbed and flickered through my brain like heat lightning, offering only brief flashes of light, but no real illumination about the future. Edmond had not wanted to discuss it, and I could see that he was right to postpone things until the idea had fully been absorbed into my still mostly stunned mind. Certain subjects between us

259

would have to be addressed, though, and soon.

I'd said I didn't give a damn about the gossip, but that wasn't entirely true. It meant little enough to me, but might prove to be a problem for this little innocent. It wasn't his fault that his mother was a murderous—

Not now, Johnny Boy.

Or ever. I'd hardly endear myself to the child by expressing an honest opinion to him about Clarinda.

Would he even *like* me?

I chewed my lower lip on that one for several long minutes.

And how in the world would I ever tell Father?

I fidgeted from one foot to the other for even longer.

Good God, what would Mother—no, that didn't even bear thinking about.

I shook myself, nearly shivering from that thought.

Well, we'd all get through it somehow, though for the moment I hadn't the vaguest inkling of what to do besides stare at the little face that so closely mirrored my own and hope for the best.

"He's a very good boy, sir," whispered Nanny Howard from close behind me.

I gave quite a jump, but at least forbore from yelling in surprise.

She couldn't completely hide her amusement at startling me, but diplomatically pretended not to notice my discomfiture.

"A good boy, you say?" I asked, my voice a little cracked.

"Yes, sir. Very smart he is, too, if a bit headstrong."

"Headstrong? I like that."

"Indeed, sir. It complements him, when it's not misplaced."

"I . . . I want to know all about him. Everything."

"Of course, I'll be glad to tell you whatever you like. We should talk elsewhere, though."

At this gentle hint from her we moved out into the hall, leaving the door open so she could keep an eye on her charges. I was eager to hear any scrap of information on the boy, but alas, just as she was settling herself to speak we were interrupted.

"*Jonathan?*" Elizabeth came hurrying toward us, brows high with alarm. "What on earth are you still doing here? You know you—" She stopped when she saw Nanny Howard.

"It's all right," I said, keeping my voice low and making hushing motions with my hands.

"But it's very late for you," Elizabeth insisted, speaking through her teeth. God knows what Mrs. Howard thought of her behavior.

"It doesn't matter, I'm staying here for the day." Now I had shocked her, a portent of things to come, no doubt.

"*You're what?* But you—"

Before her surprise overcame her discretion, I took Elizabeth's elbow and steered her back down the hall out of earshot of Mrs. Howard. My good sister was just starting to sputter with indignation at my action when I reined us up short and turned to face her.

The look on my face must have helped trigger that innate sympathy that sometimes occurs between siblings, where much is said when nothing is spoken.

"What is it?" she asked, suddenly dropping any protest she might have had. "Is something wrong? Has Edmond—"

"No, nothing like that. Nothing's wrong—at least I don't think so, but you'll have to decide for yourself, and I hope to God that you think it's all right, because I really need all the help I can get, especially yours, because this is—is—"

"Jonathan, you're babbling," she stated, giving me a severe look. "For heaven's sake collect yourself and tell me *what* is going on."

And so I did.

The haunting novel that continues
Bram Stoker's <u>Dracula</u>

**She once tasted the blood of Count
Dracula and felt his undying passion.
Now Mina's story continues...**

MINA

MARIE KIRALY

Returning to the mortal world, Mina tries to
fulfill her duties as a wife while struggling to
forget Dracula's exquisite pleasure. But her
world has changed with the first sweet taste of
blood, and Mina will never be the same again.

___ 0-425-14359-7/$5.50